"I knew your sister…
in the *biblical* sense."

A sudden piercing image of Julia and Lawrence together made Sara's stomach heave. "I…don't understand why you're telling *me* this. You know she's dead, right?"

He nodded. "I just learned of her accident. I've been looking for her for about two years." At her questioning glance, he added, "I'm thinking of running for public office and I didn't want any surprises. You know…blackmail."

"That's crazy. Julia would never do anything like that."

"I didn't know. We only spent one night together and…we didn't talk much."

"So why are you telling me this now? Why do I need to know that Julia had an affair? She wasn't perfect but she was my sister, and I loved her." Tears began to gather in her eyes. "She's dead. Isn't that punishment enough for her sins?"

He started to put out his hand to touch her, but let it drop to the bench.

"There's a chance I might be Brady's father," he said softly.

Dear Reader,

People often ask me where I get my ideas for stories. I wish I knew for sure. This particular story has been in my head for years, but it never felt right to me until last summer when my son, Jon Paul, asked me what my next book was going to be about. We were strolling down a quiet street in La Grande, Oregon, and I started rattling off my idea about a judge, his private investigator buddy and a baby. The more I talked, the more *real* the characters became. When I asked Jon Paul what he thought of the premise, he told me, "Write it, Mom." So I did.

As my heroine, Sara, came into focus, I realized she shared some of my daughter Kelly's positive attributes. Both have a ready smile and nonjudgmental attitude that make them easy to love. And both learned at a tender age that the strong go on—chin up. Or, as Sara says, "You just do the best you can."

The only problem I had in writing this book is that several of its secondary characters have very strong voices and personalities that can't be overlooked. It became apparent early on that Bo, my hero's best friend, was a hero in his own right. And to my surprise another character popped out of nowhere with a spunk and energy that seemed the mark of a heroine. You know what that means…a sequel.

I hope you enjoy reading this book and come to care about these characters as much as I do. The ending may surprise you—I know it did me.

Happy reading,

Debra

HIS DADDY'S EYES
Debra Salonen

HARLEQUIN®

TORONTO • NEW YORK • LONDON
AMSTERDAM • PARIS • SYDNEY • HAMBURG
STOCKHOLM • ATHENS • TOKYO • MILAN • MADRID
PRAGUE • WARSAW • BUDAPEST • AUCKLAND

ISBN 0-373-70934-X

HIS DADDY'S EYES

Printed in U.S.A.

For Kelly and Jon Paul, with a mother's love

CHAPTER ONE

SUPERIOR COURT JUDGE Lawrence Bishop III slammed his gavel. The three staccato repetitions dropped a curtain of silence over the proceedings. The opposing lawyers, who up to that moment had seemed poised for fisticuffs, turned to him with a combination of supplication and censure in their eyes.

As the third Bishop male to wear the black robes of a judge, Lawrence, who was "Ren" to everyone except his mother, had grown up hearing stories of courtroom theatrics. But in the two years since his father's death and Ren's subsequent appointment to the bench, he'd become weary of prima-donna headline hounds, such as defense attorney Steve Hamlin.

Hamlin, an up-and-coming name in Sacramento political circles, had a well-practiced smile that garnered female groupies. His defendant, a soon-to-be third-time offender, slumped in his chair like a lump of unformed clay.

Peter Swizenbrach represented the plaintiff—in this case, the State of California. If one believed the evidence—and Ren did—the lump was guilty of serial stupidity, which normally wouldn't be punishable by life in prison unless it included using a gun, which this did.

"Gentlemen," Ren said, his voice carrying as he

meant it to, "do either of you see a jury in this room?"

The lawyers looked at each other as if suspecting a trick question. Tentatively, each shook his head.

"Then, who the hell are you playing to?" Ren barked, nodding toward the dozen spectators. "The audience?" Three young women—obviously Steve Hamlin groupies—in the front row squirmed as if he'd called on them to speak. "Because if you can't control yourselves, then I will ask them to leave. I," he stressed the word regally, for he was king of this particular corner of the world, "am not impressed."

The two attorneys scurried to their respective tables to regroup.

Ren stifled a sigh. The bench was every lawyer's dream job—and an important step in Babe Bishop's not-so-secret political agenda for her son—but some days Ren would have traded it for a window job at the post office.

Before he could muster enough energy to begin round two, his clerk, Rafael Justis, a bright, young Hispanic who took no small amount of razzing about his name, handed Ren a folded piece of paper the size of a postcard.

Ren opened it. The familiar scrawl brought a peculiar quickening of his senses even before he read the cryptic: *Gotta talk.* Ren swore softly under his breath, then lifted his gavel a second time. "We'll take a twenty-minute recess."

REN TOSSED HIS ROBE on the brass-and-mahogany coat rack that had been his father's, then paced to his office window. The view of downtown Sacramento from the third-story wasn't impressive—no prestigious law firm's corner office with a vista of the river. But it was an improvement over his previous digs: a tiny cubicle in the basement of a fifty-year-old federal building, where he'd researched environmental law.

Ren had chosen law school because it was expected of him, but he'd wound up falling in love with the law, not the circumspection of it. Although his favorite professor had urged Ren to take up teaching, Ren couldn't bring himself to disappoint his parents, so he'd sought a compromise: environmental law. The pay sucked, but it gave him a chance to champion a cause he believed in.

For fifteen years, Ren quixotically tilted at bureaucratic windmills. Then, to his immense surprise, a small court battle over salmon spawning grounds two years ago stirred a media frenzy, and Ren became an overnight celebrity. Pretty heady stuff at age forty, but damn unnerving, too. Looking back now, Ren understood the impetus behind his crazy lapse in judgment, which no doubt was the subject of this upcoming meeting—a meeting Ren hoped would bring resolution to two years of haunting guilt.

A noise outside his chamber door made his stomach clench, and he ran a hand nervously through his hair, causing a wedge of ash-brown hair to fall across his view.

A soft knock preceded the opening of the door. Ren turned, motioning the visitor to a chair. At five foot ten, one hundred eighty pounds, with sandy brown hair and hazel eyes, Bo Lester epitomized the word *nondescript,* an invaluable trait in his line of work.

"Howyadoin', Ren?" Bo called amiably before plopping like a sack of potatoes into the leather wingback chair opposite Ren's desk.

No more grace than when we were students, Ren thought, smiling. He quickly sat down in his high-tech desk chair—a Christmas gift from Eve, his future bride, and leaned over to shake hands. "Long time no see," Ren said.

"Did I pull you out of court? I told that Mexican kid I could wait. It's your money, and you know I don't mind wasting it."

Ren grinned. Robert Bowen Lester Jr., or "Bo," as he preferred, liked to come off as a redneck hillbilly. He was, in fact, the only son of one of the country's top financial gurus, Robert B. Lester Sr. But Bo had broken with his family shortly after college when he'd chosen law enforcement over what he called "legalized money laundering." Today, Bo was one of the top private investigators in northern California.

"You have some information, don't you?" Ren asked, feeling as if he were swimming in shark-infested waters.

Bo shifted positions, hunching forward to rest his elbows on his knees so he could face Ren eye-to-eye. Ren found the posture ominous.

"You found Jewel." Ren's comment was a statement, not a question.

Bo nodded.

"Where?"

"Here."

Damn. A worst-case scenario. He and Bo had discussed this possibility from day one. As long as Jewel lived somewhere outside the Sacramento area,

Ren wouldn't feel any need to contact her. He could stay out of her life, as—*so far*—she'd stayed out of his.

But now that option was gone. This was a town that lived and breathed political scandal. What would happen to Ren's career if Jewel decided to embarrass—or even blackmail—him? His mother's hopes and dreams would be destroyed. Babe would kill him if she found out. And Eve…Ren didn't dare think what his future bride would do to Julia. But he could be sure that whatever form her retaliation took, it would probably wind up on the six o'clock report. Eve Masterson was the popular anchor of the Channel 8 news team.

Bo rapped his knuckles on Ren's desk. "Don't get too far ahead of me on this, old friend. That's only part of the news."

Ren sat back and took a deep breath. His friend knew him well. "So tell me." Ren was pleased his voice didn't betray the fierce humming in his chest.

"Well, I've got bad news, and even worse news. Which do you want first?"

"Cut the crap, Lester, just tell me."

Bo's wiry brows waggled, but his smile faded as he took a folded piece of paper from the breast pocket of his wrinkled cotton shirt. He slowly opened it. "First off, the name she gave you— Jewel—was pretty close. Does the name Julia Noelle Carsten ring a bell?"

Ren's heart thudded against his ribs. Jewel had a full name. His gorgeous sex goddess, his first-and-only one-night stand, had a name. *Julia.* Such a pretty, innocent name for someone with a body like hers.

"Julia Carsten," Ren repeated aloud. He searched his memory, which included a long list of miscreants. "Nope. Never heard of her."

Bo smoothed the paper across one knee, out of Ren's line of sight. "Her married name was Hovant," he added casually.

"Married?" Ren croaked, lurching to his feet. His chair crashed backward into the bookcase behind his desk.

Of course. Why else would she disappear without so much as a word? Ren retrieved his chair and sat down, feeling both relieved—Jewel couldn't very well resort to blackmail when her own reputation was at risk—and yet, let down.

Ren looked at Bo. The man who'd just simplified Ren's life and eased his guilty conscience wasn't looking very pleased about it.

"Oh, God," Ren groaned. "What else?"

"She's dead."

An invisible weight of some extraordinary measure pressed on Ren's chest making it impossible to draw a breath.

"She can't be dead. She's too young." Even as he said the words, Ren knew they made no sense.

Bo passed him the paper, which Ren saw was a copy of an obituary. Four inches of tiny print. A four-inch lifetime.

"How?" he asked hoarsely, trying to comprehend the unthinkable.

Bo cleared his throat. Ren felt himself tensing.

"The inquest called it—"

"Inquest? Why was there an inquest?" Ren asked sharply.

"Fancy speedboat. Too much power, not enough

lake. Rammed an exposed rock and burst into flames—''

Ren shuddered at the graphic image.

''—the inquest ruled it an accident, but the investigating officer told me Dr. Hovant was known for his temper. Some people think he might have let that temper run away with him.''

''Murder-suicide?'' Ren asked, almost choking on the words.

''Something like that, but no way to prove it.''

Ren tried to digest the information, but it wouldn't stay down. ''Her husband was a doctor? What kind?'' he asked, as if it mattered.

Bo shrugged. ''A specialist with a whole bunch of letters after his name. Julia had been a nurse before she became Mrs. Hovant.''

Questions percolated in Ren's head like toxic runoff, but Bo didn't give him time to sort through them.

''It happened last July. I asked around the marina. Everybody remembered the crash. One guy said the boat blew up like a grenade.'' Bo shook his head. ''You could ask your fiancée. They probably have it on tape. The media eats up this kind of thing.''

As usual, Bo didn't bother hiding his disdain for Eve or her job, but Ren ignored the jibe. ''Why do they think it was intentional?''

Bo shrugged. ''I guess that's what happens when you air your dirty laundry in public. According to my source, the Hovants were known to get into shouting matches. Seems their marriage had been rocky for the past few years—which, I guess, might explain why Jewel-slash-Julia did what she did with you.''

"This obituary says she was survived by her son, Brady. Stepson, right?'' Ren asked, looking up. "The woman I made love to was nobody's mother."

His comment seemed to startle Bo, who frowned and tugged a small wire notebook from his hip pocket. After flipping through half-a-dozen pages, he looked up. "You're right. She didn't have the kid when you were together. He was born later."

Ren froze. "How much later?"

Bo fumbled with the notepad. "October? November?''

Ren and Julia's tryst had taken place the Friday after Valentine's Day. *February, March, April...*he mentally counted. "I repeat—how much later?"

Bo flipped pages. "Bingo! Brady Hovant. No middle name. Born November twelfth. Eight pounds ten ounces. I forgot to mention the aunt. I talked to her, too."

"What aunt?"

"The kid's aunt. Julia's sister. Sara Jayne Carsten, age thirty-one. Runs a bookstore near the K-Street mall. She's got custody of the kid."

Ren frowned, trying to wade through a river of swirling emotions.

Bo sat forward. "Hey, man, this doesn't mean anything. Think about it. Julia obviously slept around. And she was married. There's no reason to think...I mean, you didn't...hell, man, this is the age of AIDS—tell me you didn't have unprotected sex."

"Of course not." Ren glared at his friend. "I used a condom." He frowned, trying to remember. Not that it was hard to recall with photographic—some might say pornographic—clarity the night in question. "All three times."

"My, my, aren't you the stud."

"Shut up. She's extraordinary." *Was. Jewel is dead.*

Ren picked up his phone and pushed a button. "Mr. Justis, court is over for the day. We'll reconvene tomorrow morning."

Bo looked at him, frowning. "This has rocked you."

Resting his elbows on the desk, Ren put his head in his hands. "I never met anybody like her, Bo. Cool and direct on the outside, steamy and wild on the inside. Damn. She was incredible."

"You fell hard, didn't you?"

Ren looked up. "If you mean, was I in love with her?—no. Not even close. Love and sex are not synonymous, my friend. She was gorgeous, wild and hot, and I can definitely say I've never had sex like that before or since." Bo's hoot made Ren scowl. "That was not meant to demean my fiancée in any way. You don't marry a woman like Jewel."

"Dr. Hovant did," Bo said, rising. "Fat lot of good it did him. If the rumor mill is right, all they did is fight—right up to the moment he drove his boat into a rock."

Bo crammed his notebook into the back pocket of his rumpled canvas slacks. "Well, looks like your secret's safe. Bullet dodged. Case closed."

Ren picked up a pen and made a series of hatch marks on his blotter. Nine of them. "Are you sure?"

"Why not? If Julia knew who you were she obviously didn't tell anybody, because we haven't heard anything in two years. She never even mentioned your name to her sister.''

"How do you know that?"

Bo produced a disreputable-looking cotton baseball cap from his other back pocket. "Because I'm a professional. When I visited Miss Carsten at her place of business last week, she never blinked when your name came up."

Ren's blood pressure spiked. "You asked her about me?"

Bo made a face. "I told her my friend collected first editions, which is true. I said he was pretty well known for his collection. True again. I said his name was Lawrence Bishop III, and asked if she'd ever heard of him." Bo smiled, apparently picturing the encounter. "She laughed and said, 'If any of my customers have numbers associated with their names, it's more likely the result of a problem with the law than hereditary honor.'"

Ren knew he should have been relieved, but for some reason felt more peeved than pleased. Bo turned to go. "Wait a minute. You're not done."

"Yes, I am. You hired me to find your love goddess. I did. It's not my fault she's dead." Bo wedged the cap on his head.

Ren rose and walked around his desk. "Bo, I need clarity on the matter of this child."

His friend snorted. "What kind of clarity? You used a condom. You were a good bad little boy. End of story."

"You don't find it the least bit unnerving that I spend the night in the arms of a stranger in early February and nine months later said stranger gives birth to a child?"

"But you said—"

"Condoms have been known to fail, Bo. And I was asleep when Jewel left, maybe she took the…evidence of our encounter with her. For what purpose, I don't know. Maybe hubby was sterile and she needed a sperm donor. I don't have a clue, but I'm uncomfortable with loose ends and this one seems like a big one."

"Actually, he's pretty little," Bo said, leaning down to demonstrate a height somewhere near his knees. "Cute as a bug. Curly brown hair. Big blue eyes."

Ren pictured a photograph hanging on his upstairs wall: his father leading a toddler—Ren—with curly brown hair and big blue eyes down a dock to the family boat. "You saw him?" he asked.

"Yeah. At the bookstore," Bo replied. "The aunt takes him to work with her instead of using a baby-sitter. Go see for yourself."

The idea made Ren's knees buckle. He parked his butt on the desk and gripped the edge while he forced his brain to recall the paternity cases he'd tried. "What's his blood type?"

"I don't know. *A, B* or *O,* I suppose," Bo said flippantly.

"Could you narrow that down?"

"How? Medical records are confidential."

"Come on, Bo. You hack the telephone company's records all the time. All I want is his blood type, although I suppose I'll probably need a DNA match to go to court. Maybe you could ask the aunt."

Bo's mouth dropped open. "Have you lost your frigging mind? There ain't no way that woman would voluntarily give you a drop of that baby's blood if it meant you might wind up taking him away from her.''

Lowering his voice, he added, ''Listen, Ren, get a grip. Chances are, like, one in six zillion this could be your kid. Maybe Julia and the doc had a spat, and she ran up to Tahoe to get back at him—but odds are the kid's his. If not, she'd have come looking for you as soon as she found out she was pregnant, right?''

Ren had no way of knowing what Julia would do; he didn't know Julia—only Jewel—and their relationship hadn't involved much talking. ''I never told her my last name.''

''Big deal. If she didn't recognize you from the salmon thing, she sure as hell couldn't have missed your dad's funeral or when you were appointed to the bench.''

''Maybe…''

''Not to mention the fact I see your ugly puss in the papers every few days thanks to that news bimbo you're engaged to.''

''Eve is co-anchor of the Channel 8 news, Bo— I hardly think she deserves that kind of disparagement. But you do have a point. We are photographed quite often. If Julia had wanted to reach me, she could have found a way.''

''Exactly,'' Bo confirmed. ''My old man used to tell me 'Don't trouble trouble 'til trouble troubles you.'''

Ren snorted. ''Very profound.''

''Hey, people pay big bucks to hear Robert B. Lester Sr. talk. The point is, you've got a nice life. Don't rock the boat.''

A part of him wanted to agree, but the problem with Bo's nautical metaphor was that Ren's boat was sinking fast from a broadside hit by an eighteen-month-old iceberg.

"SARA J., I'M NOT GONNA tell your sorry ass again, you can't be giving stuff to every person that comes asking!" Keneesha said with finality.

Sara ignored her friend and continued putting books into the box she was sending to the homeless shelter. Daniel Paginnini was due to arrive at the bookstore any minute to pick them up, and she wanted to be sure she included as wide a range of titles as possible.

"Leave her be, Keneesha," Claudie St. James said, rocking back and forth in the bentwood chair. "You know how she gets. Sara's a woman on a mission. And I don't mean position."

Claudie laughed at her own joke. Sara smiled, too. For her age, which Sara guessed to be twenty-five, and profession—prostitute—Claudie could, at times, be downright childlike. Perhaps that was what endeared her most to Sara.

Claudie rocked a little faster, her small feet coming off the colorful braided rug that delineated the story corner where Sara regularly read to her customers' children and to her 18-month-old nephew. At the moment, Brady was sound asleep in his soft-sided playpen behind her desk.

"Don't talk dirty in front of the child," Keneesha said, her tone surprisingly maternal. To Sara's knowledge, neither woman had children, but ever since Brady had arrived in Sara's life, the two hookers had become veritable founts of wisdom on how to raise children.

Claudie snorted. "The child's snoring like an old man, or is your hearing going?"

Keneesha drew herself to her very impressive height of six foot, her voluptuous chest swelling indignantly. "I hear just fine. I was referring to Sara J."

Both women laughed. Sara looked at them, her best—most unlikely—friends, and stuck out her tongue. The two laughed all the harder.

Sara had known Keneesha, a woman in her midforties, for almost ten years, which was how long Sara had been back in Sacramento. They'd struck up a conversation on a bus from Reno. Sara had been on the last leg of her journey, returning home after being summarily ejected from the Air Force. Keneesha, "Kee" to her friends, had been returning home after three days of partying with a group of high-rollers.

Kee had listened sympathetically to Sara's story of her aborted military career—destroyed by a boyfriend, who'd used Sara as a means to facilitate his drug sales on base. Kee had agreed wholehearted with Sara that the judicial system was deeply biased and routinely hung women out to dry.

Claudie had come along later, showing up one night, fiercely prepared to stake out her turf. Kee, who could act downright maternal on occasion, had taken the younger girl under her wing, and Claudie, too, became attached to Sara. To the casual observer, Keneesha and Claudie had only two things in common: their profession—which Claudie engaged in only to supplement low-paying jobs that never seemed to work out, and which Keneesha did when she pleased, period—and Sara. They adored Sara.

Everyday the two women would make their way from their rooms in the crummy hotel down the street to No Page Unturned, Sara's bookstore. They'd drink coffee at Sara's new coffee bar, or, on nice days, they'd sit out front at one of the three tiny tables and poke fun at the general populace.

Sara was content with her life as a single mother and small-time bookstore owner. She'd inherited the store when her long-time employer, Hank Dupertis, a gruff old widower with no children or close relatives, passed away in his sleep. Brady was a gift that accompanied the most grievous loss of Sara's life— her beloved sister's death.

The book Sara was holding slipped from her fingers, just as the bell above the door tinkled. When Sara straightened, she saw Daniel stride into the shop.

"Hello, Sara love," Daniel said, his dark eyes teasing. "Will you marry me today?"

Once—about three lifetimes ago—Daniel had proposed in earnest. Fortunately, Julia had intervened. "You and Danny both need to find out who you are before you jump into a relationship," Julia had told her. "Get out and live a little, girl."

For Sara that had meant a stint in the Air Force; Daniel had headed to college, then to a job in Seattle. He'd returned to Sacramento just after Julia's death, and although he and Sara remained good friends, both knew his proposals were in jest.

"Sara J. don't need no stinking man in her life," Keneesha said. "She's got us."

Daniel looked from the large black woman to the petite blonde, then back to Sara. "Two hookers and a bookstore—why does that not sound like everybody's idea of heaven?"

Sara laughed and pushed the now-overflowing box across the display table. "I guess everyone's idea of heaven is different. Actually, I've been very blessed. I have three wonderful friends. And business is good. In fact, *Channel Eight News* is doing a show called *The New Downtown* next Friday. They want to interview me about No Page Unturned."

"Next week?" Claudie squealed. "I thought you said next month. Good Lord, Kee, how are we going to get her done by then?"

Daniel looked confused, so Sara explained. "They think I need a new look to be on TV." She glanced down at her calf-length cotton dress, a sort of wallpaper print with a pale rose background and tiny yellow flowers. Her white sneakers were gobbling up her anklets, heel first. "Who has time for glamour?" she said, tugging up her stockings.

"You're beautiful to me just the way you are," Daniel said. He tenderly reached out and tugged on a lock of Sara's shoulder-length hair.

Sara hated her hair. Bone straight, baby fine and the color of dishwater, her mother always said. Compared to her sister's vibrant red locks, Sara's always looked washed out. The idea of being interviewed by someone as beautiful as Eve Masterson left her more than slightly unnerved, which was why she'd agreed to the makeover.

"Yeah, but you're a man, so what do you know?" Claudie said spitefully.

Sara sighed. "Stop squabbling, children. I told you you could play with my hair, so be nice."

"And a new outfit," Keneesha reminded her. "I am royally sick of those baggy dresses. You need some color, girl."

Sara looked at Keneesha's leopard-print tank top plastered over fuchsia pedal pushers, and involuntarily cringed. "Maybe."

The bookstore bell tinkled, and Sara glanced at the nondescript gentleman in a baseball cap who quickly made his way toward the back of the building. The patron seemed vaguely familiar, but since he didn't seem to require her assistance, Sara turned to Daniel, who was talking.

"...and you can have first pick."

"What?" she asked, noticing how Claudie's gaze stayed on the customer as he meandered into the cookbook section.

"Jenny just cleaned out her closet. She never keeps an outfit longer than a year and she only buys the best. I was taking the bag to the shelter, but you can go through it first."

Daniel's sister, a true fashion diva, was Sara's size and had excellent taste. "That's fantastic. Thanks!"

"No problem," he said, giving Sara a hug. "Now, where's my godson?"

Keneesha scurried around the desk to stand defensively in front of the playpen. For a large woman, she moved with surprising speed. "Back off, lightfoot. He's our godson, not yours."

"Do you have that in writing?"

"I'll show you writing, white boy," Kee said, her bluster taking on volume.

The noise woke Brady.

Sara hurried to the playpen and picked him up. "Hey, baby love," she said, kissing his soft, plump cheek. His sleepy, baby smell made her heart swell and her eyes mist. "How's my boy?"

Daniel walked over and planted a kiss on Brady's cheek. The sleepy child chose that minute to rub his eyes, and his small fist collided with Daniel's nose.

"See, there," Keneesha chortled, triumphantly, "he likes us better."

Sara saw a hurt look cross Daniel's face and impulsively drew him close with her free arm. "We both love you, Danny boy, you know that," she said softly.

"I know," Daniel replied. "I love you, too. I'll see you Sunday, right?"

Before Brady came into her life, Sara had participated on Sundays in a literacy program at a local shelter. Unfortunately, nowadays her free time was so limited, she seldom had the energy to join the other volunteers at the Open Door family shelter.

"I'll try, but Brady's cutting teeth, and my neighbors don't like the way my eaves look." She rolled her eyes. "I keep getting nasty letters from the Rancho Carmel Homeowners' Association."

Daniel gave Sara a peck on the cheek. "Don't sweat it. You've done your share." He picked up his box of books. "So? Who's going to fetch the bag of clothes?"

Claudie grumbled about being the company slave, but she followed him out the door.

Brady squirmed, so Sara knelt to put him down. His bare toes curled against the sturdy nap of the new gray-blue carpet. Until recently, the store's flooring had consisted of worn tile squares circa 1955—some black, some green, about half of them broken. Hank had refused to waste money on a building he regarded as "a piece of junk waiting for the wrecking ball." Sara never had the funds to re-decorate, but finally decided to use some of the trust money Julia's lawyer sent each month to make Brady's play area safe and comfortable.

"Mine," Brady said, reaching for the bottom drawer of Sara's desk. She'd been careful to have all the drawers fitted with locks—except one, which belonged to Brady. She made sure a healthy snack was in the drawer at all times.

She couldn't help smiling at his triumphant chor-tle when he pulled a thick hunk of toasted bread from the drawer. His ash-brown curls, as thick and lush as his mother's had been, bounced as he tod-dled to his miniature cash register and sat down to play.

Sara glanced around; she'd nearly forgotten the customer now unobtrusively tucked in a corner near the cookbooks. *That's odd,* she thought. Her occa-sional male cook usually carried the tragic look of the recently divorced. This fellow didn't strike her as needy or interested in *cordon bleu* cooking. And he definitely seemed vaguely familiar.

She started in his direction, but was deflected by Claudie's loud "Whoopee!"

"Holy sh—shimany," Keneesha exclaimed. "Look at this, Sara J. Lord God, what I wouldn't give to be size eight!"

Sara joined her friends at the counter to examine Jenny's discarded clothes. It wasn't until the bell tinkled that she remembered the cookbook man.

Bo POCKETED his palm-size camera and exited the bookstore, ducking into the alley. A mural of the store's name was painted in five-foot-tall lettering along the brick wall. *Clever name for a bookstore,* he thought. *I wonder if Sara made it up?*

Thinking of Sara made him scowl. Normally, Bo liked his job, but at this particular moment he felt like a piece of excrement wedged between the proverbial rock and a hard place.

Ren Bishop was the brother Bo never had, his one true friend, and Bo owed him more than he could ever repay—but he wasn't happy about the turn this case had taken.

I should have seen it coming, he silently groused as he opened the door of his car, a twenty-year-old Mazda with peeled paint and two primed dents in the fender. His work car, like Bo himself, knew how to be inconspicuous. "Two years without a goddamn lead," he muttered. "The only witness finally comes home after trekking through India, and what do I find? A dead Jewel and a kid that's got Bishop written all over his face!"

Lowering himself to the tattered upholstery, Bo pictured the sideswiped look on his friend's face when he'd left the courthouse. It reminded him of that night two years ago when Ren had stumbled down the gangplank of Bo's houseboat, vulnerable, exposed and all too human.

"I screwed up, Bo," Ren had confessed, pacing from one end of Bo's tiny living room to the other. "Positively. Beyond all screwups."

"Did you kill someone?"

"Of course not."

"Then stop pacing. You're making me seasick."

Bo had been surprisingly unnerved by his friend's agitation. In college, Ren had been known as Mr. Unflappable. Bo didn't like seeing him flapped.

Ren proceeded to spill his guts about the redhead who'd mysteriously disappeared after one night of passion. Bo recalled half hoping that Jewel was a blackmailer so he'd have a chance to meet her. But nothing happened. If that night clerk had stayed in India, Bo never would have had a clue to Jewel's true identity.

"That's Mrs. Hovant. Julia," the twenty-year-old clerk told him, after Bo gave her Ren's description of the woman. "She and Dr. Hovant used to come up from Sac five or six times a season, depending on the snow. Maybe they still do. I don't know. I don't work at the lodge anymore."

With a little cautious probing, Bo also found out that the day in question stuck in the clerk's memory because Julia had come to the lodge alone. "I asked her where the doc was, and she said something like 'Getting his rocks off at a medical convention.' She didn't seem too happy," the clerk told him.

The rest had been child's play for the PI.

Bo heaved a sigh, stirring the dust on his dashboard. He'd expected Ren to mourn Jewel's death, but this thing about the kid had caught him off guard. Bo had tried to downplay Ren's concern, but he had to admit the possible date of conception fell eerily close to the one-night stand.

Still, Bo had balked at pursuing it, partly because of what it might do to Sara, an innocent bystander in this little passion play.

"Even if, for argument's sake, the kid is yours," Bo had argued, "there's nothing you can do at this point. It's your word against the mother's, and she's dead.''

"As the biological father I'd have more rights than an aunt.''

"But it comes down to proof. How can you get the proof without admitting what you did? Which, if I remember correctly, was what you hired me to make sure never happened.''

"I don't suppose there's any way I can. But regardless of how it affects my political future, I still have to know.''

Bo sighed and started the car. A couple of discreet photos and the kid's blood type from his medical records. This Bo could do, but that would be it.

"You have to draw the line somewhere," he muttered to himself. "Even for a friend.''

CHAPTER TWO

REN YANKED ON THE CORD of the wooden blinds with more force than the old rope could take. The handle came off in his hand and the heavy shades crashed back to the mahogany sill with an ominous *thunk*. He sighed and tossed the yellowed plastic piece on the sideboard.

I've got to call a decorator, Ren thought. Although he seldom used the formal dining room, he knew it would be called into play more often once he and Eve were married. At present, the room reflected Babe's favorite decorating motif: Ostentatious. The opulent crystal chandelier cast an amber glow across the Regency-style table at its eight saffron brocade chairs. Without benefit of the morning light streaming through its mullioned windows, the room's musty gloom matched Ren's mood.

Ren blamed part of his foul mood on his alarm clock. If he'd remembered to set it, he would have made his weekly golf game. Instead, he'd slept in till nine-thirty. Ren pushed on the swinging door and entered his kitchen, a pristine world of black-and-white tile—the first room he'd remodeled after he moved in.

His home had once belonged to his parents, but after his father died, Babe, wanting something smaller and more luxurious, sold the house to Ren.

He loved the old beast, just as his father had, but the forty-year-old house needed work.

"Coffee," he mumbled, moving like a bear just out of hibernation. Ren took a deep breath, hoping to discover his coffeemaker was still warming his morning brew. His nostrils crinkled. No light beckoned from the stainless steel coffeemaker, but the smell of overcooked coffee lingered.

Ren microwaved a mug of the tar-like liquid and carried it to the small bistro table in the glass-enclosed breakfast nook. He sat on one of the waist-high stools covered in black-and-white hound's-tooth.

The wall phone rang before he could take a sip of his coffee. He stretched to pick it up. "Hello."

"Hi, handsome, sorry about last night. I'd have called, but you wouldn't believe how late we got out of the booth."

Ren had no trouble picturing his fiancée as she rattled off her apology. No doubt she was in her car, zipping through the light, Saturday-morning traffic on Interstate 80, headed back into town from her Roseville condo. Eve was ever a study in motion; she reminded him of a hummingbird with too many feeders to frequent.

"Don't worry about it," he told her, finally taking a sip of coffee. The brew—a shade off espresso—made him blink. "It's not like I was dying to go to the fund-raiser."

Ren heard a horn honk. Probably Eve's. She drove fast and had little tolerance for those who got in her way. "I know, but your mother won't be a bit happy. By the way, I went online and had a nice big basket of flowers delivered to her this morning with a note saying you'd be making a substantial donation to her cause—what was it, anyway?"

"League of Women Voters, I believe."

"Oh, damn. I wish I'd remembered that. Don't be too generous. They were particularly snotty to the media last fall."

Ren smiled—his first of the morning. His first since Wednesday afternoon, actually. Although he'd gone through all the motions for the past two days, his mind had been consumed by the thought of Julia. And her child.

He missed what Eve was saying and had to ask her to repeat it.

"Where have you been lately?" she exclaimed. "I'm serious, Ren. You always tell me I have too many irons in the fire, but at least I listen when somebody is talking to me. I asked whether Babe talked to you about setting a date for the wedding. She left a message on my machine, and it made me realize we really do need to sit down and talk about scheduling. You *know* what my schedule is like."

Ren knew. *Lesson One of celebrity dating: Everybody follows the schedule but the schedulemaker.* "You're right. We do need to talk." Ren recognized that although his affair with Julia had taken place before he and Eve started dating, she had a right to know what was happening, particularly if it turned out he'd fathered a child.

"Okay, then," she said. "Let's see...."

A loud engine noise came over the line, and Ren cringed, picturing her flipping through her thick dayplanner while changing lanes. "Why don't you call me back?" he suggested. "I may go out later, but I'll take the cell phone."

There was a pause. "You hate cell phones. Ren, are you okay? You don't sound like yourself."

"I didn't sleep well," he admitted. A guilty conscience had a way of conjuring up the worst scenarios. For instance, what if the reason Julia's husband had driven into a rock pile was that he'd found out the child wasn't his? What if Ren was to blame for his son's mother's death? Would the little boy wind up hating him when he was old enough to understand?

"Maybe you need vitamins. Boyd did a piece on male vitality last Wednesday—did you see it?" Eve asked.

"Nope. Missed it."

"Do you *ever* watch my show?" she asked, her voice suddenly vulnerable.

"Yours is the only news program I watch, you know that. I just happened to be with Bo that night," he said in partial honesty. After Bo had brought him the news about Julia and the baby, Ren had driven to the American River and walked along the jogging trail until dark. It was either that, or do something utterly stupid like visit the aunt's bookstore and check out the kid for himself.

Eve's dismissive snort brought Ren back to reality. "I wish I knew what you see in that man. He's such a boor."

Ren grinned. He'd never figured out why the two people he cared for most couldn't stand to be in the same room together. "Bo did a little research job for me and brought me the results. He's the best in the business, you know."

"So you say, but..." The sound of squealing tires broke her line of thought. "I'd better go, sweets.

I'm meeting Marcella this morning. We still have to go over my '96 and '97 tapes. You wouldn't believe what a fanatic this woman is. She makes *me* look laid-back.''

Her musical laugh brought an odd pang to Ren's chest. He loved this bright, beautiful woman, but he had a feeling she wasn't going to be overly thrilled at his news.

"So are we on for tonight?" he asked when he found his voice.

"Maybe. Marcella is only in town for another four days. She flies back to New York on Wednesday. Would you mind if she joins us?" Ren and Eve had a standing reservation at Hooligan's. Since she worked weeknights, Saturday and Sunday were their only nights to dine together. Usually, they ate out on Saturday, and he cooked on Sunday.

"Naturally I'd prefer to have you all to myself," he said, hoping his tone was more romantic than peeved. "Let's leave it open for now. Call me later, and we'll figure something out. Maybe we could ask Bo to join us so we'd have a foursome."

Ren grinned, picturing Eve's face at the idea of introducing her famous New York agent to the Sacramento PI. "You're right," she said. "We'd better hang loose until I have a better scope on my time. See you later, sweetheart. I love you."

She hung up before Ren could tell her the same thing.

"Exactly what kind of foursome did you have in mind?" a voice said from the doorway.

Ren spun around, nearly dropping the phone. "Goddammit, Lester," he shouted. "Don't you know how to knock?"

Bo shrugged. His sloppy green-and-gold plaid shirt wasn't tucked into his pants, making him look as if he'd come straight from the bowling alley. Brown double-knit pants barely cleared a disreputable pair of saddle shoes, which he wore without socks. His flattened-out hat was the kind that snapped to the brim.

"I looked for you on the golf course. Your partner said this was the first time on record that you were a no-show. He even thought about calling the paramedics, but didn't want to miss his tee time." Bo's lips curled wryly. "Notice your *real* friend dropped everything and rushed right over to check on you."

Ren hung up the receiver and sat down. "Thank you for your concern, but I overslept." He took a sip of coffee, then frowned. "Did I give you a key?"

Bo ambled to the coffeepot, took a mug from the white oak cupboard and poured himself a cup. He added two scoops of sugar from the bowl on the counter, then carried it to the microwave. "Nope. I picked the lock. Gotta keep in practice, you know."

Ren doubted that. More likely he'd forgotten to set the alarm. He'd been doing a lot of irresponsible things lately.

"You got anything to eat?" Bo asked, poking his head into the refrigerator. "Oh, Lordy, Revelda's apple pie," he said, referring to Ren's part-time housekeeper. "I swear I'd marry that woman if she'd have me."

"She wouldn't. She'd have a heart attack if she saw that floating hovel you call home."

"Actually," Bo said, talking through a mouthful of pie, "I found a lady to come in and clean for me a couple of times a month. Works great now that I've moved my computers to the office. Speaking of computers—'' He pulled a manila envelope from his waistband and tossed it on the table.

Ren's gulp of coffee lodged in his throat. He strove for nonchalance as he opened the envelope and withdrew a half-dozen black-and-white photographs and a single sheet of paper.

He picked up the computer printout first, but his gaze was drawn to the photos. "Is this her? This can't be her.''

Bo's mouth was full. "Uh-huh,'' he grunted.

Ren shook his head, his gaze darting from one photograph to the next. "There's no way this woman is Jewel's sister. She's so…plain.''

Bo's muffled expletive made Ren drop the printed page and pick up a photo. Leaning forward, he studied it closely. While the image was a trifle blurred, it showed a woman whom, though nice looking, he wouldn't have looked at twice. How could he reconcile this image with the one he held of her sister, an Aphrodite with flaming red hair, lush curves and flashing green eyes?

Feeling a bit let down, like a child at Christmas who'd expected a bike and got a book instead, he sighed. "Her hair's straight, her dress looks like a discount store special and her figure…'' Ren frowned, squinting. "Well, I can't tell much because of the dress, but she looks like a librarian.''

Bo made a low, snarling sound and helped himself to a second piece of pie. "Close—she owns a bookstore.''

"Owns it or runs it?''

"I didn't hack her bank records, but her business card says, Sara Carsten, Owner."

"She's pretty young to own a business," Ren said, mentally adding a point in her favor.

"The guy down the block said she's worked there since high school. In fact, she's turned it around from near-bankruptcy. The old man who owned it left it to her. She's kept up with the times—added a coffee bar and two Internet stations. And she's got a couple of book clubs that meet there." Bo made a sardonic sound. "The men's group is called The Unturned Gentlemen."

Ren added another point in her favor—literacy was a pet project of his. "Okay, she's a good person and a decent businesswoman, but I still can't believe she's Jewel's sister."

Bo scowled. Ren ignored him and rocked back, holding the photo. In the light from the window behind, he could see things he hadn't noticed before. Her smile, for one. It was a kind, gentle smile that made him inclined to smile back.

Ren focused on her eyes. Jewel's had been bright green, full of flashing sauciness and humor. If he squinted, Ren thought he could see humor in this woman's eyes, too. "What color are her eyes?"

"How the hell should I know?"

The downright angry tone could not be overlooked. "What is your problem?"

"You, man. You are my problem," Bo said, marching to the table. He ripped the photograph out of Ren's hand. "Here you are, poised to destroy this woman's life, and you don't think she's *pretty*. Well, f—"

Ren raised his hand in warning. He studied his

friend as he might a criminal with a gun. Keeping his tone calm, Ren said, "I was just surprised that I couldn't see any similarities between the sisters."

Bo's shoulders relaxed visibly. "It's not a very good picture. She was talking to that guy when I took it." He put the photo on the table and pointed at a good-looking man standing at the edge of the photograph. "She even gave him a hug, and I heard her tell him she loved him."

A funny, totally unexpected twinge caught Ren in the solar plexus. "Her boyfriend?"

Bo shook his head. "No. I got his plate through the store window. His name is Daniel Paginnini. He works in the Building." Ren had met enough congressional insiders to know that meant the Capitol. "I'd say he and Sara are old friends. She's got a lot of friends."

Ren detected an odd inflection in Bo's tone, but he let it go, although he was curious why Bo was so defensive of the woman. Ren picked up a shot of her holding the baby. Her back was to the camera, but her upper arms looked firm.

"Does she work out?" he asked. Jewel had been in peak physical condition, he recalled, her long, lean body as finely honed as an athlete's. When he'd asked about her sleek muscles, she'd said, "My job keeps me in shape." When he'd inquired about her job, she changed the subject by putting her mouth on a part of his anatomy that drained the blood supply from his brain, waylaying any questions he might have asked.

"Yeah," Bo said snidely. "She lifts weights. I'd say forty pounds, about a hundred reps a day."

"What?"

"The kid, man. She's a single mom." Bo shoved another photo in Ren's face. All Ren could see of the child was a mop of curls and a pudgy fist clamped around a soft blanket. He missed the first part of Bo's heated litany. "...gets up at dawn and works around this ugly house in Rancho Carmel until it's time to go to the store, then she runs her business and chases the kid all over the place until after the noon rush. Then, she lets one of the hookers take over while she takes the kid to the park..."

The word took a couple of seconds to register. "Did you say 'one of the hookers'?"

"Yeah."

"How many are there? And what are they doing in a bookstore?"

"Two. The big one's black. The little one's white. And they're her friends. As far as I can see, they're there every day."

Ren sat back, letting out a caustic laugh. "Oh, that's a wonderful environment for a child."

Bo leaned forward, his lips curled in a snarl. "I knew you were going to say that. Like you have any business pointing fingers."

Ren's mouth dropped open. "Okay. That does it. What the hell's going on with you?"

Bo pulled out a second stool and hopped up to sit at the table. He dropped his chin into his palm and muttered, "I like her."

"The aunt? Or the hooker?"

Bo glared. "Sara."

Perplexed, Ren reached for the photograph again. He'd never seen Bo behave in this manner. When involved in a case, Bo rigorously maintained a hard-nosed impartiality.

"Have you actually talked to her? Since that first time?"

"Yeah, yesterday."

Ren's solar plexus took another hit. They'd agreed that Bo's surveillance would be from a distance. "Was that necessary?"

Bo sunk lower in the chair. "It wasn't my idea."

"Whose idea was it?"

"The hooker's."

Ren smiled at the embarrassment he heard in Bo's tone. Bo was a professional, one of the best. Ren could imagine Bo's chagrin if someone had blown his cover.

"The big one or the little one?"

Ren almost missed the mumbled answer. "The little one, huh? Hmm. What happened?"

"She remembered me, okay? I can't tell you the last time that happened. Maybe I need to work on my disguises—they get old, you know."

Ren nodded, trying to keep from smiling.

"I didn't think anybody noticed me Wednesday when I went back to take the pictures, but yesterday, right after Sara and Keneesha—the black hooker—returned from the park, I eased in behind a couple of shoppers—and *wham*. The little one—Claudie—nailed me. I thought she was gonna demand a strip search."

Ren diplomatically covered his grin with his hand. "There's an image."

Bo shuddered as though recalling a harrowing experience. "It was so sudden. One minute I was standing in the Mystery section listening to Sara explain about some drumming group when—boom—Claudie grabs my arm and spins me around, feet apart, back against the wall. My hand was going for my piece—''

"You were carrying? Around m—a baby?'' he corrected.

Bo scowled. "No. But old habits are hard to break, and she knew what I was doing. Believe me. I saw it in her eyes. She knows people. And she pegged me.'' He sat back, shaking his head.

"What'd she say?'' Ren was surprised when a smile crossed Bo's lips.

"She said, 'What's this guy doing back again?' And then Sara and the other one came up, and Sara told her, 'We really need to work on your people skills, Claudie. Let the customer go.'''

Bo sat up straight. "You'll never guess what happened next.''

"What?'' Ren croaked.

"Sara invited me to join her *gentleman's* reading group. Meets every other Wednesday at the store. So I figure I can keep an eye on things until you decide what you're going to do about this.'' Bo nudged the computer sheet toward Ren. "Have a look.''

Ren's stomach contracted at the implication he read in Bo's words and tone. His heart thudded loudly in his ear as he skimmed the page. "*O*-positive,'' he said softly. "Same as mine.''

"Yeah, I know. I hacked your file, too.''

Neither man spoke. Ren stared out the window at a mockingbird strutting in his backyard. A black and white maitre d' against a flawless green expanse. *What does this mean? Another coincidence or am I a father?*

Over the pulsing static of questions, strategies, legal precedents, moral obligations, terror and niggling hint of joy in his head, Ren heard Bo mutter something about reading books not being part of his contract.

Suddenly, the incongruous image of Bo in a literary setting struck Ren as hysterical. Laughing, he said, "A reading group. You?" The release loosened the pent-up emotions percolating in his chest, taking him beyond humor. Gasping for breath, he sputtered, "That'll have Professor Neightman rolling over in his grave."

Bo jumped off his stool and stalked to the door. "You know what you and Professor Neightman can do, preferably in public with your fiancée watching," he barked.

Sobering, Ren drew in a shaky breath and wiped the tears of laughter from his eyes. He regretted his jest. For a man who seemingly cared not a whit what people thought, Bo could be damn touchy about certain things, and his lack of formal education was one of them. Not that he hadn't had his chance. But Bo hadn't been in study mode during college; he'd been too busy partying.

"Hey, man, I'm sorry. I appreciate what you're doing, really. I know you're not crazy about this, but is there any chance you could get some better photos?"

"Why? You think she's gonna get sexier?"

Ren flinched. "I'd like a shot of the child. Type *O* is pretty common. It could be a fluke, but if he—"

Bo shrugged. "I'll think about it."

Ren would have pressed the point, but Bo didn't give him the opportunity. The heavy door swished closed, leaving Ren in silence.

He picked up the photographs and headed for his study, intending to go through his mail and pay bills. But once there, he laid out the photographs on his desk. Maybe his calling Sara plain had come from his need to see something of Jewel in her. According to the background information Bo had faxed him, the two women had different fathers. Julia's had split shortly after her birth. Her mother had married Lewis Carsten a year later and he'd adopted Julia. He'd died when Sara was a toddler. Their mother—an alcoholic—died when Sara was 17.

Ordering himself to put aside any memory of Jewel, he studied Sara's image. Her jawline was strong but not harsh, her nose perky and small. He liked the shape of her eyes, her thick lashes a shade darker than her hair. In the black-and-white picture, her heart-shaped lips reminded him of an old-time movie heroine—innocent yet sensual.

He could tell, even in the blurry image, that she wore no makeup—a practice that set her apart from other women of his acquaintance. Perhaps he'd done her an injustice. She was pretty, and if she changed hairstyles—hers was straight and plain—she could probably turn a man's head. However, that didn't alter the fact that she projected not one iota of the sexual chemistry her sister had exuded.

A sudden knife-like pain sliced through his gut, making him bend over. Tears rushed to his eyes, and he choked back a cry that had been lurking in his subconscious for days. He lowered his head to his desk and wept—for the loss of someone he barely knew, but who'd touched his life with a kind of unfettered passion he'd never experienced before.

He hadn't loved her, this enigmatic Jewel, but on that one night she'd given him…freedom.

THE RAUCOUS SQUABBLING of two blue jays in her neighbor's sycamore tree reminded Sara of Claudie and Bo, the most recent recruit to Sara's gentleman's reading group. It had taken Sara until this Sunday morning, when the mindlessness of scraping paint freed up her random access memory, to place him—the customer who had asked about first editions for his friend. At the time, she'd brushed him off with a flip answer.

"Sara, is it okay if I give Brady a peanut butter sandwich?" Amy Peters asked. The thirteen-year-old wasn't a terribly experienced baby-sitter, so Sara only used her when she was home and needed some relatively uninterrupted time.

"Sure. You know where everything is, right?"

"Yeah, but it looks like this will be the last of your bread."

"Darn. I forgot to buy some last night. Oh, well, Brady and I will walk to the market before his nap."

Amy dashed back inside. Brady was a pretty good toddler, but he had a mischievous streak in him—he loved to be chased. And just lately he'd discovered he could send Amy over the edge by hiding.

With a sigh, Sara tackled her task. A good mile of gutters encircled Hulger's house. Unfortunately, the original painter had failed to prime them adequately; the brown paint flaked like dandruff in some spots, yet resisted her most vigorous scraping in others. Another reason she hated her brother-in-law's house.

After the accident, Sara had given up her apartment, which was within walking distance of the bookstore, and had moved into Julia and Hulger's twenty-eight hundred square-foot house because she hadn't wanted to uproot Brady. Although it meant a difficult commute twice a day, she'd welcomed the security the gated community offered. But now she was regretting her decision.

"Hello, Miss Hovant," a grave voice said.

Only one person called her that—Mary Gaines, her neighbor to the left. "Sara, Mrs. Gaines. Please, call me Sara," she said, striving for patience. Sara didn't even bother trying to correct the woman on her last name.

"I see you're *finally* getting that gutter painted," the white-haired woman said. Her emphasis was clear.

"Just scraping. I'm still waiting for a bid on the painting. The painter was supposed to meet me yesterday but didn't bother showing up." After the scathing message she left on the painter's machine, Sara doubted she'd ever hear from him again.

"I can give you the name of a man, but he's not cheap," her neighbor said, turning to leave. "I just hope you get something done before the next association meeting."

Sara waited until the woman was gone, then sighed heavily. The homeowners' association took its job seriously—too seriously for Sara's taste. But she didn't think it was right that she had to pay for Hulger's mistakes. And in her opinion, the entire house was a mistake.

Hulger had had the house built as a wedding present for Julia. Then he'd devoted the five years before his death to imposing his taste on every decorating detail, inside and out. Sara still could never understand how a woman as strong-willed and self-sufficient as Julia had tolerated such an autocratic husband. Another mystery of life, she figured.

In many ways, Julia was an enigma. Sara blamed their mother for that. When Audra was incapacitated by drink and couldn't run a can opener let alone a household, Julia had become a surrogate mother to Sara, making sisterly confidences impossible.

Julia's stormy relationship with her husband had never been open for discussion. Danish-born Hulger once told Sara his role in life was to make money and visit his parents once a year; Julia's duties, according to Hulger, included looking beautiful for his friends, entertaining in lavish style and accompanying him to Denmark.

Julia had tried to do justice to her role, working out at the gym to stay fit and taking exotic cooking courses, but she'd missed her nursing career. Sara had been privy to enough arguments between the couple to know this was a huge issue in their marriage.

Sara had hoped things would turn around once Julia found out she was pregnant, but Brady's birth seemed to add a new kind of tension to the marriage.

Sara sighed. She missed her sister every single day. Living in Julia's house was a mixed blessing—reminders of Julia abounded, but so much of her taste was overwhelmed by Hulger's bizarre, unwieldy legacy.

An hour or so later, Sara strapped Brady into his stroller and started down the street. Although she'd invited Amy to join them, the teen said she intended to use her baby-sitting money to take her mother to the movie as a Mother's Day treat. Sara had completely forgotten about the holiday.

"Well, Brady, love, what should we do to celebrate?" she asked, giving the stroller a jiggle. "Shall we buy an ice-cream cone?"

"Iceee," he cried enthusiastically.

She pushed fast to avoid looking at Hulger's unfinished landscaping. In her opinion, the empty concrete fishpond resembled a giant diaphragm, which complemented the stunted marble shaft that was supposed to support an ornate fountain. Sara had petitioned the estate lawyer—a close, personal friend of Hulger's who treated Sara like some greedy interloper—for the funds to complete the work, but he'd spouted something about long-term capital investments overriding short-term needs. Feeling utterly intimidated, she hadn't even bothered asking for help with the gutters.

Sara pressed down on the handlebar of the stroller, leaning Brady far enough back to look up at her. *"Whee,"* she said, pushing him over the speed bump. His high-pitched chortle made her heart swell. She loved the sound of his laugh. Her favorite time of the day was his bath. Invariably she'd wind up soaked, but it didn't matter because they'd laugh from start to finish.

"Fas," Brady demanded. "Mommygofas."

She took two quick steps. "This fast?"

He shook his head, his curls dancing. "Mo'fas."

She sped up. "This fast?"

He leaned forward, pushing his little body back and forth as if his movement could increase the speed. "Mo'fast."

His reward for saying the word right was an all-out run, which lasted until Sara became winded. Brushing her bangs out of her eyes, she hauled in a deep gulp of air. "No mo'fast. Mommy tired."

With a slower pace, she walked to the market, singing a silly song for Brady. *"When you're happy and you know it, shake your feet…"*

Brady's fourteen-dollar sneakers bounced just above the pavement. "Another 'short-term' need, I suppose," she muttered under her breath. *I wonder whether that lawyer would manage if he had my income instead of his.*

BO SQUEEZED OFF THE LAST of his exposures. Even through a telescopic lens, he could tell Sara looked tired, but the shots of her laughing as she pushed the kid in his stroller ought to get Ren's attention. With her hair pulled back in a ponytail, she looked like a teenager. Not exactly sex-goddess stuff, but he'd included a few shots of her nicely shaped legs displayed by snug denim shorts, for good measure.

After a stop at the one-hour processing lab, he could wash his hands of this job. It was one thing to tail a stranger, but for some reason he didn't think of Sara that way. Bo blamed that on her open, friendly manner. He had a feeling Ren would like Sara, too, but Bo doubted the feeling would be mutual once Sara found out about Ren and her sister.

Bo shook his head sadly. He wasn't the kind of guy who believed in happy endings, but this one looked worse than most.

CHAPTER THREE

THE FOLLOWING WEDNESDAY EVENING, Bo parked the Mazda a block-and-a-half from the bookstore, then hunkered down to wait. The Unturned Gentlemen's reading group was due to begin in fifteen minutes. His stomach rumbled—a two-front nervous rumble.

First, the more time he spent in Sara Carsten's company, the more Bo admired her. The duplicity of befriending her while running a background check seemed shoddy, but the longer Bo was around Brady, the more convinced he was that the little boy was part-Bishop.

Granted, Bo knew squat about kids, but Brady had an imperious manner that shouted, *"I'm important!"* Pure Babe, some Ren.

The second source of anxiety stemmed from the slim paperback resting on the seat beside him. He couldn't decide if he was more amazed by the fact that he'd actually read the thing or that he'd enjoyed it.

A rap on his passenger window startled Bo, until he saw the smiling face of Sara Carsten, who was bending down to look at him. *Busted,* he groaned silently. He picked up his volume of *Endurance: Shackleton's Incredible Voyage,* then opened the door and hauled himself to his feet.

"Hi, Bo. I'm so glad you could make it. Did you like the book?" Sara asked. At her side, a far less cordial Claudie watched him warily.

"Yeah," he admitted. "I liked it. Half the time I couldn't believe it was true, but no writer would be that cruel to his hero, right?"

Sara sobered. "True. Real life's often bleaker than fiction."

Claudie snorted. "The guy was a jerk. He deserved what he got. Why the f—heck would anybody go to Antarctica in the first place?"

"Challenge. Adventure. Accomplishment," Bo returned.

"Men things," she muttered. "Only men would be stupid enough to think those things mattered."

Before Bo could reply, Sara laughed and said, "Now, now, children, if you can't play nice, you don't get any cookies."

"Cookie?" a voice chirped from the navy-blue stroller.

Bo walked around the front of the car and squatted, eye-level with Brady. "Hey, kiddo, out for a ride?"

Brady kicked his feet and twisted to one side, shyly hiding his face in the soft fabric. "We had a picnic supper in Capitol Park. Brady walked all the way there, but petered out on the way home," Sara said.

"It was them squirrels that wore him out," Claudie added.

Sara poked at a crumpled bread wrapper stuffed in the top pocket of the stroller and explained, "He likes to chase the squirrels. Brady loves animals—but what little boy doesn't?"

"I bet *he* didn't," Claudie muttered.

Bo decided it was time to confront her. Rising, he faced her squarely. She barely came to the top of his shoulder, but she lifted her chin defiantly and met him eye-to-eye.

She wouldn't be bad looking, if she weren't so damn prickly, he thought, taking in her blousy shirt cinched at her very narrow waist by a black leather belt. Although her purple stretch pants showed every curve of her shapely legs and derriere, her running shoes were more Stairmaster than streetwalker.

"Night off?" he asked, and immediately wished he hadn't.

Her eyes narrowed viciously, and her red lips clamped together as if she'd tasted something bitter. "This ain't the safest area at night, so Keneesha and I take turns hanging out with Sara on book club nights. You got a problem with that?"

Not at all. In fact, he found it admirable. But he couldn't tell her that.

Sara relieved him of the problem. "I'm so lucky to have such great friends. Look what Claudie did to my hair. Isn't it fun?" She fluffed out her short-ened locks. The style made her hair seem fuller, and it bounced in a girlish manner near her jawline.

"I like it," Bo said honestly.

"Who cares?" Claudie rejoined waspishly.

"I do," Sara said. "I'm vain enough to be pleased when a handsome man tells me I look nice." A blush brought up the color in her cheeks. "Well, my *hair* looks nice."

Handsome? Bo nearly stumbled backward into the gutter, but he managed to get past the odd compliment in time to add, "You definitely look better than nice. I'd go so far as to say beautiful."

Claudie frowned at him and gave Sara a push. "You better open up. Your *gentlemen* don't like to be kept waiting."

Sara, who was dressed in a simple sleeveless, teal-green sheath that cupped her bosom, then fell straight as a plumb bob to the tops of her canvas deck shoes, looked at the utilitarian watch on her wrist and gave a little yelp. "Good point. Come along, Bo. You don't want to be late for your first meeting."

"He'll be there in a second, Sara J. I gotta discuss something with your new *gentleman*."

Sara tossed a concerned glance over her shoulder. "Don't hurt him, Claudie. He's a paying customer."

Bo swallowed. He didn't like the way Claudie was looking at him. Like he was a wad of gum on the bottom of her shoe. "Okay, say your piece."

Claudie waited until Sara was inside, then asked, "Are you a cop?"

Bo blinked, astounded by her perceptiveness. "No."

"You move like a cop. You're always asking questions like a cop. If you're not a cop, then what are you?"

A PI looking into ruining your friend's life. The thought made his stomach heave, nearly recycling his hastily eaten burrito.

He moved past her, noticing for the first time how fragile she seemed. *How'd you end up on the streets?* he wanted to ask. Instead, he said, "Just a guy killing time 'til I get a job, but jobs ain't easy to come by when you got a record.'' He was good at improvising.

''What kind of record?''

D.U.I. in college. ''None of your business,'' he said shortly, walking away. She dogged his heels, step for step, but stopped half a block from the bookstore. Reluctantly, Bo slowed, then turned around.

''I don't know if I believe you, but I don't really give a flying you-know-what. Keneesha and me look out for our friends, and Sara is off-limits to all losers,'' she said, her tone ominous. ''She wouldn't be interested in you anyways.''

Bo had no intention of making a play for Sara—no matter how cute she looked with her new haircut—but he didn't like being told what to do. He'd had enough of that growing up. ''Oh, really? And why is that?''

Claudie waited until the man ahead of them was through the door of the bookstore before she said in a low voice, ''Because she's…gay.''

Bo's mouth dropped open. ''Bullshit,'' he sputtered. ''I don't believe you.''

Her eyes narrowed. ''Well, she is.''

Before he could reply, Sara poked her head out the door and motioned to him. ''I need him, Claudie. The group's starting. Besides, this is your night off.''

Bo's face heated up, even though he could tell by her tone, Sara was teasing. His only satisfaction came from seeing Claudie's face flush with color, too.

SARA TUNED OUT the low rumble of masculine voices emanating from the far corner of the bookstore. Years earlier, before Hank had died, she'd hauled in a couple of old couches Julia was throwing out and some funky pole lamps to create a "reading room." Hank had called it a waste of space, but had let her have her way. Although he never admitted it, sales went up—and the reading room stayed.

Closing her eyes, Sara gently rocked Brady back and forth. If she let herself, she could drift off to sleep, too. She'd been up since five, trying to figure out how to pay for the repairs needed on Julia's house.

"Can I put him down for you?" a voice asked softly.

Sara opened her own eyes to a pair of remarkable blue ones, as deep a hue as the pair she played peek-a-boo with every morning—only this pair was attached to a stranger. A very handsome stranger, who seemed full of concern for her.

That by itself was odd, but the sudden, shocking quickening of her senses left her speechless. In answer to his question, all she could do was shake her head.

"He looks heavy. Are you sure?" His voice was cultured, rich as honey and faintly melodic. Its basic vibration caught her somewhere between her breastbone and her belly button and radiated outward in the strangest way.

She rocked forward, intending to rise, but her knees felt insubstantial, as if they might crumple if she put any weight on them. He seemed to sense this, and plucked Brady from her arms as if by magic. He didn't hesitate for a second but smoothly transferred the sleeping child to the playpen with such fluidity that Brady didn't even stir.

Sara put her hand to her chest as if to capture Brady's warmth a second longer. Tears rushed to her eyes for absolutely no reason.

"He's a handsome boy," the stranger said.

"Thank you." Sara looked at him as he stood a few steps back from the crib. Suddenly she felt a deep primal urge to push him away. She rushed to cover Brady with a knitted throw that Keneesha had made for him.

Sara straightened, forcing herself not to be intimidated by the man's size or beauty. And he *was* gorgeous. His thick, wavy autumn-brown hair had a carefree quality that made her want to touch it. His skin was a healthy tan, not too dark, not too pale.

"Are you here for the group?" The inanity of her question struck her the second she took in his fine, navy pinstriped trousers, perfectly creased above Italian leather shoes. Even without a tie and unbuttoned at the collar, his smoke-gray shirt made a fashion statement: wealthy.

He shook his head. "No, I'm supposed to meet a friend, but I got here a little early. Do you mind if I look around?"

The bookstore owner in her wanted to offer him free reign, but some other part of her remained uneasy. She tried attributing her qualms to his proximity and his maleness, but somehow that wasn't enough. She had a store full of males, and none of them made her senses peak like this man.

"Be my guest," she said, faking a smile.

When he stepped away, she let out a long, silent sigh and turned to her desk. She had a hundred things to keep her occupied while the men talked, but couldn't for the life of her recall a single one. She was about to sit down, when the stranger called to her, "Have you read this one?"

His soft, husky tone made tingles run up her skin. Rubbing her bare arms—Sara told herself it was rude to ignore him—she walked to the cardboard display case holding the latest release from a popular, prolific writer.

"No, I'm not really a fan of horror genre."

He seemed surprised by her frankness. A blush warmed her cheeks. *Smart move. Knock a potential sale to a potential customer.*

"I once heard a fifty-eight-year-old man accused of killing his eighty-year-old parents say the reason he hacked them to death with a butcher knife was that they wanted to move into a rest home and he would have had to get a job." His serious, contemplative tone took her by surprise.

"Are you a psychologist?" Her first guess would have been politician.

A smile tugged at the corner of his thin, masculine lips, suggesting a dimple in his left cheek. "It sometimes feels that way. I'm a judge."

Sara reflexively took a step back. *A judge.* The word conjured up memories of a time she wanted to be excommunicated from her consciousness.

She started to turn away, but his next words stopped her.

"In law school they tried to prepare us for some negativity." He flashed her a beguiling, boyish grin. "Do you know the difference between a catfish and a lawyer?"

Sara shook her head, intrigued by the humor in

his tone and the oh-so-human crinkles at the corners of his eyes.

"One's a scum-sucking bottom feeder. The other's a fish."

Sara tried not to smile, but did, anyway.

Oddly, his smile faded. "The antipathy changes when you become a judge," he said. "It doesn't go away—it just becomes more…judicious."

The wistfulness of his tone caught Sara off guard. The only judge she'd ever met stood out in her memory as a Wizard of Oz kind of character. A big head and commanding voice, passing judgment on things he didn't understand.

"I'm sure it's not an easy job, in fact, I can't imagine one I'd want less."

Instead of being put off by her opinion, the man stepped around the display, bringing himself closer to Sara. It made sense since they were speaking in library-level whispers, but crazy alarms went off in her head, obscuring his reply.

"It wasn't high on my list, either, but when the governor asked me to fill a vacant slot, I felt I had to accept."

Normally, Sara might have credited his amiability to good manners and responded accordingly, but for some reason her long-simmering resentment over the justice system chose that moment to erupt. "You're talking politics. I'm talking human lives. What makes you—or anyone for that matter—think you're capable of deciding someone else's fate? Doesn't that constitute supreme ego?"

His brows sank together in a more attractive way than Sara wanted to admit. "No, I don't think so. Law limits a judge's powers. Any judgment is based on evidence, and the law as it applies to that individual case.''

''But how can you read a few lines on a sheet of paper or listen to two over-priced lawyers talk for ten minutes, then decide a person's fate? Not everyone who breaks the law is a bad person,'' she added in an even softer voice.

His blue eyes were tempered with compassion, as if he knew she was speaking of herself. ''I believe a person who breaks the law and pays his or her debt to society is a better person for it. The ones who break the law—from shoplifters to congressmen—and go unpunished are the losers. They have nothing to build on but guilt. What kind of legacy is that?'' he asked.

His words touched her, as did his tone and some elusive nuance in his manner, something that made her think he might actually be capable of knowing her without judging her. How crazy was that?

''Ren?'' a voice croaked.

Sara blinked, dissolving the mesmerizing connection between them.

The stranger straightened with such unexpected hauteur that Sara had to work at keeping her mouth from hanging open. He suddenly looked like a judge, not just some handsome man lending a sympathetic and understanding ear to her old grievances. Sara's heart boomed in her chest—what had come over her?

''Hello, Bo,'' he said, turning to face Sara's newest recruit. Bo hurried forward, displaying considerable shock at seeing his friend.

''What are you doing here?'' Bo demanded.

''I had to work late and I remembered you were

going to be here. I thought we could grab a drink when it's over.''

Sounds plausible, Sara thought, *but it's not the truth.*

Bo squinted at his friend a moment longer, then looked at Sara. She read something sad in his eyes. Anxious to help, she reached out to pat his hand, which gripped his book like a buoy. ''It's a very informal group, Bo. You can leave anytime. Besides, there's always next week,'' she said. ''Did they tell you they're switching to weekly meetings? What do you think? Do you want me to get you the next book?''

His gaze flickered to his friend, whose grin provoked a snarling ''Sure.''

Confused by the antipathy between the two, Sara pulled back her hand. ''Well…um, great. Stay put, and I'll be right back.'' She tossed a semi-smile in the judge's direction, then dashed to her storeroom. She didn't understand what was going on any more than she could explain what had come over her, but Sara cultivated new readers like flowers in a garden; she wasn't about to let this one wither on the vine. Not without a fight.

REN EYED THE BOOK in his friend's hand, damn glad it wasn't a gun. Prudently, he backed up a step, which also afforded a better view of Sara as she hurried toward a doorway marked Employees Only. His gaze followed the lithe form in the pale green dress. She moved quickly but with grace, back straight. Bo's last photos showed her to possess a very shapely body with sleek calves and a trim derriere, but her business dress was of Shaker simplicity.

"What the hell is this about?" Bo growled, taking a step closer.

Ren raised his hand defensively—not that it would have done any good if Bo Lester took it in his head to beat him senseless. Ren had seen him in action more than once during Bo's drinking years. "Pure impulse. I can't explain it. I guess I needed to get it over with."

"You could have warned me."

Ren shook his head. "I didn't know myself. I was supposed to meet Eve for dinner—she took the day off to drive her agent to the San Francisco airport, but she called from her car. Some big toxic spill up near Lake Shasta. I started home, then changed my mind."

Ren had only intended to peek inside the store, but something had come over him the instant he saw Sara Carsten—eyes closed, lips whispering a lullaby, rocking the sleeping child. The image was so ecumenical, so Madonna-like, that he felt drawn inside as if propelled by a force outside his body.

And then Ren took the biggest leap of faith in his life. He'd picked up the baby. A child that could be his own flesh and blood. It was an idea so staggering and life-altering that he should have run in the other direction, but holding that compact little body seemed the most natural thing in the world.

"Let's get one thing straight. You hurt her and you'll regret it." The threat was so serious, so unexpected, all Ren could do was nod, as Sara hurried to join them, a cardboard box in her arms.

"Sorry 'bout the wait. I've been hoarding these

so long I couldn't remember where I put them." As she neared, she faltered a step as if sensing the primitive, masculine energy between them.

She set the carton on a display table and picked up one small paperback. "The title is *A.P.B.* It's a little police procedural—the first in a series. The rest of the group voted for something light this time."

Bo put out his hand. "I like crime novels. The good guys always win. The bad guys either end up dead or in jail. Right?" He shot a pointed look at Ren.

She glanced from Bo to Ren. "Umm...yes."

Ren regretted causing her added disquiet. "My friend's not a big reader," he said, picking up a book. "I can't tell you how great it is that you've been such a positive influence on him."

One slender brow lifted. "Bo may not read a lot, but he must like books. He's been here pretty often."

"Oh?" Ren asked.

She nodded. "In fact, the first time he came in was to ask about a rare book for a friend." She clapped her hand over her lips, a blush claiming her cheeks. "This is your friend, isn't it. The rare book collector. I've ruined the surprise, haven't I?"

Bo seemed momentarily taken aback, but he recovered. "Actually, this *is* that friend, but since I'm not sure he deserves a Christmas gift this year, don't lose any sleep over it, okay?"

She was obviously puzzled by Bo's response, but chose not to question him. Instead, she smiled. "My sister used to tell me I was notorious for speaking before my brain could catch up with my mouth."

The word *sister* caught Ren by surprise, and he

almost missed a step as he followed her to the counter. Now would be the perfect time to segue into that subject, but he found himself mute. So, apparently, was his private investigator.

While Bo paid for his new book, Ren studied the child sleeping so peacefully in the playpen behind Sara's desk. The little boy had turned slightly, curled protectively around a stuffed elephant he'd somehow found in his sleep. This image, as much as the one of Sara rocking the baby, wrapped itself around Ren's heart and squeezed.

"What's the baby's name?" he asked, not having known he was going to.

"Brady," Sara answered guilelessly.

She glanced over her shoulder and smiled. Ren, who was studying her face, saw something that had been missing from her photographs, even the ones from Sunday afternoon. A luminous quality that enhanced Sara Carsten's quiet beauty.

"Brady," he repeated. "That's…different."

She flashed him a grin that made him blink. "You're very diplomatic. Of course, that probably comes with the job. My sister, Brady's mother, had the name picked out even before she knew she was having a boy, but she could never decide on a middle name."

The duplicity of his inquiry made his throat dry and his jaw ache. "You're his aunt," he said, as if not framing it as a question could absolve the guilt he was going to feel if he took this inquiry forward. Since Armory, his lawyer, wasn't due back from Hawaii until tomorrow night, Ren had put off formulating a legal strategy.

Her lovely face changed. In sorrow it became vulnerable. "My sister died," Sara said simply. "She was killed in an accident, but she left me Brady."

Tears glistened in her eyes. Hazel, not temptress-green, but beautiful nonetheless. *And I thought she was plain.*

When she looked down to count Bo's change, Bo shot Ren a dark look. It hadn't been easy convincing Bo to stay on the job, but Ren's promise to approach the matter slowly had helped. His impulsive decision tonight might have jeopardized things.

"Well, there you go," she said, tucking the book in a sack. "Thanks, Bo. I'm glad you came. And it was…um, interesting talking with you…"

"Ren Bishop," he added. "It's Lawrence, actually, but only my mother calls me that."

He held out his hand, and she took it, just a trifle reluctantly. Her hand was small, her grip slightly reserved. "Sara Carsten," she said, dropping his hand to reach for a card from a plastic basket beside the cash register. Her blush told him she'd used that as an excuse not to touch him any longer.

Ren took the card she offered. "I don't carry first editions," she said. "But I might be able to help if you tell me what you're looking for."

Ren was within a heartbeat of telling her the whole sordid story when the sound of men's voices indicated the readers' group was over. "We gotta go," Bo said, starting away.

As Ren followed his friend out of the store, he glanced back once and was surprised to find Sara's gaze still on him. She had a puzzled expression on her face. He lifted his hand to wave goodbye, but Bo grabbed his arm in one plate-sized fist and dragged him bodily out the door.

"You bastard," Bo muttered, stalking off down the sidewalk. "There's a right way and a wrong way to do this."

Downtown's daytime hustle and bustle had given way to an empty-theater kind of quiet. Miniature lights peeked through the new-growth foliage of the well-pruned trees. A gold-hued street lamp spotlighted Ren's Lexus while ignoring Bo's Mazda one space ahead of it. The two cars seemed a metaphor for the contrast between their owners.

Ren stopped beside the Mazda. "This wasn't planned, Bo. It probably wasn't smart. But I needed to see him." *I held him—the child that might be my child.*

Suddenly Ren's knees felt disconnected from his body. He reached out to steady himself on the blistered hood of the car. "Is there a bar around here? I really could use a drink."

Ren's response seemed to take some of the heat out of Bo's anger. "Around the corner," he muttered, leading the way.

Bo didn't speak again until they were seated at a small table. After the waitress delivered a light beer and a cola, Bo said, "Okay, suppose you explain to me what happened tonight. I thought I was the inside guy, and you were going to let the suits make contact when we all decided the time was right."

Ren took a long draw on his beer. "I was in my office looking at the pictures...the ones you took Sunday." He paused, knowing there was no way to explain the sense of urgency that had been building in him ever since Bo had delivered the color photos of Sara and the child. Yes, he saw a resemblance in some of the shots, but this need to connect went deeper than that.

He shrugged. "It had to happen sometime, right?"

Bo took a sip of cola. "This means you're going forward with the paternity suit, doesn't it?"

Ren couldn't meet Bo's gaze. He didn't want his friend to guess the truth: that deep down, Ren wanted the child to be his. He *needed* the child to be his. As much as he loved Eve, Ren knew her career was her primary focus. It might be years before she was ready to have children, if ever. Ren was ready for fatherhood now.

"Do I have any choice, Bo? Would you walk away? Live the rest of your life wondering?"

Bo looked ready to argue, but in the end shook his head. "I guess not, but what about Sara?"

Ren's heart lifted, then fell oddly. He hadn't expected to like her, but he did.

"She's a good person and a wonderful mother," Bo said. "She doesn't deserve what this is going to do to her. It's bound to get messy. If she's smart, she'll scream bloody murder and hire some media shark like Steve Hamlin to make you squirm. Even if you ultimately win, you'll be scarred for life."

Ren took another swallow of beer. Bo's prediction threw him, but he pretended to shrug it off. "I wouldn't blame her for going on the offensive. She obviously loves the child, and I saw what mentioning her sister did to her." Ren's voice faltered; Sara's unshed tears had touched him deeply. "I don't want to hurt her, Bo, but I have to know. What if he's my kid?"

Ren didn't really expect Bo to understand. Bo's

relationship with his own father was practically non-existent. Ren doubted they'd exchanged more than a dozen words in the past year.

"Yeah, I get it. My old man may be a well-dressed rat, but I know he'd give his last dime to help me out," Bo said, surprising Ren with his insight.

Before Ren could respond, a voice said, "Don't tell me you actually have a friend."

To Ren's surprise, a woman in tight purple leggings and a blousy shirt pulled a chair from a neighboring table and straddled it, dropping her chin to the arched metal back. Her unsteady gaze flicked from Ren to Bo.

Bo groaned. "Go away, girl. Didn't you give me enough trouble earlier?"

"That's why I came over. To apologize." Her words were slightly slurred.

"Apologize for breaking my balls for nothing?"

Her eyelashes fluttered coquettishly. "Did I have my hand on your balls? I must have missed that."

This has to be one of the hookers. Claudie? And she's been drinking.

She turned her attention to Ren. "Oh, my, aren't you hunky—"

"You're off duty tonight, remember?" Bo barked.

"Working girls never pass up an opportunity to…work."

A sad little smile crossed her lips, and Ren was reminded of Sara's words. *How can you know the person behind the crime?* If Claudie were brought before him, what would he see?

"Not tonight, Claudie. Besides, he's taken," Bo told her.

"You could still introduce us. I don't bite. Well, I do, but it costs extra."

Ren put out his hand. "Ren Bishop."

"Claudine St. James. My friends call me Claudie," she said, giving him a suggestive look that came off totally fake. Ren decided he liked her pluckiness.

Bo coughed. "So what's the apology for, Claudie?"

She drew herself up fairly straight and said solemnly, "I told Keneesha what I told you, and she called me a dumb f—person. She said Sara would never forgive me if she found out, and I'd better tell you myself or she would."

Ren couldn't keep from asking. "Told him what?"

She shot him a poisonous look. "This is private. Just between the cookbook man 'n me."

"It's okay. Just say what you want to say." Bo brushed her arm with his fingertips.

Her automatic flinch made Ren's stomach clench. Men probably weren't very nice to her. He had heard his fair share of horror stories in the last two years; hers was probably no different.

"I lied," she said soberly—her intense scowl obviously a ruse to keep tears at bay. "Sara's not gay. I made that up."

"Hell, I knew that," Bo said gruffly. "I never believed you for a minute. You're a terrible liar."

"I am?"

"Yeah. And when you're that bad of a liar, it's

like it never happened, so just forget it.'' Bo rose and motioned for Ren to follow.

She stood, catching the edge of the table as if her equilibrium had been shaken. ''You know, cookbook man, you're not that bad, after all.''

''Cookbook man?'' Ren asked, as they exited the bar. He inhaled deeply, the brisk delta breeze a welcome change from the smell of stale beer and cigarette smoke.

Bo growled. ''When I was taking your damn pictures the first time, the best view was from the cookbook aisle.''

Ren studied his friend in the light from the neon Budweiser sign. Bo was a successful investigator who traveled all over the world, but in his private life he was a recluse who favored fishing and satellite TV over dating. Obviously, these women had somehow touched him. Ren didn't question his friend's loyalty, but he wondered if his decision to pursue the paternity issue would change their friendship.

They walked in silence. Ren used his remote to unlock his car. The double *beep-beep* pierced the quiet. ''Bo, this isn't malicious,'' he said somberly. ''I wish there were some other way, but I sure as hell don't know what it is.''

Bo looked skyward. ''Yeah, I know.''

Ren waited a minute, then asked, ''Do you have that background information on Sara yet? I'd like to read it before I see Armory on Friday morning.''

Bo unlocked his car the old-fashioned way. The door gave an unhappy groan when he opened it. ''It's at home. I wasn't expecting your surprise appearance tonight, remember?''

Before Ren could reply, Bo climbed into his car. Ren watched him start it and pull away. Obviously, Bo didn't understand the primal urge that had pulled Ren through the bookstore door. Ren wasn't sure he understood it himself.

He glanced up the street. A yellow glow spilled from the windows of the bookstore. *Why is she still there? She should be home, tucking Brady in bed.* Ren longed to walk back to the store to make sure she was okay, but the lawyer in him warned against it. *You're poised to change her life forever. And she's never going to forgive you.*

SARA EASED BRADY'S sleeping form to her left shoulder to better manipulate the key. She'd waited as long as she could for Claudie to return, but still had a long drive ahead of her.

"I'll do that," someone said behind her.

Sara recognized her friend's voice and immediately gave a huge sigh of relief. "Thank God, you're okay! I was worried about you," she said, giving the younger woman a quick, one-armed squeeze. The smell of alcohol and cigarette smoke made her recoil. "You are okay, aren't you?"

Claudie kept her head down as she took the key and finished locking up. "Yeah, I'm fine. Had one too many at Jake's, is all."

Sara's brows went up. "How come? You never drink."

Claudie handed her the keys with a look of profound weariness. "I drink. Just not when you're around. How else do you think someone like me lives with all this shit?" The last word was part whisper.

Sara put her arm around her friend's slim shoulders. "I didn't mean to sound condemning. I was just surprised. I know you're doing the best you can—so am I. That's why we're friends, remember?"

The two walked down the dark alley toward the employee parking lot. "Do you want to talk about what's bothering you?" Sara asked.

Claudie held her tongue until Sara had Brady strapped in his car seat in the back seat of her Toyota wagon. When Sara closed the door, Claudie melted to the curb like a marshmallow over an open flame. "I suck, big time," she wailed.

Sara sat beside her. "You don't mean that literally, do you?" she said, purposely injecting a spot of humor. Sara knew her friends liked to think of Sara as angelic, so her occasional forays into the ribald always cracked them up. This time the jest went over Claudie's head.

"I told the cookbook man you were gay," Claudie cried.

Sara grasped the odd confession immediately, but it took a second or two longer to figure out how she felt about it. Bo, her newest recruit, was a nice guy, but Sara felt no attraction to him. And even though she was attracted to his friend Ren Bishop, she'd never get involved with a judge, so what did it matter?

Sara shrugged. "Did he believe you?"

"No. I don't think the other guy did, either."

Sara's heart took an unwelcome jump. "The other guy? Tall? Wavy hair? Really handsome?"

Claudie looked at her strangely. "You met him?"

"He came into the store while he was waiting for Bo. Where'd you see him?"

"At the bar." Claudie turned to face Sara. "I 'fessed up like Keneesha told me. And Bo said he never believed me, anyway, because I was a terrible liar so it wasn't like what I said even counted. But Keneesha said a rumor like that could make trouble for you with Brady. If social services proved you were an unfit mother, they could take him away. They do that, you know."

Her solemn anguish touched Sara's heart. *Did that happen to you, my friend?* Sara wondered. She didn't ask; Claudine St. James never spoke of her past. Never. "Nobody's out there trying to take Brady away. Why would you worry about something like that?"

Claudie shook her head. "You know what life's like, Sara. Every time you get a sweet thing going, somebody comes along to mess it up."

An odd shiver passed through Sara's body. She prayed her friend was wrong. Life without Brady was unthinkable.

CHAPTER FOUR

REN SCANNED THE JAM-PACKED reception area located on the second floor of the courthouse. Potential jurors milled about waiting for instructions, praying, no doubt, for a quick release. To pick Bo out of such a crowd was like looking at a Where's Waldo? puzzle, Ren thought.

"So, what's the plan, Stan?" a voice asked beside him.

Ren glanced to his right. Typical Bo. Baggy, tan canvas pants. Navy T-shirt with some engineering firm's logo on the breast pocket. Scruffy running shoes.

"Lunch," Ren said shortly. "Let's beat the mass exodus."

They took the stairs, hurrying past the uniformed guards at the entrance. Neither spoke until they reached the plaza.

"Where do you want to eat?" Ren asked, jogging down the concrete steps to the street.

Bo shrugged. "The noodle shop?"

The thought of food made Ren queasy, but the instant the white hand appeared on the stoplight, he took off—a sprinter in street shoes. Dodging slow-moving pedestrians, he hurried toward the J-street locale, not paying attention to Bo until his friend grabbed his arm and hauled him to a stop in the shadow of the Union Bank building.

"Slow down. Sara doesn't get back for another hour, and we need to give her time to get Brady down for his nap. Tell me what Mason said."

"I gotta give him credit," Ren answered. "He didn't even blink when I told him about Julia."

Armory Mason, Ren's lawyer, had been his father's closest friend. Telling Armory of his affair was almost as bad as confessing to his dad.

He'd called Bo right after the meeting with Armory. They'd discussed the timing of this upcoming confrontation, and he'd asked Bo to accompany him to smooth the way with Sara.

"I'm a little nervous," Ren admitted.

"Well, duh. Who wouldn't be? But you gotta eat." Bo grinned. "Actually, I gotta eat. I don't care about you. You want moral support—it's gonna cost you lunch."

He started off at a more sedate pace which Ren matched. The four blocks to the café brought them closer to Sara's bookstore, as well. *Sara*. He'd thought about her almost nonstop since Wednesday night. Sara…and Brady.

Earlier, Armory had confirmed what Ren had deduced on his own. Before there could be a custody suit, they had to determine paternity. In other words, he needed a DNA test.

"I suggest you talk to the aunt first," Armory had told Ren. "You say Bo's obtained the child's medical records so you know the little boy's blood type is *O*, which is the same as yours. But that's a very common type. In fact, I'm type *O*, and we both know I'm not *your* father."

Ren smiled politely at Armory's attempt at levity.

"Perhaps if you explain the situation, she'll be agreeable. If she's unreasonable, I'm sure we can get a court order, but that will take time."

Unreasonable, Ren thought. What constituted "reasonable" when a child was involved?

Armory looked thoughtful. "You said she's a single mother. Do you know what her financial needs are? Maybe she'd be receptive to an offer of some sort of monetary incentive."

Ren knew his lawyer was only doing his job. But Armory didn't know Sara Carsten. Of course, Ren didn't know her, either, but he didn't think she'd take a penny from him. The only way she might consider his request was if she believed it was in Brady's best interest.

At the small restaurant, both men ordered teriyaki noodle bowls—Bo's with chicken, Ren's with broccoli. A smiling Asian woman took Ren's money, then told them "Number twenty-two." After filling their drinks, they sat down at a small table. Ren chose a chair facing the large, plate-glass window. Foot traffic surged and ebbed on the sidewalk. People carried take-out meals to the park across the street.

Does Sara ever take Brady to that park? Ren wondered.

Bo kicked Ren's shins to get his attention. "Lordy, they must have loved you in court today. Let any murderers go free?"

"All I did today was listen to lawyers with motions. Boring, long-winded motions." He sighed. "I don't know what's wrong with me, Bo. I used to love that part of the game—finding the best argument to prove my point. It took me back to my high-school debate team days.''

Bo snorted. ''Don't tell me you were that kind of geek.''

''It was fun. Besides, the debate team got to travel all over the state.''

''So did the football team, but we didn't have to wear sissy jackets and ties.''

Ren couldn't help looking down at his Ralph Lauren suit. He poked his paper napkin at a faint spot on his red-and-navy striped tie. The lax dress code was one of the things he missed most about his days as an environmental lawyer. Tucked in a basement, no one had cared what he wore. Once he went public, dressing became a contest that both Babe and Eve insisted on his taking part in.

When their number was announced, Bo rose. He returned moments later with two steaming bowls. The aroma tempted Ren despite his unsettled stomach. Ren half listened to Bo's tale of his struggle with an elusive catfish that had gotten away, but his nerves were slowly getting the better of him.

''Am I doing the right thing, Bo?''

Bo chewed, appearing thoughtful. He looked at Ren a long time before answering. ''I've been trying to put myself in your place, and I guess I don't see how you've got any choice. But I'm not sure Sara will see it that way.''

Ren's appetite vanished. He pushed his bowl aside and took a sip of iced tea.

''What else did Armory say?'' Bo asked. ''What are your chances of gaining custody if she fights?''

Ren shook his head and looked around, hoping Bo's words couldn't be overheard. ''Paternity issues

aren't his specialty. He's going to call a friend.''
Ren hated the idea of people talking about his life,
speculating about what made him do something as
foolish as having sex with a stranger.

''What did your mother say when you told her?''
Ren took a sip from his glass to avoid answering.
''You haven't told her yet, have you?''
He shook his head. ''I need to tell Eve, first.''
Bo stopped chewing. His look made Ren fidget
with his chopsticks, poking at a blob of spilled teriyaki sauce. ''I haven't seen her in over a week. She
took her agent wine-tasting in Napa last weekend,
and then she covered that big chemical spill up near
Shasta. This isn't the kind of thing you discuss on
the phone.''

Bo's expression said he recognized an excuse
when he heard one. ''I thought you were staying at
her place on weeknights,'' Bo said.

Ren stifled a sigh. While he and Eve had discussed moving in together, neither wanted to be the
person to make the move. Ren felt her condo was
too small, and she called his home a mausoleum.
''Off and on. She didn't want me around when her
agent was there.''

He couldn't stifle the bitter chord in his tone. Eve
had been so wrapped up in her plans, she didn't have
a clue about Ren's impending crisis. During one of
their infrequent phone conversations, she'd seemed
to pick up on his tension, but attributed it to lack of
sex.

''Don't worry, sweet thing,'' she'd told him. ''I'll
be home Friday night, then we'll have the whole
weekend to play. We could go back to Napa. I have
a coupon for a mud bath. Marcella loved it.''

Ren hadn't liked Marcella, Eve's agent; he'd found her pompous and demanding. Eve, who called her a cutthroat deal-maker, was hoping the woman could steer her career to bigger and better markets— maybe even network television.

"Hang tough, honey," Eve had told him before hanging up. "We'll be back on schedule in a day or two." Everything was a schedule to Eve. When life was on track, everyone was happy. Being off schedule meant chaos. What would a paternity suit do to Eve's elaborate and carefully considered plans?

"I'll tell her tonight," Ren said decisively. "First Sara, then Eve, then my mother." A good, logical order.

Ren didn't try to interpret Bo's look; instead, he swiped his friend's half-finished bowl of noodles and carried it to the busing area. "Hey, man, I'm not done," Bo complained.

"Close enough. Let's go."

Despite his grumbling, Bo followed Ren outside and plunged into the throng. A few doors down the block, they passed in front of the bar where they'd talked two nights earlier. "Hey, cookbook man," Ren called, when Bo got sidetracked by an attractive young brunette in a tight skirt, "I thought you liked blondes."

Bo frowned. "Don't call me that. Claudie does it to get under my skin. I stopped by the bookstore yesterday to pick up the new reading list, and she went on and on about my culinary prowess—only she made it sound like I was cooking in the bed-room." He shook his head. "For a high school drop-out, she's pretty snappy with the insults."

"How do you know she's a dropout?"

"Sara was quizzing her for the equivalency test when I was there. Sara says once Claudie has her GED, she'll be able to take some junior college courses and get off the streets permanently."

Ren paused. "Are you interested in her?"

Bo's face flushed red and he put on his sunglasses. "Of course not. She's a mixed-up kid, and I feel sorry for her, that's all."

They walked on in silence. A glance at his watch told Ren they were still too early, so he slowed his pace. A display in the window of an antique store caught his eye. "See that music box? Eve bought Babe one like it for Mother's Day."

Bo shrugged. "So?"

"She bought it for *me* to give Babe. Signed my name. Had it delivered. I got the bill this morning."

"How much?"

"That's not the issue. The point is, she didn't ask me first. She just did it."

Bo cocked his head. "Babe doesn't like music boxes?"

"It's not the music box." Ren sighed. "I might have picked it out myself. It's just…" He wasn't sure he could explain why this had him so pissed off. Eve was doing what she did best—organizing.

"Let me guess. You feel as if your life is out of your hands."

Surprised by Bo's insight, Ren turned. "I wouldn't go that far. I still have control over my life—" he ignored his friend's skeptical snort "—it's just that everything is a challenge with Eve. She has her agenda, and if you want to be involved you have to stay on schedule." *Right down to having sex,* he added silently.

Bo cuffed him lightly. "Hey, man, welcome to the real world. Eve's a modern woman. She makes good money. She's got the car, credit, connections. If you think about it, she doesn't really need you. You're...what's the word?"

"Superfluous?"

Bo snickered. "Yeah, that's what Claudie called me the other day. She said once doctors figured out how to make test-tube babies, men were about as useful as tits on a boar."

Ren leaned one shoulder against the building and squinted at Bo, who had a bemused look on his face. "What about love?"

Bo's arched look summed up his opinion on that matter.

"Well, what about family, then? Children? Continuity?"

Bo shrugged. "I said the same thing to Claudie, and she pointed to a magazine with Rosie O'Donnell on the cover. Single and just adopted her third kid. Traditional families may not be a thing of the past, but there's a lot of single parents out there doing a better job than some of the dysfunctional mom-and-pop families."

Bo rolled his shoulders and took a step away. "The point is, you're engaged to a career woman and you haven't even told her you might have a kid. Eve's a beautiful woman, but she doesn't strike me as the motherly type. Am I right?"

Ren felt himself tense. "We've talked about kids. Nothing specific, but..." He tried to recall Eve's exact words on the subject. Something to the effect of "Everybody wants kids, right? Someday. But I'd have to be at a secure place in my career. Television viewers have short attention spans and very little loyalty."

Bo began walking but stopped. "Have you asked yourself what you'd do with Brady if Eve dropped out of the picture? I mean, Sara's a terrific single mother. Do you think you could do that well?"

Ren had wondered the same thing, and he wasn't nearly as confident as he wanted to be. "I don't know, but I had a great role model growing up, right?"

Bo's attitude softened and he smiled. "Yep, that's true. They don't come much better than Larry."

Ren's father had taken Bo under his wing at a critical time in Bo's life. If not for Larry's intervention, Bo might never have kicked the booze.

The two walked in silence until they reached the entrance of the bookstore, where a circular emblem two feet in diameter and inlaid with mosaic tiles in the shape of an open book was imbedded in the sidewalk. Ren hadn't noticed it before. "I like that."

"Sara had it put in. She thought it would be a way to lure people. She said most people walk with their heads down, and they don't see the sign overhead unless they're looking for a bookstore. The mosaic catches their attention and makes them look up."

Before Ren could comment, Bo yanked open the door and marched inside. "Lucy, I'm home," he called in a pathetic imitation of Ricky Ricardo.

Ren squared his shoulders and took a deep breath. Best-case scenario, he told himself, she won't call the police and have me arrested. Worst-case? Years of litigation, family profiles, home studies, lawyers, judges, he thought, sighing. But in all honesty, he couldn't blame Sara. Any good mother would go to great lengths to protect her child.

THE TINKLE OF THE BELL over the door seemed to set off a frenzy of activity—an anthill gone mad, Ren thought as he stepped inside. Claudie and three strangers, two men and a large, colorfully dressed black woman, were moving chairs, tables and display racks to one spot, then picking them up and moving again. In the center of this chaos stood Sara, Brady in her arms.

At least, Ren thought it was Sara, although she certainly looked different. Instead of a shapeless dress, she wore a fitted suit of silver-green with a white silk blouse, shimmering hose and black pumps. Her hair was pulled back by a woven metallic band that emphasized her high cheekbones and arched brows.

"Hi, Bo," she called, glancing over her shoulder. She acknowledged Ren with an extra widening of her eyes, but turned away when Claudie called her name.

"Where do you want this one, Sara J?"

"Over there." Sara pointed to the far wall, below a poster that read, Read Now, Before You Forget How.

"What's going on?" Bo asked, walking to her side. Ren followed, unable to keep from cataloguing the changes he saw in her. Instead of soft and demure, this was a woman who knew what she wanted and had no trouble voicing her demands.

"Move the table a little more to the left," she

ordered a harried-looking gray-haired man. "The gal who called said the more spacious a place looks, the more inviting it is. We want to invite people here."

When the change was made to her apparent satisfaction, she turned to Bo and Ren. "Isn't this exciting? The camera crew should be here any minute."

Her breathless, flushed excitement made her look younger. Her enthusiasm lifted Ren's spirits, making him want to grin, even though this wasn't at all what he'd expected to find. "What camera crew?"

"*Channel Eight News.* They're doing a feature on downtown businesses." Her cheeks bloomed with color. "I told Claudie we'll be lucky to get a sound bite—but every bite helps."

Ren's stomach turned over. "Channel Eight, huh."

She shifted Brady to her other hip. "Eve Masterson herself. It's so exciting."

Ren and Bo exchanged looks. *Exciting* was not Ren's first choice of adjective.

"Hi, Brady," Ren said, smiling at the little boy who promptly buried his face in his mother's shoulder.

"Don't be shy, honey," Sara coaxed. "Can you say hello?"

Brady shook his head. His hair was lighter than Ren's and held a faint tinge of red, but the springy waves seemed so familiar that Ren almost reached out to touch them. Before he could, however, Brady squirmed to be let down. When Sara bent over to set the little boy on his feet, Ren couldn't help noticing the way her skirt outlined her shape.

"How's that?" Claudie asked, flashing a critical look from Bo to Ren. She handed Sara something, then pointed to the wall behind the coffee bar where a slightly lopsided banner was hanging.

"Wonderful," Sara exclaimed. "Is that the last of the reading posters?"

Claudie rolled her eyes. "Lord, I hope so."

Sara gave her a light cuff on the shoulder, then sent her off in another direction. To Ren, she said, "Are you here for moral support?"

He didn't understand the question, but before he could ask, she was called to deal with another crisis. Over her shoulder she called, "You're welcome to browse, of course, but we're closing down the register until after the interview."

"Actually..." Ren stopped when he felt a warm little body attach itself to his right leg. Smiling, he looked down. Brady had wrapped both arms around Ren's thigh like a monkey. He squeezed his arms tight, making a sort of grunting sound.

Ren's laugh was aborted by a low bark of agony that stopped everyone mid-stride. "Argh..." He reached for his leg just as the little boy jumped back, a satisfied smirk on his face. "He bit me!"

No one moved for a full five seconds, then Sara leapt between Ren and Brady as if separating two prizefighters. "Brady," she cried, dropping to one knee. "Did you bite?"

The little boy's face immediately registered his mother's distress. Instant tears appeared at the rims of his Delft-blue eyes. His bottom lip unfurled like a flower petal. Before she could reach for him, Brady darted away and crawled under her desk.

"I am so sorry," she said, rising. "He's never done that before. I can't…" She shook her head.

Ren rubbed the throbbing spot on his thigh. "Don't worry about it," he said, but a dozen thoughts clamored for attention. *Does he hate me already? Do I really want to be a father?*

Sara lightly touched his sleeve, then dashed after Brady. "He's had all his shots," she called before ducking behind the desk.

Ren looked at the other spectators. The older man picked up a Raiders cap from the counter and headed for the door. "Guess you don't need me no more, Sara. See you Wednesday. 'Bye, Bo."

"See ya, Frank," Bo called, as the man left.

A tall, good-looking man in a white shirt rolled down his sleeves and lifted his suit coat from a chair. "Sara, love, I'm leaving, too, but I'll stop by after work to watch you on TV, okay?"

Sara's head popped up above the desk. "Great, Daniel. Thanks so much for everything. See ya tonight."

Ren exchanged nods with the man as he left.

Claudie finished straightening a display, then walked to Ren. "I'd be happy to check out that bite for you if you want to take off your pants."

"No, thank you. I'll be fine."

"Honey, you *are* fine," the large black woman said, pushing Claudie aside. "My name's Keneesha. I'd give you one of my business cards but I'm out right now."

"Better not," Bo said, giving the woman a dry look. "The man's a judge."

She eyed Ren skeptically before turning to Bo.

"Cookbook man, what are you doing here?" Keneesha asked.

"I asked him to come," Sara said, joining the little group. Brady was plastered to her, his head pressed against her chest. "Remember? I wanted some of the readers to be here in case Miss Masterson had time to interview any of the Unturned Gentlemen."

By the look of horror on Bo's face, Ren felt it safe to assume Bo had forgotten about that little detail.

"And Claudie, you could talk about the books you've been reading to prepare for the equivalency test," Sara told her.

"Oh, no. In fact, I just remembered something I gotta do right this minute. What about you, Kee? You wanna be on television?"

Keneesha's eyes grew big. "F—Forget that action. I'm outa here."

Sara's face fell. "Come on, don't go. I need you. I can't face that woman alone. Claudie..."

Ren turned to watch both women scurry through the door. He realized at the same instant that Bo had disappeared, as well.

Sara looked momentarily dismayed, then sighed and hugged Brady. "Oh, well, we can do this, can't we?" she whispered softly. "But first we have to apologize to Mr. Bishop." She looked at Ren, as if to confirm his name.

Ren couldn't help smiling. She looked so earnest, so fresh and real. "Please, call me Ren. You, too, Brady, even though we haven't been formally introduced."

He tried to keep his tone light, but could tell she

was embarrassed. She stepped closer and turned so Brady's face was visible. The child immediately turned his head the other way. She bent her head and said in a low voice, "Brady, you need to apologize. We don't bite. Ever. You hurt Ren and you need to say you're sorry."

The boy turned his head and looked at Ren. The child's blue eyes—a dark, almost sapphire color—were luminescent with tears. He blinked twice and rattled off a string of gibberish made more unintelligible by the wet fist he kept in his mouth.

As the long explanation continued, Ren looked from Brady to Sara—her heart plainly on view as she watched the little boy's animated apology. Sara wiped her son's tears and kissed the top of his head.

"Very nice, love," she said. "You're a very brave boy to admit when you made a mistake," she told him, then looked to Ren. "I don't suppose you got that." He shook his head, mesmerized by the connection he saw and felt between the two. "Brady said he was sorry. Your pants are nice but they don't taste good."

She smiled. "I think he wanted to touch your pants and just got carried away. I'm very sorry. We both are."

She might have said more, but at that moment the door opened and a battering ram of mobile news equipment surged inward. At the hub of the onslaught stood Eve, who scanned the interior in a three-second sweep before focusing on Ren and Sara.

Eve's beautiful face, an exotic combination of Mediterranean skin tone, English cheekbones and Indo-European eyes, lit up with surprise and pleasure. "Ren," she cried, pushing past her colleagues. "What are you doing here? Did you call and get my schedule from Gloria?" Gloria was her secretary, with whom Ren spoke quite regularly—*too* regularly.

She gave him a brief squeeze, being careful not to mess her makeup. Her trademark waist-length blue-black hair shimmered beneath the high, overhead spotlights. "Actually," he said, drawing her to one side just as a young man with an armful of electrical cords bounced by, "I came with Bo, who, it appears, has developed sudden-onset stage fright."

The noise in Ren's head had little to do with the chaos Eve and her crew had brought to the bookstore. His instinct was to take the coward's way out, just as his ex-best friend had. "Um, Eve, have you met Sara Carsten?" he asked, taking a step back. "She's the owner of this fine establishment. The person you're here to interview."

"Hi," Sara said. "This is my son, Brady." Brady perked up with all the activity and looked around like a turtle poking his head out of a shell. "I'm afraid my baby-sitters have all disappeared. I...um..."

"No problem," Ren said, seeing his chance to melt into the background. "I'll take care of him."

He snatched Brady out of Sara's arms before she could protest. Brady looked too surprised to cry. "Don't worry, big guy. No hard feelings. Let's play."

One quick look over his shoulder as he walked to the carpeted children's area told him both women were speechless. But Ren doubted he could count on that kind of luck for long.

SARA DECIDED if anyone asked her what it was like to be interviewed by Eve Masterson, she could sum it up in one word: *smooth.* Watching a professional as experienced and polished as Eve was like watching a surgeon at work.

Sara had no trouble answering Eve's questions, except when they turned personal. When Eve asked her something about Brady's father, Sara deflected the query without thinking. She'd answered enough probing questions after Julia's accident, when reporters were trying to make more out of the story than was there. "I'm a single parent," Sara said, nervously manipulating the small tube of glue Claudie had handed her.

Eve nodded, her long black hair moving like an exotic animal. "It must be quite difficult raising your son alone while running a business. How do you do it?"

Sara wondered if she detected a hint of condescension in the woman's tone, but for some reason Eve's attention had shifted toward the reading area, a pensive look crossing her brow. "Nothing in life is easy," Sara answered. "I'm lucky because I can keep my son with me while I work, and he's exposed to something I love—books. I read to him and patrons' children whenever I can."

Eve's eyes were the darkest brown Sara had ever seen. On television she was beautiful; up close, China-doll perfect. When Eve gestured toward the coffee bar, Sara spotted a very large, glittery diamond on her finger, which jogged Sara's memory. Something about a judge.

Eve Masterson and Judge Lawrence Bishop. Of course.

Sara's small, involuntary *peep* made Eve look at her intently. "Let's cut, fellas. I've got plenty here," she said, reaching behind her waist to remove some kind of remote microphone. Her tailored suit, a smart black gabardine imbued with tiny flecks of silver, would have looked severe on anyone else.

To Sara, she said, "Thank you. That was very nice. I'm particularly impressed with your reading groups. You have that in common with my fiancé." She glanced toward the play area where Ren and Brady sat. "Ren started a tutorial program in juvenile hall last year."

Her words confirmed what Sara had already guessed, making her feel all the more foolish about the steamy dream she'd had last night. Sara had tried to blame it on the *Braveheart* video she'd fallen asleep watching. Somehow her dream lover had changed from Mel Gibson into Ren Bishop.

"How well do you know Ren?" Eve asked, her reporter instincts undoubtedly making her home in on Sara's attraction to Eve's fiancé.

Sara started to set the woman straight, but a rather vivid image from her dream made Sara stutter, "We don't—he just—I…" Her cheeks turned hot.

Eve's focus moved to Ren, who sat cross-legged with Brady in his lap, their heads bent over a big, colorful book. "He looks pretty cozy with your son."

He does, doesn't he, Sara thought, flinching from the twinge in her chest. To Eve, she said candidly,

"That's probably because Brady bit him. Must be a guy thing."

As if sensing their observation, Ren looked up. Oddly, his gaze went to Sara first. His smile seemed ingenuous and a little worried. Sara's heart reacted in the strangest way, making her clasp the tube of glue to her breast defensively.

Eve started toward him but was waylaid by a tall man in a turban of dreadlocks. "Sorry, Eve, but we gotta run if you want this by six," he said, taking her arm.

Eve seemed torn. With a sigh, she called to Ren, "My place? Tonight?"

He nodded solemnly.

She blew him an air kiss then dashed away. "Thank you, Sara. It was…enlightening."

Bemused, Sara watched the door close. "Enlightening?" she repeated to herself, slipping the glue stick into the pocket of her jacket. Before she could decide whether to ask Ren what his fiancée had meant, the bell over the door tinkled. Three people strolled in, trying to look nonchalant. Only Keneesha managed to pull it off. She parked her rather large bottom on the corner of Sara's desk and said, "How'd it go?"

Bo and Claudie mumbled some kind of apology as they walked past Sara.

Sara put her hands on her hips and made a clucking sound. "Cowards," she teased. "I don't know what I'd have done if Ren hadn't entertained Brady." She shuddered in mock horror.

They stumbled over each other's excuses and apologies until Ren interrupted them. "If you're back for good, I'd like to borrow Sara a moment."

He passed Brady—who seemed totally at ease in Ren's arms—to Keneesha, then looked at Bo and asked, "Can the three of you manage the store for a few minutes?"

The seriousness of his tone made Sara's stomach turn over. "What's going on? Is something wrong?" Dire thoughts of lawsuits and legal horrors filled her head. Her panic must have shown on her face, because Bo leaned over and touched her shoulder. "It's okay, Sara. You can trust him."

That oblique endorsement puzzled her so much that Sara almost missed the fact Ren had taken her elbow and was escorting her toward the exit. When he let go to open the door, she balked. "Wait. This is crazy. I barely know you. Where are you taking me? I don't care what you do for a living—you can't just kidnap a person."

He tilted his head in a gentle, reassuring way. "I'll explain everything in a minute. I just don't want an audience."

Behind her, Sara heard Bo placating Claudie and Keneesha, who sounded poised for pursuit. "Stay calm, ladies. He won't hurt her."

With a quick glance over her shoulder, Sara made up her mind. She shoved her hands in the pockets of her jacket to keep them from trembling. "Okay," she said, walking past him. "But I'm warning you— I have pepper spray." She thrust the tube of glue against the silk fabric of her jacket pocket.

He closed the door carefully. "Really?" His brows scrunched together in a judge-like manner that pumped endorphins into Sara's system. "Can I see it?"

Her mouth went dry. "No."

"You know it's against the law to carry a concealed weapon. You'd be better off cooperating." His tone sounded teasing, but his words took her back to one of the bleakest moments of her life. The officer who'd arrested her had said the same thing, and, being young and naive, she'd believed him.

Angry beyond reason, she jerked the small tube from her pocket and waved it in his face. "There— glue. I lied. Are you satisfied? You've made your point. I was feeling intimidated, and I bolstered my confidence by pretending to be able to defend myself, which we both know is a joke since you are the long arm of the law and I'm just a person who…"

Ren's stunned look took some of the fuel out of her fire. "I was only kidding," he said in a soft, even voice. "I'm sorry I upset you."

Sara's mortification grew when she glanced behind him to the three curious faces in the storefront. Blowing out a long sigh, she shook her head. "No, I'm sorry. That was nuts. I'm a little stressed. What did you want to talk to me about?"

"Could we go to the park?" He gave her an encouraging smile. "I promise not to mug you."

She nodded, trying to smile. He probably thought she was a lunatic, but she'd been edgy ever since Claudie's suggestion that something might happen to Brady.

They didn't speak until they reached Cesar Chavez Park. "Can we sit?" he asked, pointing to an empty bench. The grass was littered with gum wrappers and cigarette butts. The quiet of the deserted inner square was outlined by the buzzing traffic that surrounded it.

Sara smoothed her silk skirt primly across her knees, then stiffened her spine and said, "I'd like to think you're about to tell me some long-lost relative died and left me a million bucks, but that frown tells me this isn't good news. Why don't you just get it over with? My sister used to make me take cough syrup by telling me 'What's the worst that can happen? You throw up.' So, tell me quick in case I have to barf."

The smile that tugged up the corners of his lips eased some of Sara's fear for a second, until he said, "Sara, I knew your sister."

It wasn't what she was expecting, either the words or the tone, which sounded like a confession. "You knew Julia?"

He nodded hesitantly.

"You don't seem too sure about that."

He blew out a sigh and hunched forward. "I did. And I didn't. Maybe the most diplomatic way of putting this is that I knew her in the biblical sense."

The starchy, formal words sounded ridiculous. But a sudden, piercing image of Julia and Ren together made Sara's stomach heave. Maybe she'd throw up, after all.

"I...don't understand why you're telling me this. You know she's dead, right?"

He nodded. "I just learned of her...accident. Bo has been looking for her for two years."

"Bo? What's Bo got to do with Julia? Are you working for the insurance company?" She'd dealt with a series of investigators after the accident, and it wasn't an experience she cared to repeat.

He crossed his legs and leaned closer. The breeze

sent a whiff of his cologne her way. An expensive, intimidating scent. Sara's breathing sped up.

"Bo's my friend," Ren said, "but he's also a private investigator. I hired him to find your sister."

"Find her? What do you mean? She lived here practically all her life."

"I know that now. Bo did a complete background check, but at the time I didn't know her name."

Questions popped into her head too fast to ask. Julia had never mentioned knowing a judge. "Why were you looking for her?"

"Primarily to make sure there weren't any surprises if I ran for public office. You know—blackmail?"

Blackmail? Julia? "Are you saying you and Julia had an affair and you were afraid Julia would use that against you? For money? Are you crazy?" Sara cried, half rising to her feet. "Julia would never have done something like that. She valued her privacy more than anything. And she and Hulger had more money than God. It's ludicrous. Why would you think it?"

He shook his head; he didn't meet her gaze. "I didn't know her. I didn't know what she was like. We spent one night together. We didn't talk much."

At least he had the grace to sound embarrassed, Sara thought, sitting back down. But that was small succor for her outrage on Julia's behalf. "Why are you telling me this? Why do I have to know if Julia had an affair? She wasn't perfect, but she was my sister and I loved her." Tears began to gather in her eyes. "She's dead. Isn't that punishment enough for her sins?"

Ren started to put out his hand to touch her, but

let it drop to the bench. He swallowed and looked so serious that Sara's blood started racing, making it hard to hear his words. "There's a chance I might be Brady's father."

The words barely made it into her consciousness before she was up and running. *I have to get my baby. We have to run. As far away as possible.*

"Sara, please, wait."

"No. Go away. I don't want to hear this."

He put his hand on her shoulder. "You have to."

She shrugged it off and tried to run, but her new shoes tripped her up. She stumbled, then recovered her balance before he could help her. "I don't believe you. I don't know why you're doing this, but it's not true."

When she started off again, he dashed into her path and held out his arms like a scarecrow to keep her from going around him. "Why would I do that? Invite scandal into my life? This is a political town and I have a political job. Why would I go out of my way to make trouble for myself?"

Her gaze darted to a figure atop a sorrel horse at the far end of the park. She sometimes brought Brady to this park when the Farmer's Market was in session, just to see the mounted police. Maybe, for once, the police would be her ally. She started to hail him, but the sun's glint on the man's badge stopped her. *Fool,* she silently castigated herself. *Ren's a judge. They play for the same team.*

Drawing on strength she didn't know she possessed, Sara took a deep breath. "I don't know you. Apparently, I don't know Bo. In fact, it seems as though there's some kind of conspiracy going on here."

Ren dropped his arms. "It's not a conspiracy, Sara. After I found out about Julia's death and Brady's birth, I asked Bo to check you out. See what kind of mother you are. What kind of life Brady has."

Sara's anger surged. "And what? The two of you decided I wasn't good enough to be Brady's mother? That I'm not providing the kind of life a judge could provide? So you thought you'd just drop in and take over?"

He ran a hand through his hair, sending it tumbling across his brow. "No. Of course not. You're—"

Sara didn't let him finish. She knew all about empty promises and kind-sounding lawyers. "I don't know what you want from me, but let me tell you something. If you're after custody of Brady—a child you'd never even seen until last week, you'll have a long and difficult fight. He's *my* son. Julia gave him to me." She pushed past him, praying she could make it to the bookstore before her tears started.

CHAPTER FIVE

"So WHAT'D HE SAY after that?" Keneesha asked.

Sara rested her elbows on her desk and cradled her throbbing head in her hands. She'd been over the whole scene a dozen times, at least, but her friends seemed incapable of grasping the idea that she might wind up losing Brady. Her baby. Yes, he was Julia's son, but Sara had been in that delivery room, too. She'd held him moments after his first cry. How could she possibly give him up to a stranger who showed up on her doorstep?

"After what?" Sara asked, drawing on all the patience she could muster.

"You asked him if you should be talking to a lawyer instead of him and he told you what?"

Sara looked at the playpen where Brady was sleeping—completely spent after missing his nap. "He said that until they did a DNA test this was just supposition. It might just be a coincidence."

Keneesha nodded with passion. "Yeah, that could be. Maybe Brady was premature."

Sara rocked back in her chair, picturing the squalling, eight-pound ten-ounce baby boy who'd peed all over the front of Hulger's surgical gown before the nurses could wrap him up. "Nope. Full term," she said, closing her eyes.

"At the moment all Bishop is asking for is a blood test, right?" Daniel asked.

"DNA. He says it's a simple procedure. No needles. You know how much Brady hates needles." Just saying Brady's name made her eyes fill with tears.

"I say we take him out," Claudie snarled, smacking a bookshelf with the heel of her hand.

Keneesha, who was perched on a plastic chair, jumped up. "I know a guy. Just got out of prison. He's a mean mother. He'd do him cheap."

Daniel stopped pacing long enough to ask, "How cheap?"

Sara surged to her feet. "Cut it out. We're not 'doing' him, no matter how cheap." Then she voiced her worst fear: "What if he *is* Brady's father?"

"Girl, don't even think it," Keneesha groaned. "Maybe this is some kind of scam. Rich people are weird—they do crazy things."

Sara didn't waste her breath arguing that they didn't know enough about Ren Bishop to gauge either his finances or his possible motives. From Daniel's quick, superficial scan of the Internet—Sara was too shaky to type—they'd learned about Ren's prison literacy program; his victory on behalf of the salmon; his appointment to the bench in the wake of his father's death. Each entry confirmed Sara's worst fear—he was for real.

The front door opened. Instinctively Sara tensed, ready to grab Brady and run. She sank back into her chair when she saw Bo walk forward, a rumpled white handkerchief extended in supplication. "Don't hurt me, please. I know I'm scum, but I have a low threshold for pain.''

"Yeah, you're a man. Tell me something I don't know,'' Claudie snarled.

Sara looked down. She liked Bo, and it hurt to think he'd befriended her only to spy on her. When he started toward her, she spun her chair the other way. ''Go away, Bo. You don't belong here.''

"Yeah, Rat Boy, we exterminate rats around here,'' Keneesha muttered, stepping in his path.

"It was my job,'' he said gruffly, his voice loud enough for Sara to hear. ''Sometimes I wish I'd paid more attention in college, but at the moment this is what I do. And yeah, at times it sucks. Surely you can understand that?''

Sara swiveled back around in time to see Keneesha stand aside. Bo walked straight to Sara. ''I'm sorry, Sara. I mean it. I wouldn't have followed through on this if I didn't think it was the right thing to do, but maybe we went about it the wrong way. I know you don't trust me, but I want to help.''

Daniel made a hooting sound. ''How? Like you did by hacking confidential medical records?''

Bo frowned but his focus didn't waiver. ''Sara, I tried talking Ren out of pursuing it, but he convinced me the coincidence was just too great. He did sleep with your sister, she did give birth nine months later. Can you really blame him for wanting to know?''

Sara covered her ears with her hands. If Julia had been there, she'd have laughed at the futile, childish response. Julia always told her, *You can't hide from reality, Sara girl. Mom's a drunk. Pretending it isn't so won't make her sober.*

"Human gestation is not exact," Daniel said.

Bo nodded. "That's what I told Ren, and he agreed, but you gotta admit he's in the ballpark." He looked at Claudie and said, "Not to be crude, but either she was pregnant when she went to Tahoe, or she got knocked up as soon as she went home, or one of the rubbers sprang a leak. Unless you know something I don't, those appear to be the options."

All eyes turned to Sara, who waved her hand in a gesture of futility. "Julia never talked about her sex life. Not to me, anyway."

Bo placed both hands flat on the desk and looked at Sara. "Ren's not doing this on a whim, Sara. He's an honorable man. Responsible. He has to know one way or the other, even if it means bad publicity that might adversely affect his career."

Keneesha elbowed Bo out of the way so she could rest her butt against the desk. "So what? Are we supposed to feel sorry for him?"

"Hell, no. Although I do. I hate to think what his fiancée's going to do to him when she finds out."

Over Claudie's boisterous vote for castration, Sara asked, "He hasn't told her?"

"He wanted to talk to you first—but he's there now."

Sara wondered how the intensely focused woman who'd been in her store this afternoon would handle the news.

"They weren't actually dating when Ren...you know, but I don't think that little detail's gonna help his case," Bo added.

Keneesha snorted. "Well, he should have thought of that before he knocked her up."

Sara flinched. "We don't know that, Kee. This is exactly what Ren warned me not to do—get too far ahead of this thing. All we know for sure is that he and Brady are both Type *O,* and that's a pretty common blood type."

Daniel walked around the desk and squatted beside her chair. He put an arm around her shoulders. "We can fight this, Sara. Jenny knows a lot of lawyers. We'll find one who specializes in custody cases. Even if it turns out he is—"

Claudie pushed him away. "Don't say another word with Mr. Big Ears here."

Bo rolled his eyes. "Don't you get it? I want to help. I can, too. I've known Ren for years. I know how he thinks."

Claudie walked up to him and poked her finger at his chest. "You're a man. You think the same way. That's why we can't trust you."

Daniel hastily moved to separate them. "Hey, watch it. I'm a man."

"Couldn't prove it by me," Keneesha chimed in.

While the four argued, Sara put her head in her hands. She didn't want to think of Ren Bishop as the enemy. Even while he'd been telling her the most potentially devastating news she could imagine, he'd remained kind and gentle, almost apologetic. "I don't want to hurt you, Sara," he'd told her, when he'd caught up to her half a block from the bookstore. "I know what a great mother you are because Brady's a terrific kid. Smart. Independent. Good strong teeth." His lopsided grin—so Brady-like—had sent a shiver of fear down her back.

When she'd threatened to get a lawyer, he'd sighed and said, "I can recommend several, but I wish you'd consider getting the results from the DNA test before we call in the artillery.''

Sara's antipathy toward lawyers ran just about as deep as her distrust of judges.

"What would you have me do, Sara? Walk away and pretend it didn't happen?'' he'd asked. His tone made her stop and look at him. She probably shouldn't have, though, because his earnestness moved her in a way she didn't want to acknowledge.

"What if he's not your son?''

"What if he is?''

The question had echoed through her head with every pulse beat as she hurried toward the bookstore. He'd stopped her again before she could flee inside. "I have to know, Sara. There's no way I could go through life without acknowledging my son. Never being a part of his life. Never holding him, watching him grow up. I couldn't live with myself if I just walked away.''

Sara knew Ren had no idea how his plea touched her heart. Even if Bo had given him every single piece of information available about her, Ren couldn't have guessed how not having a father had shaped her life. No one, not even Julia, knew how badly Sara had craved a father when she was growing up. In a way, Hank Dupertis had become a surrogate father in her teens, but that didn't make up for all the years without a dad.

Keneesha's voice brought Sara back to the present.

"If you want to help so bad,'' she told Bo, "then tell us where he lives. I've got some payback in mind.''

Bo snagged a pen off the desk and, with a flourish, scribbled a few lines on the back of an envelope. He held it up for all to see as he read the address and phone number aloud. "It's only about a mile from here. I'll lead the way if you want. He should be home by the time we get there. But if he's not, there's a spare key under the flowerpot by the front door."

"Yeah, let's do it," Keneesha cried.

"Is this a trick? Are you telling me he doesn't have a fancy alarm system?" Claudie asked suspiciously.

"Most times he doesn't bother setting it," Bo replied. "Let's go."

Sara shook her head. "Absolutely not. No violence. I still have friends back East. Brady and I could go—"

Claudie nodded. "I'll go with you. We could leave tonight."

Bo groaned. "Don't even think it, Sara. Trust me, running away doesn't solve anything. I've met people in the FBI witness relocation program. It's a terrible way to live—always looking over your shoulder."

Sara knew he was right. This wasn't something she could run from. "I'll call the estate lawyer first thing Monday. If he won't handle it, then I'll find somebody who will. Right now, Brady and I are going home. I'm shot."

With four extra sets of hands, the transition of closing up the shop and moving Brady to his car seat went smoothly. It was only when she started to get into the car that Daniel said, "Sara, we forgot to turn on the television. We didn't get to see you on the news."

Sara's laugh sounded harsh to her ears. "That seemed kinda important for a few minutes, didn't it?"

Claudie sighed. "I doubt if Sara got much on-screen time, anyway. I have a feeling Eve Masterson wasn't too thrilled to see her boyfriend hanging out at a bookstore with a kid who has the same big blue eyes."

At the group's sudden silence, Claudie slapped her hand over her mouth and whimpered. Sara touched her shoulder. "It's okay. It's the truth." She said her goodbyes and left.

Before she'd gone three blocks, her hands were trembling on the steering wheel and tears obscured her vision. She hastily pulled over, giving in to her emotions. Fear. Anger. A sense of impending loss. "It's just not fair," she cried. Ren's resources and connections seemed limitless. How could she fight that kind of power? How could she not at least try with all her might?

Wiping her tears with her hands, she put the car in gear and stepped on the gas. Recalling Bo's directions, she turned the steering wheel sharply at the next intersection, barely acknowledging the red light.

Sara had one stop to make. She knew she'd never be able to sleep tonight without letting Ren Bishop know that where Brady was concerned, the judge was in for the fight of his life.

"IT HAPPENED BEFORE we started dating, Eve," Ren said for the third time. For some reason his infidelity, not the child's paternity, seemed to be the focus of Eve's anger. "I haven't been with another woman since we started going out, and certainly not since we got engaged. What kind of man do you think I am?''

Eve, who'd kicked off her shoes and dumped her suit jacket on the sofa the minute she'd walked into her condo, marched across the white-on-white living room like a Polynesian princess, black eyes ablaze with indignation. ''I know what kind of man I *thought* you were, but now I'm not so sure. Tell me, Ren, what kind of man sleeps with a stranger in this day and age? STDs and AIDS aside, have you forgotten about Frank Gifford and the hooker? Or Bill Clinton, for that matter? It's called scandal, Ren, and you can't afford it. No one in public office can.''

Ren, who'd been watching for her car from the large, arched window that afforded a view of the condominium's tastefully landscaped parking lot, lowered the mini-blinds. His private life would go on display soon enough without giving the neighbors a ringside seat. ''I wasn't in public office at the time,'' he told her, trying to be patient. Eve was flash and sizzle; she blew up easily but didn't stay angry for long. ''I'd just won the salmon verdict. You know what the climate was like—you were one of the reporters dogging me.'' At her indignant pout, he added, ''I'd won one for the planet. I wanted to celebrate but I couldn't walk outside without half a dozen reporters in my face.''

Her eyes narrowed. ''Are you trying to blame your peccadillo on the media?''

''No,'' he cried, exasperated. ''I'm explaining my mental state at the time. I went to Tahoe to get away, and maybe live it up a little.''

''By having sex with a stranger.''

Ren gave up trying to make her understand. He certainly didn't blame her for being mad, but he had hoped to be able to reason with her.

"So tell me again where the pretty little shop-keeper comes in? A *ménage à trois*, perhaps?" she asked snidely.

Ren was floored by Eve's hostility toward Sara. "Sara is Julia's sister. We've never had sex," he said, perhaps a bit more loudly than was necessary. "Brady is Sara's nephew."

"She called him her son."

"Julia died—Sara's his legal guardian."

Eve turned away, but not before Ren caught the quiver of her chin, a brief glimpse of vulnerability. Eve had been adopted at birth. And while she publicly celebrated her undefined ethnic heritage, she occasionally admitted harboring doubts about her lineage.

Standing in front of her antique oriental bureau, she fiddled with a flower arrangement a moment before turning to look at him. "I saw you staring at her while I was doing the interview."

Ren walked to the bar that separated the dining area from the living room. He poured himself a second glass of Merlot and downed a big gulp. Without looking at her, he said, "I may have looked at Sara, but I didn't stare." *Liar.* In fact, he'd been mesmerized by the poise and candor she'd displayed. "I was curious. All I know about her is what Bo's been able to dig up, which isn't much. She's raising a child that could be mine—I need to know what she's like."

Eve walked over to him and put her arms around his waist. "So you say. Maybe you even believe it.

But a woman senses things, Ren. There was some-thing between the two of you. Why do you think I assumed right away that you were the father of her baby?''

Ren remained rigid. He refused to believe she'd seen anything. Besides, he wasn't interested in Sara. Except where Brady was concerned.

Her soft sigh penetrated through the cloth of his suit and shirt. He set down his glass, then put his arms around her. ''I'm sorry, Eve. I never meant for any of this to happen.''

The top of her head came to the middle of his chest. She didn't look up. ''I know, Ren. In spite of what I said earlier, you are a good man. I'm sure you used precautions, and if that little boy is yours, it's purely by accident. But…'' He felt her take a deep breath. ''I have to say, the timing really sucks.''

''You mean there's actually a good time for something like this to happen?''

She looked up, gave him a half smile and then walked to the sofa where she opened her briefcase. From the upper compartment she withdrew a sheet of paper. ''Marcella faxed this to me today. I was hoping we'd be celebrating tonight.''

''What is it?''

''My proposed itinerary for next week. She's al-ready got two interviews scheduled—ABC and CNN. She expects the others to get interested after she stirs up a little buzz.''

Ren knew how important this was. For all her outward confidence, Eve needed constant reinforce-ment and success to validate her self-worth.

He moved to the sofa and sat down, drawing her

into the chair across from him. "You have to go to New York, Eve, and I have to stay here and take care of this."

She lifted her chin proudly, as if defying tears to come. "I'd hoped you could go with me. See a few shows. Shop. I'd even go to a museum or two if you insisted."

Her attempt at humor made him smile, but only for a second. "I can't put this off, Eve. I need to know. If Brady is my son, I'll probably have to go to court for custody. I'm sure Sara won't give him up without a fight."

Her bottom lip trembled. "Do you have any idea how damaging that will be to your career?" He lifted one shoulder carelessly, which made her scowl. "Then think about what it'll do to *my* career. There's bound to be spillage."

"'Spillage'?"

She looked at her lap. "This is going to sound terribly self-absorbed, but it's the truth. If there's bad publicity, it'll spill over on me, too, and I can't afford that right now, Ren. I'm going into these negotiations with a blemish-free life—former Junior Miss, a popular radio personality who became an award-winning television anchor, a model citizen engaged to a judge. What happens if word of this gets back to the networks?"

Ren's heart felt pinched. A prickly sensation buzzed in his sinuses. The pathos of his being dumped for a spot on *Good Morning, America* would make Bo fall down laughing.

"So, you want to call off the engagement," he said gruffly.

"No," Eve exclaimed, taking his hands. "God,

no. Not yet, anyway. You said yourself this might all be a false alarm. Get the test done. Then we'll talk." She tilted her head, looking into his eyes imploringly. "Just try to keep it quiet."

Ren studied her a long moment. In his heart he knew their relationship was doomed, and it had nothing to do with Brady. Maybe they were both too self-absorbed to make it work.

Eve squeezed his hands and in a soft voice said, "We have something good here, Ren. I honestly hope things work out okay. No baby, no problem. Right?"

"Right," he said, a sour taste in his mouth. "I'll call you tomorrow."

She let go of his hands and sat back as if surprised. "You don't want to stay? I taped our six o'clock show. You could see your friend Sara."

He rose to leave. The muscles in his neck felt as though they might squeeze tight enough to pop his head off. "I'd better go. I still have to break this news to my mother."

"Oh, God," Eve said, adding a low moan of sympathy. She walked him to the door. "I don't know who to feel more sorry for, you or Babe. She isn't going to be happy. We were supposed to meet for brunch tomorrow to set a date for the wedding. I don't think we dare do that until we know if there's going to be a paternity suit."

When Ren didn't say anything, she sighed and said, "Don't worry, honey. It'll work out. When Marcella was here she told me about her fabulous spin doctors. These guys are publicity magicians. If it turns out he is your child, I'm sure they'll find a way to make it look like you were the victim."

When she rose up on her toes to kiss him good-bye, Ren stopped her. Instead, he gently brushed her cheek with the backs of his fingers. ''I'll call you tomorrow,'' he said and left, never looking back.

''HOW THE HECK LONG does it take to tell your girlfriend you might have a kid from an illicit affair?'' Sara muttered under her breath, pounding the steering wheel with the heel of her hand.

The inanity of her question struck her after the fact and made her shake her head. She didn't know the first thing about Ren Bishop or Eve Masterson. Maybe he could persuade her it was a huge mistake that he regretted with all his heart. Maybe she loved him so much she could forgive him, and they were, at this very moment, making mad passionate love.

For some reason, the idea made her stomach heave. She knew she should go home but she'd waited too long. The bottle of warm diet soda Keneesha had left in her car, which Sara had finished half an hour earlier, was causing all sorts of discomfort in her bladder.

Squeezing her legs together, Sara sat up straighter and looked around. The neighborhood sported wide streets, gracious front yards and mature trees that bespoke a slower period when wealthy people grouped together to outdo each other face-to-face instead of on half-acre lots in the suburbs. Ren's house—by no means the most luxurious on the block—fell into what Sara believed was called the neoclassical revival period of architecture.

A spasm of discomfort made her groan. I need a bathroom, she thought, and quick. A pair of headlights brought a flash of hope. *Ren?* The car slowed, but a reflection off its bank of patrol car lights made Sara sink down in her seat—not a good position for her bladder.

When the car was gone, Sara opened the door. *If I have to choose between unlawful entry and indecent exposure, I'll take my chances with Ren.*

She tucked her purse under her arm and, with nonchalance borne of desperation, walked to the house. Two decorative coach lights illuminated the wide, covered porch. She pretended to drop her purse, spilling out Brady's crayons like Pick-Up-Stix. While kneeling to retrieve them, she peeked under the smallest flowerpot to the right of the ornately carved door. To her relief, a single brass key was, indeed, where Bo had said it would be. She snatched it up and, as casually as possible, strolled back to the car.

Brady made a few soft protests when she picked him up. But he was a sound sleeper and dropped his head back to her shoulder as she carried him up the brick walkway. The key fit. The door opened. And Sara, who'd been holding her breath expecting some kind of alarm to sound, let out a sigh of relief. "Bo was right."

With the aid of the hallway light, which was already on, Sara was able to see into the room to her left—a large, very masculine-looking office. A handsome leather tufted sofa occupied the wall closest to the door. She slipped inside and lowered Brady to the cushions. He stirred but didn't wake. Just to be safe, she whispered, "Stay right here, honey. Mommy needs to find a potty."

She dashed into the foyer and turned at the foot of the L-shaped staircase. "There has to be a guest bath down here somewhere,'' she muttered. She got lucky. First door to the right. A charming little room with an illuminated seashell above the porcelain basin, so she didn't have to turn on the overhead light.

She peed, flushed and washed her hands in record time. Hurrying back to the office, she had herself convinced she could return Brady to his car seat, rehide the key and be on her way with no one the wiser. Her daydream dissolved the moment she stepped into the office and spotted an empty sofa.

''Brady?'' she called, her voice betraying her panic. She turned on a bank of lights just inside the doorway, momentarily taken aback by the formal elegance of the room, with its rosewood paneling, leaded glass bow window and massive antique desk that cried money.

Sara checked behind the heavy velvet curtains and under the waist-high globe stand. ''Brady, honey? We don't have time to play. Where are you, sweetheart?''

''Sara?'' a puzzled-sounding voice asked.

She spun around, instantly registering the policeman at Ren's side. ''Don't just stand there,'' she cried, torn between utter mortification and fear. ''Find Brady before he breaks something.''

He dumped his coat and briefcase on the sofa and motioned her to follow. At the base of the staircase, he said, ''You check down here, we'll go up.''

Sara's heart was in her throat as she dashed toward the back of the house. Unless a house was equipped with childproof latches, a kitchen was a dangerous playground. As she paused to flick on the light in the drab, unattractive dining room, she heard

Ren tell the policeman, "He's eighteen months old, and he loves to hide."

For some reason, Ren's calm demeanor helped stave off Sara's panic, particularly when she zipped around the showy, red-and-white kitchen without encountering the toddler. She noticed a fenced-in pool with the gate standing open in the well-manicured backyard, but the sliding door to the patio was securely locked. "Brady?" she called, checking the pantry. "Where are you, sweetie?"

In the distance, she heard Ren's voice. "Sara, I found him."

Relief—with a measure of hysteria—drove her toward the sound. She grabbed the solid walnut newel at the base of the stairs and hurried toward the muffled voices on the second floor. Ren and the officer met her at the landing where the staircase turned to the right.

"Where is he?" she cried.

"Sound asleep on my bed," Ren said, subtly positioning his body to keep her from moving past. "He's okay. I covered him up."

"Did you forget to reset the alarm when you came in, ma'am?" the policeman asked her.

"A-alarm?" Sara grabbed the banister for support. "Uh…"

"It's a new unit, Officer Rivaldi," Ren said, coming to her rescue. "Sara doesn't have it down pat, yet. Half the time I forget to set it myself. We'll go over it again as soon as you leave. Judge's honor."

The cop laughed and trotted down the stairs. "Better safe than sorry. Had a burglary right down the street last month, you know."

Although Sara's instincts told her to snatch Brady

and run, she sensed Ren was waiting for her to descend the staircase. Reluctantly she turned and slowly trudged downward, Ren right behind her.

When they reached the tiled floor, Ren leaned past her to shake the officer's hand. His torso bumped her shoulder, making her flinch.

"Thanks again. Sorry to have bothered you."

The man touched two fingers to the brim of his hat. "No problem. Have a good evening."

Ren walked him to the door and closed it securely. When he turned to face her, he nodded toward a discreet white box on the wall. "Alarm," he said, his voice kind and slightly amused.

Sara suddenly felt a little light-headed, and her knees started to give out. She sank down on the bottom step and covered her face with her hands. "I can't believe this happened. You must think I'm some kind of nut." She looked up, fighting tears. "I just needed to use your bathroom."

Ren, who'd hurried to her side as if fearful she might faint, burst out laughing. "My bathroom?"

She couldn't bring herself to meet his eyes as she tried to explain. "I came here to talk to you. I waited as long as I could, but you took so long and I had to go to the bathroom, then Brady…"

Taking a deep breath to stop her rambling, she pushed off from the step and lifted her chin. "Where *is* Brady? We need to go home."

Ren graciously held out his hand, indicating she should go up the stairs ahead of him. "Do you mind telling me how you got in?" he asked.

Sara watched her feet to keep him from seeing her blush. "No, I just gambled that you might hide a key under the mat out front. Lucky me, there it was,'' she said, unable to keep the sarcasm from her tone.

Ren's low chuckle made her stagger slightly. ''A key. Hmm...next time I'll have the person who put the key there leave operating instructions for the alarm with it.''

Ren was being very understanding about this fiasco. An unpleasant thought crossed Sara's mind. If he planned to use mental instability as an argument against her in the future, she was certainly giving him fuel.

At the top of the *U*-shaped landing, Sara paused, her gaze drawn to a collection of framed photographs on the wall. Unconsciously, she studied the faces, searching for familiar features—and hoping she wouldn't find any. A black-and-white snapshot in a silver frame showed a tall man and a little boy walking hand in hand down a boat dock. Except for the clothing and unfamiliar background, the shot could have been of Ren and Brady.

''Me and my dad,'' Ren said, noticing her interest. ''Our family has a cabin up at Lake Almanor. That's up near Mt. Lassen.''

Sara thought she detected a slight wistfulness in his tone. ''You resemble your dad,'' she said.

Ren stared at the picture a moment longer. ''He died about two years ago. I miss him a lot—he was a good man.''

As if embarrassed suddenly, he turned sharply and led the way down the hall to the left. The double doors were open and a bedside lamp gave off a low, comforting glow. Brady's tiny body beneath an emerald-green cashmere throw barely made a bump in the king-size bed.

Ren stood to one side to let her walk past him. Sara liked the room at once. Although both masculine and functional, right down to the NordicTrack facing the balcony, the color scheme of navy, emerald and plum was warm and inviting.

"I wonder what made him come all the way up here?" Ren whispered. The intimate sound made gooseflesh cascade down Sara's neck.

"Brady loves stairs. Our house is a one-story, so anytime he has the chance he goes for the stairs." Sara walked to the bed and sat down beside her son. She brushed a stray curl from his forehead. "Naturally," she said softly, "he scares the heck out of me every time he starts climbing, but I guess he's got to learn."

Ren approached but didn't crowd her. She looked at him. He might be a judge and a lawyer, and he might hold her future in his hands, but he'd been amazingly decent about finding her in his house. She smiled.

In an instant something changed. His eyes narrowed as if he didn't recognize her—or maybe he recognized something in her she couldn't hide. He closed the distance between them. The lamplight cast his face into relief. His eyes—Brady's eyes—looked more black than blue as they stared at her.

Hesitantly, he extended his hand, bringing the palm to her face, cupping her cheek and jaw. Sara tried to make herself move away, but there was something so warm, so nurturing in his touch that she tilted her head against his palm. The scent of warm skin mingled with a trace of cologne from his bed—a scent she'd noticed from that first evening when he'd lifted Brady from her arms.

The instant Sara sensed him moving closer, she pulled back in panic. His eyes were hooded, his lips slightly parted. Sara knew he intended to kiss her. She couldn't let that happen. She couldn't...

Ren's hand gently tilted her chin. His head lowered, lips touching hers. Not tentatively, as she expected, but squarely, as if returning to a familiar book at the exact place he'd left off. Despite her prudent mind crying otherwise, Sara closed her eyes and absorbed the feel of his soft, persuasive warmth. His fingers stroked the lobe of her ear, the side of her neck. She liked his touch, his kiss.

Where it might have led, Sara didn't dare guess. Fortunately, a ringing sound in the distance brought her back to her senses. She pulled away. "Your phone is ringing," she said, grateful to find her voice still functioning, since her mind obviously wasn't.

Ren eyed the silent cordless phone beside his bed skeptically, then tapped his forehead. "I turned off the ringer the other day." He cocked his head to listen. Below them an angry woman's voice was blaring from an answering machine. "Lawrence, are you there? Pick up the phone."

CHAPTER SIX

REN SNATCHED UP the portable receiver and walked to the glass door that opened to his private deck. *I kissed Sara.* "I'm here, Mother. Just walked in the door. Can I call you back? I'm kinda busy at the moment."

An angry huffing sound foretold Babe's frame of mind. "Don't you dare hang up on me. I want to know what's going on with your health. Good Lord, Lawrence, are you ill? How serious is it?"

Ren leaned his forehead against the cool glass. *Why? Why did I kiss her? As if this damn thing isn't complicated enough!* "Mother, I'm fine. Can we talk about this tomorrow?"

"No," Babe shrieked. "I just spoke with Eve, and she was very upset. She said we couldn't set a date for your wedding until you cleared it with your doctor. What does that mean, Lawrence?"

Ren blew out a long sigh that left a foggy mark on the glass. Behind him, he heard Sara moving about. He turned and saw her carefully folding the blanket he'd used to cover Brady. "I feel great, Mom, really. Believe me, there's nothing wrong with my health." *My mind is a little screwed up, but...* He tuned out his mother's reply when he saw Sara bend over to pick up Brady. The image caught him mid-chest, and he felt a sudden, unreasonable urge to wrap them both in his arms and beg Sara to stay.

He covered the receiver. "Wait. Please. We need to talk."

"Are you listening to me?" his mother wailed.

Ren held the phone back a few inches. "Along with all the neighbors," he told her.

The sympathetic look in Sara's eyes made him smile. A mistake. She suddenly hefted Brady to her shoulder and turned away. He followed as she walked toward the door. "Please wait."

His mother let out a cry of frustration. "Lawrence, are you listening to me? Is someone there? Is it Bo? It's Bo, isn't it. I should have known."

Ren looked to the ceiling. "No, Mother, it's not Bo. But I do have company and I have to go. I'll tell you everything tomorrow. Lunch at Fats?" he asked, naming her favorite restaurant.

"Well, all right. One o'clock. Don't be late." The moment she hung up, Ren pitched the phone toward his bed and raced after Sara. He had no idea what to say, but he needed to make amends. He knew she didn't trust him, had little reason to like him and was fearful of his motives. What that unplanned, unprovoked kiss was all about, he didn't have a clue, but he had to make her understand he wasn't some sort of lunatic who made a habit of lusting after women he barely knew. Jeez, first her sister, now Sara.

You are an idiot, Bishop, he silently groaned.

SARA REPOSITIONED BRADY against her shoulder before starting down the stairs. She'd stayed in the bedroom as long as she could, but the shrill sound of his mother's voice—just the tone and pitch were enough to produce an unpleasant sensation in her gut—had made her snatch up Brady.

Sara's mother had died the summer after Sara graduated from high school. Audra Carsten had been a dynamic personality, even when she was reduced to tugging around oxygen. Sara remembered her as the kind of mother who could be loving and concerned one moment, raging and cruel the next—depending on her level of intoxication. Angry voices brought back memories Sara went out of her way to avoid.

When Ren had noticed her leaving, he'd quickly moved from the window and mouthed *Wait.*

Focusing on his lips had been even more unnerving than the sound of his mother's anger. *He kissed me. I let him kiss me. What was I thinking? I should never have come here in the first place,* she told herself. She thought she heard Ren set a date to meet his mother, and a part of her heart felt sorry for him.

As she began to descend the stairs, Brady shifted restlessly, knocking her slightly off balance. She grabbed the railing with her free hand, but her hip collided with the newel. She let out a soft "Ouch."

"Why don't you let me carry him down for you," Ren said, coming up behind her.

She shook her head. "I can do it. I carry him all day long."

Centering Brady's weight as much as possible, she slowly and carefully descended. The arm that supported the bulk of his weight was quivering by the time she reached the black-and-white marble squares of the foyer.

Ren hovered like a mother hen the whole way down, making Sara more nervous than she already was. He let out a big sigh when they reached the foyer. "I'll walk you to the car, but let me get a flashlight first. Those paving stones out front are tricky at night."

Sara was independent but not foolish. "Okay."

While she waited by the front door, she studied the green-and-red lights of the alarm. "Fink," she muttered, just as she heard the *clip* of Ren's shoes on the floor.

He waved the flashlight triumphantly, then leaned past her to open the door. "Whoa, that breeze turned cold. Do you want to borrow a jacket?" His nearness and smell made her heart flip-flop.

Sara shook her head, desperate to put as much distance between her and Ren Bishop as possible. Drawing on Brady's warmth, she hurried to the car, grateful for the beam of light Ren kept trained ahead of her. She maneuvered Brady into his car seat, then pulled his soft, much-loved blanket from his backpack. She tucked it around him and kissed his forehead. His breath, warm and sweet, smelling faintly of bubblegum—his favorite toothpaste flavor— brought tears to her eyes. She loved being his mother. It would kill her to lose him. She had to make Ren Bishop understand that.

Taking a deep breath, she straightened and turned to face her enemy—the man whose kiss had opened doors inside her she hadn't known existed. No matter how wonderful it had felt, she wasn't about to let it happen again.

"I came here for a reason," she said, drawing strength from her fear. "My friends and I are prepared to fight to the death—I hope it won't come to that, but you need to know how I feel about this.''

A gust of wind zipped under her skirt, making her shiver.

"You're cold. Let's go inside," he said.

She shook her head. "No. I'm exhausted. I have to go home, but I want to tell you something first," she said stubbornly.

He placed the flashlight between his knees and shrugged out of his suit jacket, then draped it over Sara's shoulders. Its warmth and subtle scent enveloped her. The gallantry of the gesture touched her.

"Thank you," she said in a small voice, hoping her emotions weren't broadcast on her face.

"I apologize for making you wait. When my mother gets going, sometimes it's best just to let her rant. I think that's why she doesn't have high blood pressure."

"And you do," Sara said softly, covertly rolling her shoulders against the silky lining of the coat.

He cocked his head to one side. "How do you know that?"

"I saw the prescription on your bedside table. A friend of mine used to take the same thing. You know, it's not safe to leave pills sitting out with children around."

"I didn't know Brady was going to be around, but I'll be sure to keep them in the medicine cabinet from now on. I don't actually take them," he added.

She blinked. "You just keep them there for appearance?"

His quick smile made her inch back. He was just too darn handsome for someone as vulnerable as she was at the moment. "Hypertension runs in my family. My blood pressure was a little high after my father passed away.''

Sara, who witnessed her own mother's painful death, wanted to reach out to touch his forearm, but she kept her hands in her pockets and waited for him to speak again.

Ren was silent for a moment, then in a low serious voice he said, ''Sara, about what happened upstairs. I apologize. It was unprofessional and…not very smart, given what we'll be dealing with in the future. Do you think we can put it behind us?''

Even though Sara agreed with him, perversely, his apology struck her as too lawyer-like. ''Is that how it happened with my sister?'' she said without thinking. ''Just a quick kiss, then *wham, bam,* you're in bed?''

He stepped back as if slapped. In the light from the street lamp she saw a stark, judicial mask settle over his features. The narrow squint of his eyes reminded her of Brady's reaction when scolded. On a toddler it was cute; on Ren Bishop it was intimidating.

Instead of scurrying to her car, Sara screwed up her courage and said, ''That is, if anything actually happened between you. I only have your word that you even met her. And until you prove otherwise, I won't agree to a paternity test. Period. *That's* what I came to tell you.''

His face changed, but Sara couldn't tell what he was thinking. She thought she read disappointment, not anger.

''I can get you an affidavit from a hotel clerk who saw us at the lodge, and I can subpoena the hotel's records.''

Court words. Lawyer-speak. Sara's old antipathy surged. "Can you find a witness who saw you make love to her? Someone from the room next door who will testify that she called out your name on climax?" She snorted facetiously. "You probably could—I've heard money's even better for the memory than ginkgo biloba."

Her anger obviously took him by surprise, but he didn't back down. "No, I can't. All you have is my word."

"And because you're a judge, I'm supposed to believe you. I'm supposed to listen to what you say and hear what's in your heart and make a decision that might affect the rest of your life, right?"

He nodded slowly.

"Then I guess that makes me a judge." She tapped her chest and lifted her chin. "And I'm sorry, Mr. Bishop, but I don't believe you. Your evidence is flimsy, your key witness is dead, and, frankly, I'm not convinced you're truly repentant enough to be a productive member of society, let alone a father."

His mouth gaped in amazement. "What?"

Sara's eyes filled with tears and she blinked fiercely. On the rare moments when memories of her trial and judgment decree flashed through her mind, she usually fought them down. Bile rose in her throat. She hated everything about the judicial system, but she'd learned a great deal from her brush with the law. She knew she could use the court system to drag this out for months, probably years. It would cost a fortune, but she'd sacrifice her business, her house—whatever it took—to keep Brady.

She shrugged off his jacket and passed it to him.

"I have to go. You can expect to hear from my lawyer next week."

Suddenly drained by her memories and all that had happened tonight, she took a step, but misjudged the distance to the gutter and fell against the fender of her car.

"Sara, you're in no condition to drive. You're exhausted, emotionally spent and you probably haven't eaten all day, have you?"

Sara couldn't recall eating anything after finishing off Brady's toast at breakfast. Her head did feel a bit out of focus. The idea of her forty-minute commute sounded daunting.

"Let me call you a cab."

"I live in Rancho Carmel."

He nodded. "I know."

She felt a twist in her stomach. "That's right. You had me investigated."

He drove a hand through his hair. "Sara, I explained about that. Please, let me get you a cab. For Brady's sake."

She looked at her son curled up so peacefully in his car seat. She wouldn't let her pride put him in danger. "Okay. Call a cab."

He passed his coat back to her, saying, "Why don't you pull your car into my driveway, while I make the call. It'll be safer than leaving it parked on the street."

Sara stared at her nine-year-old wagon a moment. Julia and Hulger both had driven leased cars—always brand-new. The estate lawyer didn't seem to think Sara needed a newer car, and Sara hadn't bothered arguing the point.

Expelling a long sigh, she shrugged on Ren's

coat, then climbed into her car and pulled into the space beside his Lexus. A motion detector's bank of floodlights momentarily blinded her, but she was grateful for the illumination when she dug through the mess on the floor of the back seat to find the paraphernalia she'd need in the morning. She stuffed all she could fit in her backpack, then carefully unhooked Brady's car seat.

Ren met her before she'd made it two steps. "Let me," he said, taking the awkward plastic contraption from her hand. His fingers were warm; hers felt like Popsicles. "It'll be a few minutes. Some game is letting out and all the taxis are tied up."

Instead of leading the way to the curb, he headed for the front porch. He'd donned a vintage fisherman-type cardigan that made her think of John Kennedy, Jr.

"I put down a blanket and made you some cocoa," he told her.

"Cocoa? You had time to make cocoa?"

"Just some instant stuff I zapped in the microwave."

She chose the far end of the blanket. Her legs were numb from the chilly breeze, and she fought to keep from shivering. Once Ren had set down the car seat at her feet, he reached behind them to pick up a steaming mug. Sara latched on to its warmth with a murmur of thanks. Its sweetness and heat seduced her. She inhaled deeply. The first sip reached all the way to her toes.

They sat in surprisingly comfortable silence. "Are you being nice to me because you're hoping I'll change my mind?"

"Sounds like a lawyer kind of thing, huh?" His tone held a note of humor.

"Yes, actually."

He flinched as if dodging a bullet. "You don't like lawyers, do you?" He held up a hand. "Don't answer. It was a rhetorical question. But in answer to your first question, yes, I do hope you'll change your mind."

"I—"

He didn't let her finish. "Because if you do, we might be able to avoid dragging in a whole fleet of very expensive lawyers." He grinned. "I mean, since you don't like them."

The cocoa loosened her up enough to ask, "How?"

"Simple. Do the test. If I'm not Brady's father, then the whole thing's over. I fade away like a bad dream. Of course, I'd be happy to reimburse you for any expenses you incur during this ordeal, the cost of the doctor, the mileage, time off work…"

His spiel was exactly what she'd expect from a lawyer.

"And if you are…" She couldn't bring herself to finish.

He took a deep breath and let it out slowly. "Then, naturally, I'd want to be a part of his life." Gently, he added, "I imagine that would mean some kind of joint-custody arrangement."

The words hurt her ears. She set her cup aside and pulled the lapels of his jacket around her neck as if she could just shut out the sound. It was a childish gesture, she knew.

"Sara, please, think about it," he pleaded. "I've seen what happens when a child becomes a negotiable point of contention in a courtroom. Only the lawyers come out ahead. I'm asking to add to the quality of Brady's life, not take away from it.''

Sara couldn't think about that right now. His tone was very persuasive, but that was to be expected— he was a lawyer. He'd had her investigated. He probably knew just what to say to sway her. He couldn't be trusted—she had to remember that.

Fortunately, a pair of car lights broke the long dark expanse in front of them. The car slowed and turned into the driveway.

Saved by the cab, she thought minutes later, taking a deep breath of stale air. A country-and-western station played on the radio. After securing Brady's seat, Ren had shoved a wad of bills at the driver with instructions to return for her the next morning. Sara didn't meet his gaze when he told her goodbye. Instead, she muttered a weak ''Thank you,'' then wrapped her arms around the hard plastic shell of Brady's car seat and closed her eyes.

REN WATCHED until the taillights were out of sight, then he walked to the porch and picked up Sara's mug and the blanket. His jacket was draped over one arm. He'd argued that Sara should wear it home, but she'd insisted the taxi was heated and she would be fine.

''Stubborn woman,'' he muttered softly.

''Talking to yourself these days, old man?'' a voice asked.

Ren almost pitched his entire load into the bushes as his instincts prepared him for battle. Only the familiar chuckle that accompanied the droll accent saved him the embarrassment. "That does it, Lester. You're fired. Go hound some other client."

Bo followed Ren up the steps like a puppy. "Can I have cocoa, too?"

Ren stopped mid-stride. "How long have you been here?"

His tone must have made an impression, because Bo, who was dressed like a cat burglar complete with black stocking cap, paused and looked at his watch. "Four minutes, thirty-eight seconds."

"I meant, how much of our conversation did you hear?"

Bo looked him square in the eyes. "None. I was walking up when the taxi arrived. I parked half a block away when I saw Sara's car in the drive."

Ren relaxed. He proceeded into the house, pausing to drape his jacket over the banister. "Why are you here?" he asked, when Bo followed him into the kitchen.

"Thought I'd see if Eve left any skin on your hide." He opened the refrigerator and withdrew a can of flavored tea. After a couple of healthy guzzles, he burped.

No wonder Eve found his manners so appalling, Ren thought, putting away the box of instant cocoa.

"So, is Eve bootin' your ass or what?"

Ren walked to the far end of the counter and selected a bottle of brandy from his liquor cabinet. He poured a small amount into a snifter. "Let's go to the den. I'm weary, my friend. Very weary."

Before Ren settled into the chair behind his desk, he punched the message retrieval button on his answering machine, out of habit. The first message was a cheery reminder from his dentist of an upcoming appointment. The second was his mother's voice. He erased both.

"Babe sounds healthy," Bo said, dropping to sprawl on the couch.

Ren took a long sip of his brandy, savoring the smoky, robust bite as it went down, then he rocked back, kicking his feet on top of the desk. He was tempted to call Sara to make sure she got home okay.

"Do we have Sara's home number?"

"Why do you want to know? Did I mention I'm changing sides in this battle? I'm gonna work for Sara from now on."

Ren ignored the threat. "I just want to make sure she got home safely."

"You seem kind of interested in her—beyond just the custody thing. I thought she wasn't pretty enough for you."

Ren pictured the moment before he had kissed her. Sara's lips had trembled—whether from fear or anticipation he didn't know. Her eyes had been luminous, her cheeks flushed. Pretty? Not even close. More like phenomenal. "I would appreciate it if you forgot I ever said that."

Bo regarded him shrewdly. "It'll cost you."

"Are you blackmailing me?"

"Wouldn't that be against the law?" Bo asked innocently.

"Yes."

"Then no, Your Honor, I'm not. I'm just suggesting that a pie might, on occasion—shall we say, once a week—find its way from your unworthy and unappreciative kitchen to my very worthy, very appreciative kitchen."

Ren wasn't in the mood to laugh, but he chuckled, anyway. "I would have thought a cookbook man like yourself could bake his own pies."

It was Bo's turn to frown. "Don't call me that. Sara's a soft touch compared to Claudie and Keneesha."

Ren shook his head. He ran his fingernails along the faint bristle of new growth on his chin. "I think it's safe to say that as far as the females of our acquaintance are concerned, neither one of us could get elected dog catcher."

Bo nodded. "Not even dog-poop catcher."

Ren laughed and Bo joined him. When his friend rose to leave, Ren told him, "Your first payment of hush money is in the fridge. Take it with you."

Bo grinned and said, "Thanks. By the way, Sara's number's in the book. See ya' around, pal. Don't hang anybody I wouldn't hang." With that he disappeared.

Ren listened carefully. He heard the suction of the refrigerator door, but after that only silence. He started to snap off the light, then reached into the lower cabinet and withdrew the phone book. He found the number and wrote it on a Post-it note. With the little yellow flag attached to his finger, he reset the exterior alarm, turned off the lights and walked upstairs.

I won't call, he decided. She's fine. They're fine.

He prepared for bed, doing the yoga and meditation that gave him an edge over hypertension. The biofeedback techniques he'd learned told him his blood pressure was within the acceptable range.

When he walked to his bed, Ren spotted the slight indentation in the covers where Brady had slept. He

ran his fingers over the spot, then pulled back the
spread and crawled into bed. When he reached over
to turn off his lamp, his gaze landed on the little
yellow note. He snapped off the light. *I'm not calling. She's probably already asleep.*

He rolled onto his stomach. As he scrunched his
pillow into a ball, his hand encountered something
hard. Raising up on his elbows he clicked the light
back on. His phone.

SARA SPIT AND RINSED, zombie-like. The forty-
minute snooze she'd had in the taxi had helped take
the edge off her fatigue, but she still felt shell-
shocked. The driver had been helpful and had insisted on carrying Brady to her door. He had even
waited until she was inside with the lights on before
backing out of the drive.

Brady, bless his heart, went right back to sleep
after she changed his diaper and put on his pajamas.
She'd rocked him for a few minutes—more for her
peace of mind than his—although even that simple
gesture almost brought her to tears. How often
would she be able to rock her little boy if Ren
Bishop turned out to be Brady's father?

After wiping her mouth with a towel, she looked
in the mirror. The eye makeup Claudie had insisted
she wear for the camera had left dark smudges under
her eyes. In the glow of the overhead lights, Sara
thought she looked half dead. Surely that's what
she'd be if she lost Brady.

The jingle of the telephone made her jump. Probably Daniel, she thought, dashing across the cold tile
to the plush carpet. She vaulted into bed and drew
up the covers. "Hello?"

"Sara, it's Ren. Did I wake you?"

A lump formed in her throat. "N-no."

"I just wanted to make you sure you got home safely."

His voice did weird things to her equilibrium. She felt small and vulnerable around him, and that wasn't a very smart way to feel if he were about to become her enemy. "I'm fine. Just exhausted. You were right, though."

"I was?" He sounded surprised to hear her say anything positive. "About what?"

"The cab. I was in no condition to drive. I slept the whole way home," she admitted.

He was silent a moment. She could picture him smiling. He had such a warm smile...for a judge. "Good," he said. "I'm glad I could help since I was at fault for causing you..." His voice trailed off as if he didn't want to bring up a sore subject. "Will you be able to go back to sleep now?"

Sara smiled. One good thing she'd retained from her military experience was the ability to sleep on command. "Yes."

"Good."

"What about you?"

Sara wondered if his pause meant he was surprised by her question. "I doubt it. Fortunately, my golf partner loves it when I'm not at my best."

Sara smiled. He was teasing. She could tell by the softening of his tone.

The pause between them lengthened. "Would it be all right if I stopped by the bookstore tomorrow, Sara? Maybe if you got to know me, you might—"

Sara interrupted. "No. I mean, no, don't bother stopping by. I won't be there. I'm opening up, but

Claudie and Keneesha are taking over in the afternoon so I can meet with a contractor. My eaves need painting."

"Why do you live so far out?" he asked. "That commute must get old."

Sara looked at the cathedral ceiling above her bed. Spiders were spinning condo-webs.

"I wasn't thinking too clearly right after the funerals. It seemed logical that Brady should stay in an environment he knew, so I gave up my apartment and moved in. But you're right, the commute can be pretty awful. Fortunately, I go in a little later than the white-collar commuters."

She snuggled down, for some reason reluctant to break off the conversation. "How'd you manage to find such a convenient location?"

His low chuckle made her shiver. "I was born."

"I beg your pardon?"

"I grew up in this house. My parents lived here until Dad passed away. Then Mother moved into a condo on the golf course and offered me this place."

"Must be nice," Sara said.

His sigh caught her by surprise. "Actually, it was a tough choice. I was in the process of restoring a 1906 Victorian in Folsom—a true money pit, but I loved it."

"So why did you move?"

"Mother pointed out that this place fit all three real estate criteria—location, location, location." There was a pause. "If you met my mother, you'd understand. She should have been a lobbyist."

Sara's grin faded when Ren continued, "I've been thinking about what you asked me—about how I became involved with your sister. Would you like me to tell you what happened? I guarantee you'll be under no obligation to believe me.''

Sara's heart moved into her throat. ''I'll listen.''

''Okay—''

She heard him draw a breath. She closed her eyes and focused on his voice.

''I truly can't explain why it happened. Believe me, nothing like this had ever happened before. All I know is I was running away from my life at the time. I figured fresh air and fast skiing would help me find some perspective. Then on the very first trip up the hill, I found myself sitting next to the most beautiful woman I'd ever met.''

Julia was good at catching men's attention, Sara thought, smiling.

''We flirted. I was flattered.''

Sara made a snorting sound.

''No, I mean it. I'm no Don Juan. I've dated very few women in my life, actually. I attended an all-male high school. The girl I dated in college broke my heart when she chose medicine over me. Law school was all-consuming, then I went to work for a government agency that frowned on fraternization among colleagues.''

''You're engaged to a very beautiful woman,'' Sara felt obliged to point out.

''I wasn't when I met your sister. I'd met Eve that January, but we hadn't been out on a date.'' He sighed. ''Anyway, Julia and I skied together all day. She was great—bold, a little crazy. I was utterly infatuated. I invited her to dinner. She said, 'Let's order room service.' When I woke up in the morning she was gone. Not a note, not a clue. All I knew was her first name—Jewel.''

Sara frowned. "Our mother sometimes called her that. 'My little Jewel.' I thought Julia hated that name."

Ren blew out a breath. "Maybe that's why she used it. If she went there intending to have a fling, she might not have liked herself very much at that moment. I really can't say. To me, she seemed very up, spontaneous, poised. Totally in control. It was always her call."

"Nobody made Julia do anything she didn't want to do."

"Why do *you* think she did it—went to Tahoe that weekend alone?"

His subtle phrasing disarmed her; she forgot her fear of saying something that might be used against her in court. "I don't remember that exact weekend, but I know she was restless. She pretended to be happy living the life of a wealthy doctor's wife, but she really missed her job, her friends, the sense of accomplishment she got from nursing."

"Maybe she got tired of pretending," he suggested.

"Maybe," she agreed. "Too bad we'll never know."

Ren ended the conversation a few minutes later, telling her she needed to rest.

Sara hung up feeling oddly torn. She could have liked this man under normal circumstances. She could certainly understand how her sister might have been attracted to him.

Tears filled her eyes as she rolled on her side and pulled her pillow to her belly. "Did I fail you, Julia?'' she softly cried. ''Were you so lonely, so sad, you turned to a stranger for consolation? Or did you sleep with him for another reason—to get pregnant?''

CHAPTER SEVEN

"AHOY, MATES, come aboard," Bo hailed, employing a hearty pirate voice that made Brady dig his fingernails into Sara's bare thigh. She took his hand to reassure him and also to lead him safely across the metal dock to the end berth where Bo's houseboat was moored. "Happy Memorial Day," he called, waving a Brady-size flag.

"Hi, Bo, thanks for inviting us," Sara called back, hoping to ease her son's trepidation. On the drive to the Delta, Brady had jabbered nonstop about boats, but now seemed frozen in either terror or wonder—Sara wasn't sure which.

"Glad you could make it. How's my little fishin' buddy?"

Brady ducked his head behind Sara's leg, almost knocking her off balance. Bo gallantly cleared the short distance between them and relieved her of her overstuffed backpack. "So, tell me again why the Cowardly Hooker, I mean Claudie, isn't with you," Bo asked, ushering them aboard the boxy-looking vessel.

Sara had never seen a houseboat up close—with horizontal vinyl siding and metal awnings, it resembled a mobile home on pontoons. She looked around, taking in the small harbor outlined by banks of dense, bushy trees, and counted a dozen vessels, from rowboat size to canopy-topped residences like Bo's.

"Claudie said to tell you she had to wash her hair," Sara said, her nostrils crinkling at the fishy scent in the warm, humid air. "I told her she could do better than that, so she said to say it was cramps. Take your pick."

As Bo led the way to an exterior patio at the rear of the houseboat, Sara's free hand clamped tight to the waist-high metal railing that encircled the vessel. The decorative upright columns seemed too far apart to keep Brady from the water. *This might have been a mistake.*

After plunking her bag down atop a round picnic table covered in a cheerful geranium-print tablecloth, Bo scratched his head. His wrinkled Hawaiian-print shirt topped baggy cargo shorts. His feet were bare except for dime-store thongs. "Humph. I'll tell you whose butt I'm gonna kick on Wednesday night."

"She charges extra for that, you know," Sara quipped, smiling when his mouth dropped open.

"Never underestimate the quiet, demure type," he muttered, as if filing away an important fact.

She herded Brady away from the exterior corridor. "Actually, Claudie's trying hard to turn her life around, Bo. She's taking an online study course to help her pass the GED, and Sundays and holidays are the best days to study."

Bo looked unconvinced. "Why lie about that?"

"She doesn't want anyone to know, in case she fails. This is pretty shaky ground for her. Someone went to a lot of trouble convincing Claudie she was dumb, and when you're taught that as a child, it's hard to make yourself believe otherwise.''

Bo nodded sagely. ''I'm glad she's climbing out of the pit. Maybe I'll go a little easier on her.'' He frowned. ''Naw, that would just make her mad. Anyway, Brady's here and you're here—that's what counts, right?''

He squatted low and held up a high five for Brady, who studied the hand as if it were an interesting piece of art. Bo sighed. ''We'll work on your good ol' boy camaraderie, but first we gotta get you a life jacket, bud. Only way I'll have a moment's peace.''

She still felt a little uncomfortable socializing with the person who has investigated her, but Bo had stopped by the bookstore several times in the past week to convince her of his sincerity. He'd even volunteered to help her scrape paint next weekend.

And when Sara needed a favor from Ren—to hold off trying to get a court order for the DNA test until Hulger's estate lawyer returned from his two-week vacation—she'd used Bo as an intermediary. He'd returned her call saying Ren would wait, if she'd promise to reconsider doing the test without a court order.

Sara vacillated between standing her ground at any cost and giving in to the inevitable, but Daniel and Keneesha adamantly opposed any concession. ''Only a fool would believe a political player like Ren Bishop,'' Daniel had told her. ''His fiancée is going to be the next Jane Pauley. Do you think she's going to stick around Sacramento just so you can help raise that little boy?'' He'd read in a gossip column about Eve Masterson's reputed talks with the networks.

Bo's offer of a relaxing day on the water seemed like just the break she needed.

After giving a quick tour of his home, Bo showed Sara to the room where she and Brady could change clothes. "Don't forget the sunscreen," he warned, pulling the door closed behind him.

A short time later, Brady—bright and pudgy in his coast-guard-approved life vest—worshipfully held a small plastic fishing rod in his hand. "Let's catch dinner, pal," Bo said, leading the way to a fishing platform attached to the rear of the houseboat.

Sara—frosty mug of beer in hand—watched them from a lawn chair. Her heartstrings twanged. Brady not only responded to this kind of male camaraderie, he gravitated toward it like a moon. It was odd, Sara thought, how in a few short days she'd come to see something was missing in both their lives—when they had seemed pretty complete before.

Sara leaned her head back and closed her eyes.

"Where's Ren today?" she asked, despite her best intentions to the contrary. Sara hadn't seen him since that Friday night when he'd called her a cab, although she'd spoken to him several times on the phone.

"Some political fund-raising bash. Very posh," Bo told her. When he named the host of the event, Sara choked on her beer. Only the wealthiest, most influential of Sacramento's upper echelon. "He said he might stop by later. If that's okay with you."

Sara shrugged as if it didn't matter one way or another. But, her stomach jumped.

"I wasn't sure how you'd feel about him coming here," Bo said, looking at her. "Claudie's kinda backed off from hating him so much, but Keneesha's still ready to hire a hit man."

Sara nodded. "She's like a mother bear protecting her cubs—me and Brady. I've warned Ren to take precautions—bodyguards, bulletproof vest, whatever," she joked.

"I'm sure that went over big."

"Actually, he burst out laughing. I guess he doesn't consider an angry hooker a big threat."

Bo looked up and grinned. "I doubt if Kee's even a blip on his radar screen compared to Babe and Eve—now, those two have fire power."

Sara wanted to ask about Ren's fiancée, but managed to fight the temptation. Instead, she watched as Bo helped Brady bait his hook and cast his line into the water. Its bright red-and-white plastic bobber fell close enough to the platform for Brady to cheer triumphantly.

Sara savored the moment. In the distance, jet skis and powerboats raced on the river's main thoroughfare—the noise a mere mosquito buzz in her ears. The sun made her drowsy; her eyes closed.

"You haven't heard from Ren's mother, have you?" Bo asked.

Something about his tone made her stomach clench. She sat up straighter. "Should I have? Ren said she was less than thrilled about the news—but who could blame her? Why? Is something wrong?"

As if sensing her disquiet, Bo frowned. "Babe Bishop is a battle-ax—I mean, ship. I can't see her letting this thing go without a skirmish."

"What could she do?"

"Make trouble between you and Ren."

"You make it sound like we have a relationship. We're just opposing sides in a custody battle. I'd expect Babe to be in Ren's corner."

Bo ruffled Brady's curls. "It's too damn—I mean darn—bad you two can't work this out without going to court. I'm not saying this for Ren's benefit, but I've been thinking about it from Brady's point of view, and I think he'd want to know the truth— I know I would. After that, if Ren is his daddy, then you could work out what's fair for the three of you."

"What about Eve? As Ren's fiancée, wouldn't she have a say?"

Bo's broad shoulders rose and fell. "Frankly, I think Eve's a long shot at this point, but that's just my opinion."

Sara would have asked what he meant, but Brady's sudden cry of joy made her lunge for her camera to record her son's first catch.

Although it was a long way from a keeper, Bo made a big deal about the wonderful prize, then he solemnly explained how to release the fish back into the water. Brady wavered, his bottom lip quivering, but after some coaxing leaned over the water and let it go. Sara watched for several heart-stopping seconds until the fish got a second wind and sped away. Brady cheered, ran to her and gave her a big hug.

When Sara looked at Bo, she was surprised at the tender look on his face. For a man who usually kept his emotions hidden, he couldn't conceal how he felt about children. Before she could ask why he wasn't married, though, Bo said, "Who wants to water-ski?"

A GLANCE AT THE SPEEDOMETER made Ren ease his foot off the gas. He purposely relaxed his fingers on the steering wheel and filled his lungs with a deep, calming breath. His stomach still churned from the mixture of political rhetoric, rich food and poisoned glances courtesy of his mother and fiancée. Babe had been outraged that he planned to cut out early from the lavish affair he'd paid royally to attend, but Ren didn't care. The only place he wanted to be at the moment was on Bo's houseboat.

He exited the freeway, thankful for the twenty or so miles of country highway that would give him time to decompress after the rarefied atmosphere he'd just left. Although he and Eve had put on a good front, he was sure he'd seen a few raised brows, no doubt a result of the gossip column revelation that Eve was up for a network job.

Ren, too, wondered where he stood with his fiancée, but her frantic schedule since her return from New York had inhibited any face-to-face discussion. His one chance to see her alone at dinner the previous evening had been sabotaged by her pager.

"Sorry, honey," she'd told him, gathering up her purse and cell phone. "I know we were supposed to talk, but I'll see you at the fund-raiser tomorrow. I took the night off, so maybe we can go to my place afterwards."

When he'd mentioned Bo's fish fry, Eve's eyes had narrowed angrily. "Naturally Bo takes precedence over our plans for the future."

"It's not Bo. Sara is going to be there, and she's bringing Brady. I've been keeping my distance to give Sara time to think, but I want her to get to know

me, so she'll see I'm not some kind of ogre just out
to steal her kid.''

"Sara," she'd hissed, pettishly. "The woman
you've never made love to but whose child you
covet.''

Ren, who'd already spent a week dealing with his
mother's chastisement, had answered with a sigh.
''This has more to do with Brady than Sara, but
she's his guardian. I have to go through her to get
him.''

Eve had leaned close and said, ''I talked to Marcella about this when I was in New York, and she
said the child's actually not such a bad idea. If it
turns out he is your son, then you won't need me to
take time out of my career to give birth. Right away,
I mean. I'd like to have a child of my own some
day, but not anytime soon. I have too much to ac-
complish career-wise.''

After she'd left, Ren had digested her words instead of dinner. He'd even contemplated going to
her place so they could try to work things out. He
and Eve had good history together—but he couldn't
help wondering if they had a future.

Ultimately, he'd chosen to go home instead,
where he'd surfed the Internet, learning about paternity issues and DNA testing kits. He learned that
no DNA test devised could prove with one-hundred-
percent accuracy if a man was a child's father, but
it could prove with a 99.6-percent accuracy rate if
he wasn't.

Ren glanced down and adjusted his speed once
more. The profusion of trees and advent of levees
told him he was getting close. Biofeedback told him
his heartbeat was speeding up, but it didn't worry

him. He was looking forward to seeing Brady and Sara.

He'd talked with her several times by phone but hadn't seen her or Brady since that Friday night when he kissed her. He'd stopped by her bookstore the day after the disastrous lunch with his mother. As Sara had told him, Claudie was in the store on her own. Ren had hoped to use the opportunity to mend a few fences with Sara's friends, but it proved a bigger challenge than he'd imagined.

As he drove down the winding country road, he pictured the exchange.

"Let's get one thing straight," Claudie had said, plunking a cup of coffee in front of him. "I don't trust you and I don't like you."

She'd paced back and forth behind the coffee bar agitatedly, then stopped across from him and added, "You mighta scared me into shuttin' up when I was workin' the streets, but I been done with that for a couple of months, so you can't do nothing to me. I know it's against the law to threaten a judge, but you better believe, if you do anything to hurt Sara, I'll…"

Ren had saved her the trouble of naming a torture. "I have no intention of doing anything to hurt Sara."

"Taking away her baby don't hurt?" she'd shouted. Resuming her pacing, she'd orated with all the power and passion of a senator. "What is it with you men? Maybe you think you know about being a mother because you had one, but it ain't the same for men as it is for women. Nature planned it that way—she gave us more hormones and a bigger heart. You could never know what it's like to lose a baby.''

Ren had felt castigated by the young woman's words. "You're right. I don't know what Sara is feeling. I only know what I've felt ever since I first learned about Brady. Wonder. Hope. Anticipation. Like I might have won the lottery but I'm waiting for that last number to appear. It's scary and exciting at the same time.''

She'd studied him a long time before saying, with a sigh, "Why can't you just go away?''

"Because *if*—and that's the big word here—*if* I'm Brady's father, then he deserves me as much as I deserve him." Ren had had to blink against the sudden moisture that filled his eyes. "This doesn't have to be a bad thing, Claudie. I know I can add to his life. I have money put away that could pay for his college education. I could teach him yoga—show him how to golf, how to ski." Her sudden frown had made him bite his tongue. "Maybe not skiing.''

Her lips had flattened as if trying not to smile, and Ren had decided to leave while he was slightly ahead.

Before he could reach the door, Claudie had called, "Sara called a few minutes ago. She said the car fairy had washed, waxed and vacuumed out the inside of her car while it was parked at your house.''

Ren had shrugged nonchalantly. "Imagine that.''

"She sounded happy. Real happy," Claudie had added, her tone remarkably free of rancor.

He'd smiled, gratified to know his small act of kindness meant that much to Sara, but it also made him realize how alone she was and what a heavy burden she carried.

Three gaudy flags, weathered almost beyond recognition, alerted Ren to the location of Bo's dockside residence. Ren liked to give his friend a hard time about his floating hovel, but in truth Ren envied Bo. Ren's house was too big and austere; despite his renovations, it was still a long way from his dream home. Bo's little home was cozy and personal.

Ren parked, grabbed his gym bag from the seat and hurried toward the houseboat. A quick scan told him Bo and his guests were out on the water in the speedboat, so Ren stripped off the layers of the outside world, pulled on a pair of navy swim trunks, then dashed to Bo's fishing platform and dove into the water.

"Ren." He heard a voice call as soon as he surfaced. A sleek ski boat—Bo's pride and joy—trolled toward him. Bo killed the inboard engine, and the boat coasted to within an arm's length. Ren grabbed the chrome railing at the rear of the boat and hauled himself aboard, shaking the water from his hair. Brady squealed with laughter.

Sara handed him a towel, which he accepted with a smile. The appreciative look in her eyes surprised him and warmed him. She liked his body.

"So how was your snooty party?" Bo asked, once Ren was sitting down. He gave the throttle a nudge and the boat surged forward, heading for the main channel.

"Predictably elegant, lavish and boring," he said, smiling at Brady who was hanging over the side, his hand trailing in the water. Sara, Ren noticed, had a firm grip on the child's life vest. "The only halfway entertaining part was when Mandy Hightower's boy-friend stumbled over Edith Sherwood's walker and sent a table full of crab puffs airborne. I caught one in midair,'' Ren said, winking at Sara.

He helped himself to a beer from Bo's cooler. The speedboat was one of the newer models that offered wraparound seating. Sara and Brady were directly across from Ren; her bare feet were almost touching his.

"Did Eve accept her award on behalf of all the little people she had to step on—I mean over?'' Bo asked.

Ren shrugged, his attention fixed on the way Sara's hair glistened in the sunlight. "I don't know. I left before that.''

Bo choked on the soda he held to his lips. "You left? Holy sh—Sheryl Crow, I bet Babe liked that.''

Ren's focus was drawn to the way Sara's slim body filled out her swimsuit. Swigging his beer, he moved to the copilot's seat beside Bo. "I lucked out. Neither Babe nor Eve is speaking to me. So I have no idea how they feel.''

Bo gave a hoot, then looked over his shoulder and called, "Hang on tight, Sara, I'm gonna open her up.''

Sara pulled Brady back and settled him on her lap. Now Ren could appreciate the way her swimsuit displayed her curves. He realized, suddenly, that he liked her body, too.

"WOULD IT HAVE HURT HER to act a little curious, Bo? My God, we're talking a possible grandchild—her own flesh and blood. All she cared about was how I've jeopardized my future. 'What will this mean to your judgeship?' she kept asking. My political viability.''

Ren's voice penetrated the houseboat's thin walls to the room where Sara was trying to get Brady to nap. After their exciting ride in the speedboat—with Ren and Bo taking turns water-skiing—Sara had sensed Brady's fatigue. Naturally the little boy didn't want to miss a minute of fun with his big friends, but she'd finally calmed him by lying down beside him. She'd been on the verge of dozing herself, when Ren's voice had seeped into her consciousness.

''She asked me why I couldn't have a normal middle-age breakdown like other men. 'Buy a sports car,' she said. 'Get your ear pierced like Harrison Ford.'''

''Did she ask for names?'' Bo asked.

Sara's breath caught in her throat.

''Of course. I'm sure she thought if I'd dallied with someone famous, she could make that work in my favor.''

Bo snorted. ''You didn't tell her about Sara, did you?''

''God, no. Sara has enough on her plate without dealing with Babe.''

His tone made Sara shiver. She'd heard enough. She rose, walked to the adjoining bathroom and splashed water on her face.

Her head throbbed from too much sun. She found some aspirin in her purse and took two, then closed her eyes and leaned forward to rest her forehead on the cool mirror. Too much sun, too much fun, too much Ren, she thought, picturing the incredible jackknife dive he'd made into the water—clean and elegant like an Olympian. As she'd deduced from their encounter the previous Friday, Ren Bishop was built with broad shoulders, narrow waist and long, well-muscled legs.

I have to stop thinking of him, she told herself. *Just remember that he has his own agenda and I have mine. Julia left Brady to me—he's my responsibility. Period.*

"Where's Bo?" Sara said a short while later, opening the screen door to the rear patio area. She'd changed out of her swimsuit into shorts, T-shirt and sandals.

Ren was alone, sprawled in a chaise longue. He started, and she realized she'd awakened him.

"Oh, sorry I woke you."

He hid a yawn behind his hand. "No problem. Bo ran to the store. I was just relaxing. That's the problem with a desk job. If you play too hard on the weekend, you pay for it all week."

"You ski well. Jumping wakes—pretty impressive."

He'd put on a gray tank top over his swimsuit. He shrugged one shoulder. "I like the water. How come you didn't try it?"

Sara walked to the railing and looked at Bo's speedboat moored a few feet away. *Julia died in a boat like that.* "My brother-in-law tried to teach me, but I just couldn't get it. Maybe I'm dyslexic when it comes to skiing. Hulger wouldn't give up—'round and 'round he'd go trying to get me up. But I couldn't do it. After a while I just quit going out with them. When Brady was born, I had the perfect excuse—baby-sitter."

Ren was silent a long time. "Did it bother you to be in the boat today? It hadn't occurred to me..."

She turned to face him. "I had a great time. Brady was ecstatic. He loves the water, and I haven't made much of an effort to take him swimming or anything. There are a couple of lakes at Rancho Carmel and a nice big pool, but there never seems to be enough time to do everything."

Sara bit her lip. Maybe it wasn't a good idea admitting her shortcomings as a parent to the person who wanted to be Brady's other parent.

"He doesn't strike me as deprived," Ren said, smiling warmly. "He's inquisitive, spontaneous, fearless, willful, kind... He really is a great kid, Sara."

She couldn't believe how good his praise made her feel. She smiled back. "Well, just don't let me forget to wake him. If he sleeps too long he'll be a bear to get to bed tonight."

"Brady?" he said with staged disbelief.

"He's going to be two in November. He's a little boy. Need I say more?"

Ren's chuckle strummed a chord deep inside her. She flattened her hand against her tummy, trying to place it.

"Are you hungry?" Ren asked, leaning forward to push a basket of chips her way. "Bo's picking up steaks. He said the only good-size fish they caught was Brady's, and you made them put it back."

Sara laughed. She held up her hand, spreading her index finger and thumb about four inches apart to show him the size of the fish. His throaty chuckle made Sara think of rich chocolate sauce. Decadent.

Still smiling, she walked to the chaise adjacent to his and sat down. She nibbled on a chip and stared at the play of shadows on the water. "Ren, I didn't mean to eavesdrop, but I overheard you talking with Bo about your mother. Maybe she's right to worry about what effect this could have on your career."

He inhaled deeply, then sighed. "To tell you the truth, Sara, my career is not *my* career. I've heard people say you should wait a year after the loss of a loved one to make big, encompassing changes in your life. My dad died, and a month later I was up for appointment to his seat. I don't really remember ever making a conscious decision that this is what I wanted to do with my life."

Sara was intrigued. She'd assumed every lawyer wanted to be a judge. "What about the money? The power?"

He sat up and faced her, his feet on the floor between them. "Superior Court judges in California earn $120,000 a year—$10,000 a month. That's not chicken feed, but—" he looked her squarely in the eye "—I learned the fine art of investing from my father. It got to be kind of a competitive game between us—to see whose companies did best. I like to win at games. So frankly, I don't need the money."

Sara stared at him, mute. Her budget was so bare bones that some months she didn't think there'd be anything left over.

He went on. "As for the power...some people might enjoy holding a person's life in their hands— I don't. Sometimes I don't know whether or not I've made the right decision. I'm just thankful there's an appellate court that can correct my mistakes if I've made any.''

His intensity made Sara's heart expand in her chest.

''My father didn't become a judge until he was fifty-nine years old. I'm forty-two. Maybe if I had another seventeen years of experience...''

Sara felt oddly moved by his revelation. ''What would you do if you weren't a judge?'' she asked.

Ren rose and walked to the railing where she'd been standing. The sun was beginning to set, and his face was shaded. Just as well, Sara thought. I can't look in his eyes without remembering our kiss.

''I used to think about teaching. I do a little tutoring a couple of nights a week at the jail. It feels good when a person connects with what you're teaching him.''

''What would your fiancée think about your changing professions?'' Sara asked.

Before Ren could answer, Bo's noisy arrival signaled an end to their intimate talk. Sara told herself she was only asking because of what it might mean to Brady, but a part of her knew she was curious for other reasons. Foolish reasons.

BO TOSSED A MATCH on the pile of charcoal, then jumped back. The minute he'd walked in he'd felt something just as combustible between Ren and Sara—even if they pretended otherwise. He shouldn't have been surprised—things had been brewing all afternoon. Overly casual stares. Contrived accidental touches.

He'd debated about getting involved or minding his own business the whole time he was shopping.

Basically, except for giving Ren a hard time about Eve—who wasn't a bad person, just not the right person for Ren—Bo stayed out of people's romances. But this was different. Sara was an innocent; she wouldn't last a minute in a Bishop sea— not with Babe and Eve circling.

"Sara, shouldn't you wake Brady? Ren promised to help him fish some more."

Sara bolted toward the bedroom, and Ren followed Bo into the kitchen.

"Something bothering you?" Ren asked.

"Yeah, there is. You said you were coming by today so Sara could get to know you better. I want to know how much better."

Ren's eyes narrowed. "I like her. Is that a crime?"

"Depends on who's the judge."

Ren gave him a steely stare, then turned away to catch Brady who barreled past like a runaway pumpkin.

"Whoa, kiddo, slow down you'll scare the fish." He picked up the little boy and smiled. Both sets of midnight-blue eyes flashed with joy, and Bo felt himself chagrined with envy.

Ren hiked Brady to his hip, then gave Bo a stern look and muttered, "Stay out of this, Bo."

A minute later Sara emerged from the bedroom and joined Bo at the counter. He started to hand her a tomato, but stopped. She looked at him questioningly. Her nose was a little sunburned, her hair windblown. She looked sixteen. He wanted to warn her not to get involved with Ren, to arm herself in any way possible against a possible attack from

Babe, and to prepare herself for Ren's inevitable victory.

Instead, he asked, "What kind of salad dressing does the kid like?"

"WHEN BO WOULD COME HOME with me for holidays—Thanksgiving, Christmas, Easter—he and Dad would take off and disappear for hours. Drove my mother crazy."

"Now, you can't pin that one on me," Bo argued. "Babe has always been crazy. Larry was just too nice to point it out, and she's got you pussy-whipped."

"Baloney."

"Gentlemen," Sara interjected, thoroughly regretting her innocent question that had somehow turned best friends into antagonists. "Whose turn is it to push?"

After dinner, they'd walked to a nearby playground, where the three adults took turns entertaining Brady. Bo took over swing duty from Sara.

"Sorry," he mumbled under his breath.

Sara sat down on the empty swing beside Brady's and watched the little boy's face light up with joy as Bo cautiously pushed him. "So," she said carefully, "the bottom line is you were roommates in college, you spent holidays together—Bo partied, and Ren was the dignified one."

A pair of hands touched her waist, making her jump. "Pretty close," Ren said softly, gently giving her a push. "After graduation, Bo stopped drinking, joined the police department and eventually became a PI. I went to law school."

Sara lifted her feet and closed her eyes, reveling in the unexpected sensations.

"And Ren continued to be his dignified self—except for one small indiscretion, which is how we all came to be here tonight."

Sara, caught up in the dual pleasure of Ren's touch and gliding upward, let Bo's comment drift past her. She used her legs to pump higher, anticipating the solid warmth of Ren's hands against the small of her back when she returned to earth.

"What about you, Sara?" Bo asked. "Who was your best friend growing up?"

Maybe the freedom of near flight made her answer with uncharacteristic candor. "Julia." The name seemed to float on the air, as if Sara had conjured up her presence. "My father died when I was three, and my mother had a problem with alcohol, so mostly it was Julia who took care of me. She was part mother, part best friend."

On her next upward arc, Sara leaned back to view the world upside down. "We fought like you guys—ongoing arguments over nothing, but we always made up. I knew I could count on her for anything, and she knew I'd always be here for her. I don't know if that made us better sisters or better friends, but we were both."

The breeze kicked up, and Sara realized it was nearly dark. "Bombs away," she called, jumping into the air. "It's getting late, Brady boy. We have to go. Tomorrow's a workday."

Ren and Bo took turns giving Brady piggyback rides. Sara knew from the tenor of Brady's shrieks of laughter that she was going to be in for a difficult time getting him to leave. Her head began to ache just picturing the long drive home with a crying, whining child in a car seat.

"Sara, what if I offered to drive you home?" Ren said, startling her with his empathic abilities.

"My car's here."

"Bo could pick you up in the morning and have Claudie run him home later. I have an early morning docket, or I'd do it."

She looked at Bo, who seemed less than thrilled by the idea. "It's really not necessary," she said, sorry she couldn't put more force behind her words.

"I know, but you had wine with dinner and it's a long, unfamiliar drive. What do you think, Bo?"

Bo looked at Sara intently. She was certain he intended to say no.

For some reason he said, "Okay. Whatever."

CHAPTER EIGHT

"THAT'S ALL WRONG, lamebrain. If you put that strap there, where does this one go?" one voice snarled.

"Get out of my face," the other growled. "How can I see when you're hogging all the space?"

Sara took Brady's hand to lead him away from the Lexus, half expecting it to blow up from the tempers brewing in the back seat. Once Bo had agreed to Ren's suggestion that he drive her and Brady home, Sara had assumed it would be a simple matter of transferring Brady's safety seat to Ren's car, then they'd be on their way. Apparently, she'd underestimated the potent mixture of male ego and technology.

Brady pulled on her arm, whining to help the men. The little boy had reached his limit even without the undercurrents of tension between Ren and Bo. "What, love?" she asked, trying to calm him with her touch. "No, you can't help them. They're having enough trouble as it is."

He pushed her hands away and flung himself to the ground, sobbing as though his world were coming to an end. "Brady," Sara soothed, squatting beside him. "We're leaving in just a minute." That promise seemed to upset him even more, although she couldn't understand a syllable of his weepy diatribe.

Sara sensed a presence at her side and looked up to see Ren, his concern obvious even given the fading light. "Can I help?"

She nodded. "He doesn't get like this often, but he's exhausted. Just pick him up and let's get him strapped in the car seat. Is it in?"

"I hope so." He lowered himself to one knee, focusing on Brady, who'd rolled onto his back and was kicking his feet against the dusty concrete floor of the parking lot. Eyes squeezed shut, his face almost apoplectic, his tantrum raged. Sara would have been mortified by this public behavior under normal circumstances, but for some reason—maybe Ren's calmness—she simply watched as Ren picked up her screaming child. Walking beside them, she tugged off Brady's heavy shoes to keep him from inflicting bodily harm.

Ren tried cajoling, but the child was beyond words. When they neared the car where Bo stood holding open the rear door, Brady tried to fling himself out of Ren's arms toward Bo, but Ren held fast. Sara chose not to watch the actual wrestling into the car seat. Instead, she gave Bo a quick hug and thanked him for the wonderful day, then slid into the passenger seat of the elegant car.

A moment later Ren joined her behind the wheel. The noise from the back seat filled the air, but Ren flashed a thumbs-up and started the car. They'd only gone half a mile before Sara groaned, "That's it. I can't take it anymore."

She unbuckled her seat belt.

"He's going to run out of steam eventually," Ren said, his voice full of concern.

"I'm afraid he'll make himself sick before that happens," she told him. "I think I can get him to calm down now that the car is moving. I have to try."

She climbed over the seat as gracefully as possible, careful to avoid touching Ren. She already regretted her decision to ride home with him—his proximity reminded her of his kiss…and the countless erotic dreams it had spawned.

"Brady, my sweet, remember your fish? Your big fish? Where do you think he is right this minute?"

Her singsong voice seemed to reach him. He stopped crying and looked at her, although his huffing little sniffles continued like a broken train. "I bet he's home with his mama under the water. I bet he's telling her about the nice boy he met today. The nice boy who let him go."

Brady's bottom lip shot out, and he looked ready to cry again, so Sara hurriedly added, "You're such a good boy, Brady. I love you. Someday when you're bigger you'll be swimming in the river and that fish—he'll be bigger, too—will look up at you and tell his buddies, 'Hey, guys, that's my friend, Brady.'"

The nonsense made Brady smile. She took a moistened towel packet from the backpack and wiped the streaks of dirt, tears and ketchup from his face. "Should we sing Ren our night-night song?"

Brady suddenly looked up, as if remembering the other adult in the car. He waved to Ren, who apparently caught the motion in the rearview mirror and waved back. "How'ya doing, Brady? Time to sleep?"

Brady responded by asking if Ren was going to sleep at their house so the two of them could play in the morning. Sara felt herself blush.

Fortunately, very few people aside from Sara could understand Brady. "He wanted to know if you'd read him a bedtime story," she ad-libbed.

"Sure, big guy. Anything you want."

Yawning, Brady reached out and took Sara's hand. "Mommy sing."

Sara laid her cheek against the soft padding of his seat. In a low, soothing voice, she softly sang the lullaby Brady liked best. He popped his thumb in his mouth and closed his eyes. Sara closed her eyes, too, intending to rest them just a second or two.

"Sara, wake up." Ren's voice was gentle. "I need your authorization to get in."

Sara sat up, startled by the bright lights outside the car. She realized in an instant where she was—the back seat of the Lexus, parked at the Rancho Carmel security gate. "Oh, my gosh, I slept all the way. Oh…" she groaned.

The rear passenger window slithered down. "Don't worry about it. We're here now, so check us in." His tone was kind, almost amused.

She swallowed her embarrassment and leaned out the window to wave at Clark, the night guard. He handed Ren a visitor's pass, and Ren pulled ahead.

"So, where to?"

She directed him to her house. At night, the rambling, angular building didn't look quite as hideous as it did by day. As soon as he was parked in the driveway, Sara scrambled out and dashed to the door to unlock it and turn on lights. Before she could return for Brady, Ren was there, child in arms. "Lead the way," he said.

Brady's nursery was the one room in the house Sara liked. She flipped on the light switch and pointed to the crib nestled in an alcove replete with skylight.

"Leave him on his back. I need to change his diaper and put on his jammies," she said, taking both from a built-in dresser.

"Won't he wake up?" Ren asked, his low whisper sending crazy messages up her spine.

"I doubt it. He was wiped out."

"So were you," Ren said softly, moving aside to give her space.

His closeness made her nervous. "I know, but I still can't believe I zonked out like that. How rude! I'm so embarrassed."

"Don't be. You needed the rest. I'm glad I was there." He moved away a step. "Besides, I'd had a pretty hectic day myself. The drive gave me time to think."

Sara didn't ask about what. As she changed Brady, Ren walked around the spacious room. "Great room," he said, studying the mural on the walls. "Who did the paintings?"

"Julia found a struggling young artist from Sac State. She lived here for six months while going to school. It's Julia's design."

Ren whistled under his breath. "Your sister was very talented."

"Yes," Sara whispered back. "But her true talent was nursing."

She kissed Brady and turned him on his side, tucking his stuffed elephant beside him.

Sara motioned Ren to follow. "How about a cup of coffee? It's decaf." At his nod, she led the way to the kitchen. A vast, humorless room, its steel-and-chrome motif resembled the control panel of a space capsule.

"Wow, can this thing get us to Mars?" Ren asked, looking around.

Sara laughed. "Amazing, isn't it? State-of-the-art everything. Hulger always bought the best."

Ren walked to the wall of glass at the far side of the breakfast nook, where Sara and Brady ate all their meals. He cupped his hands on either side of his head and looked outside. When he looked back, his face remained impassive, but Sara knew what he was thinking.

"Big, huh?"

"Did it come with a zebra and giraffes?"

Sara burst out laughing. She didn't stop until Ren touched her shoulder. "Sorry," she said, wiping the corners of her eyes. "Most people say things like, 'Were all those rocks here or did you bring them in?'"

She lowered her voice. "Do you know what? Hulger did have the rocks moved in. They cost a fortune. Julia almost divorced him over it."

When the coffee was ready she handed him a cup and directed him to what Hulger had called his "Valhalla."

"Oh," Ren said, lifting his chin to take in the massive fireplace of rock and mortar. "That's some fireplace."

Sara sat down on one of the leather couches, arranging a multicolored throw so her legs weren't touching the white leather. She disliked the feel of the cold leather against her skin.

Ren, who was also wearing shorts, didn't seem affected by the modernist leather-and-chrome sling he chose to sit in. "This décor doesn't suit you," he said, sipping his coffee.

Sara smiled at his diplomacy. "I know. None of the furnishings are mine. I was living in a three-room apartment before I moved in here. My stuff is stored in one corner of the garage." She pictured the small pile of boxes and half-dozen antiques she'd been carefully acquiring—none of which would have jibed with Hulger's taste.

"You don't have to live here, do you?"

She took a deep breath. "I often think about moving, but it's complicated. Like I told you, I moved in because I thought this would be less stressful for Brady." She shook her head remembering those hectic, heartbreaking weeks after Julia's death. "It was pure chaos after the accident. I had two funerals to plan…Hulger's parents came from Denmark. You can't imagine how crazy it was."

Sara could tell by his frown that he wanted to ask her something. She took a guess. "You're wondering if I heard any of the speculation about the accident, aren't you?" His brow crinkled as he nodded. "People will always talk, Ren. Even at the memorial service I heard someone say Hulger drove the boat into a rock on purpose, but that isn't true."

"You sound pretty sure."

"For one thing, the inquest ruled it an accident, but above that, I knew Hulger. He was selfish, brash, impulsive and temperamental, but, above all, proud.

He would never have given Julia the satisfaction of getting to him.'' She massaged the muscle at the base of her neck. ''Maybe that doesn't make sense to you, but it does to me. Hulger was a very vocal, demonstrative person—he could rant and rave like a two-year old, but within seconds of blowing up he'd be smiling, acting the congenial host. That was one of the things that drove Julia crazy.''

''So you think he might have been caught up in the heat of the moment and missed seeing the rock, but that he didn't purposely aim for it,'' Ren said, keeping his gaze on her face.

''Exactly. He worshiped Julia, and he loved this stupid house. Plus, he was very good at his job. He had a great future ahead of him. I know he'd never have committed suicide. Never.''

''What kind of father was he?''

Sara took a drink of coffee; it tasted bitter. She rose. ''I'm going to freshen this up. How 'bout you?''

He shook his head. The look on his face told her he knew she was avoiding his question.

''I'll be right back.'' She'd never particularly cared for her brother-in-law, but she didn't think it prudent to speak of his shortcomings to Ren. Maybe Hulger's petty jealousy—even toward his baby son—could be used against her in court.

Plus, it didn't help matters that she was feeling more and more attracted to Ren as a man. Her friends would be horrified if they knew she felt drawn to him—his kindness, his flaws and especially his touch. Sara hated to admit it, but she liked Ren Bishop.

REN ROSE AND WALKED around the vastly unattractive room. What a horrible house! Poor Sara, he thought. The more he learned of her sister's life, the easier it was to picture Julia escaping to Tahoe for a weekend of fun and games. The man who had designed this room was looking to impress people, not enjoy life.

He paused before a painting. Ren recognized the artist's scrawl but not the work. The unframed canvas of grays and browns sported a diagonal dissecting streak of red.

"Hulger paid a fortune for that painting," Sara said, joining him.

"Hulger was an idiot," Ren said shortly.

"Actually, the estate lawyer had that piece appraised and it's tripled in value. I asked him if we could sell it so I could use the money to finish the yard, but he said he'd prefer to see the estate stay intact."

"He's an idiot, too."

She laughed, and he had the urge to kiss her. "I should probably get going."

She nodded. "It was a busy day. I haven't had so much fun in a long time, and I know Brady will be talking about it for days."

Ren still hadn't figured out how anyone could understand anything that came out of Brady's mouth. His doubt must have shown on his face, because Sara said, "He does speak English, Ren—it just comes out so fast nobody can understand him but me. It's normal. Trust me."

"I do. You really handled him well in the car. I'd have just let him cry."

"That would have been okay, too. I'm probably

too softhearted. Keneesha says I spoil him, but it breaks my heart when he's upset.''

''It must be tough to be both the caregiver and the disciplinarian.'' He'd meant to sound supportive, but he could tell by the way Sara's chin came up that she interpreted his words as condescending. He decided to change the subject. ''How long were Julia and Hulger married?''

''Four or five years, I think. I can't remember. They dated several years before that. Julia had been a nurse at the hospital where he worked. She always said people accused her of marrying for money, when in truth Hulger probably married her to avoid deportation.''

''Really?''

She lifted her shoulders. ''Who knows? I never asked.''

''Bo said people at the marina claimed they fought a lot.''

''That's true,'' Sara said, looking down. Her toes curled against her leather thongs. ''But it wasn't all bad. They had fun, too. They traveled all over the world. They threw lavish parties—he was a terrific dancer, and Julia loved to party.''

''Had they been trying for long to have children before Brady was born?''

She let out a breath. ''I think so, but I can't say for sure. Julia was intensely private about some things. She was a complex person, and she hated anyone to second-guess her decisions. She prided herself on being in control at all times.'' Sara tilted her head and gave him a serious look. ''You know, it occurred to me earlier when Bo was describing your mother that she sounds a lot like Julia—no-

nonsense, forward action, perhaps a little self-absorbed.''

Ren couldn't picture the slightest resemblance between the woman he knew as Jewel and his mother. ''Hmm…'' he said, trying to sound agreeable.

''In fact,'' Sara said, looking introspective, ''now that I think about it, your fiancée is that kind of person, too, isn't she?''

Ren took a step back, surprised by her question. ''Are you suggesting a pattern here?'' he asked, trying to be amusing.

She shook her head, giving a harsh, unhappy little laugh. ''No, I'm the last person who should be giving advice about dating. I…''

She looked at him, and Ren could tell she was remembering something painful. He ached to pull her into his arms and comfort her, but he'd already made the mistake of kissing her; he wasn't foolish enough to compound it.

He said good-night and walked to his car, conscious of her gaze following him. As he pulled away, the porch light blinked off, removing the single dab of cheerfulness from the hulking fortress.

SPEEDING DOWN Highway 16 toward town, Ren pushed a preset button on the built-in car phone and listened to the remote ring. There was no answer at the houseboat. ''That's weird. Where'd he go?'' Ren mumbled. He punched a different button. *Maybe he has his cell phone on him,* he thought.

After four rings, a voice said, ''Yeah?''

''Hi. Where are you?''

''None of your business.''

Ren wasn't put off by his friend's bluntness. "I tried the house and you didn't answer."

"I'm talking to you now, aren't I?"

"Listen, after you drop off Sara tomorrow, would you come to my office? I want you to look into the trust that controls Julia's estate. There's no reason Sara should have to live in that godawful house. Have you seen it?"

There was a pause, and Ren heard Bo murmur something to another person. Ren realized he must have intruded on a personal moment. "Are you with somebody?" he asked.

"Yeah, as a matter of fact, I am."

"Oh. Sorry. I just wanted to get this settled. Do you want to call me back later? I'm on my way to Eve's right now."

Bo made a muffled comment to whomever was with him, then asked, "You're calling from your car?"

"Yes, I'm taking the back way to Eve's."

There was another pause that made Ren think he'd lost the connection. He was about to hit Redial, when Bo said, "Listen, buddy, I should warn you. Eve called my house looking for you, and Claudie said she called here—at the bookstore, too."

Ren's mouth fell open. "You're at the bookstore?"

The connection started to crackle. "Yeah," Bo returned testily. "Wanna make something of it?"

Ren grinned at his friend's contentious tone. "No. Not at all. I know what a big reader you've become." Snickering, he added, "Give my regards to Claudie." But the line went dead.

Ren wasn't sure what to make of Bo's interest in

the young woman. Granted, she'd given up working the street when Sara hired her to work at the bookstore, but that didn't mean she was right for Bo. Ren shook his head. He had more pressing matters to think about, namely what was he going to say to Eve.

He wasn't surprised to see the lights on in his fiancée's apartment. She was a night owl. He parked and hurried up the steps to her door. She opened it before he could knock.

"Hi," he said, stepping into the foyer. "I heard you were looking for me." His shin encountered a large black suitcase. "Going somewhere?"

"Yes," Eve said shortly. She was dressed in workout clothes: black leggings and a jade-green sports bra that left her midriff exposed. Her feet were bare. Her hair was twisted into a knot atop her head.

He stuck his hands in the pockets of his Dockers and waited. He'd learned to respect Eve's sense of drama—whatever kind of scene this was, it was going to happen her way.

"Ren, I'm taking the job in New York."

"Is there a reason why you're going so soon?"

Her black eyes flashed in anger. "Damn right. When you chose that woman and her brat over me, I knew then and there our relationship was over."

Ren frowned. "I told you I was going to Bo's."

"Yes, but I didn't know you couldn't even wait long enough to see me receive my award. If I mean that little to you, if my feelings are so far down on your list of priorities…"

Ren stepped toward her. "I'm sorry, Eve. I didn't

realize it was that big of a deal. You get those kinds of awards all the time. What's one more?''

Tears clustered in her eyes, and she turned away. ''Nothing to you, obviously, but it meant something to me. And it meant something to the people who came up to me later asking where you'd gone and why you weren't there to congratulate me.''

Ren grimaced. ''I should have stayed until after the ceremony. I apologize.''

Eve turned around slowly. ''It doesn't matter now. I'm leaving in the morning.''

Ren started to walk past her to the living room. ''Can't we talk about this?''

She placed her small, perfectly manicured hand on his arm. ''Why subject ourselves to the ordeal? It won't change anything. You know this is the way it has to be.''

Ren's heart felt heavy in his chest. A rash of wonderful memories—Eve on Valentine's Day wearing strategically placed construction-paper hearts; the two of them making love on the beach in Maui; their Sunday mornings together sharing bagels and the *New York Times*—chased across his vision, momentarily blinding him.

''Are you sure this is what you want?'' he asked, covering her hand with his. ''I'm sorry I hurt you today, but there's nothing going on between Sara and me. Unless that DNA test proves I'm Brady's father, I won't have any reason to ever see her again.''

Eve pulled her hand back and walked to the door. ''I'm sure you believe that, Ren, but I don't. I know you. Probably better than you know yourself. She's your escape, your get-out-of-jail-free card.''

Ren shook his head. ''What does that mean? I'm

not trying to escape from anything. You're the one who's leaving."

"But you left first. Why else have sex with a stranger? Why go to such desperate lengths to prove you're the father of somebody else's child? Why else would you give up on a wonderful relationship that could take you right to the top?"

"Maybe I don't need my relationships to take me anywhere, Eve. Maybe I like where I'm at."

She made a scoffing sound. "If you liked where you're at, you never would have gone looking for Miss Bookstore. A lawyer could have handled any responsibility you feel toward her child, but you hired Super-Snoop to track her down. You're involved with her, Ren, whether you want to admit it or not." She took a breath. "I have an early flight tomorrow."

Stunned by Eve's slicing summary of his motivations, Ren moved cautiously back into the foyer. He stepped around her suitcase. "What about all your stuff?" He made a sweeping motion with his hand.

"The movers come Thursday." She lifted her chin proudly. "Marcella got me a full relocation package, great benefits and stock options. It's everything I ever wanted—career-wise."

Ren heard a softening in her tone. She was hurting, too. He moved to her and put his arms around her, drawing her close. Bending low, he pressed a kiss to the top of her head. He breathed in her scent—exotic and spicy.

"I'm proud of you, Eve. You're living your dream. I'm sorry I can't be a part of it anymore."

He felt her shoulders shake, and she clasped him tight. "Me, too," she whispered softly.

After a minute she broke away and took a deep breath. "I have a lot of packing to do."

He started toward the door.

"I already called your mother and told her good-bye. She seemed pretty upset. You might want to call her when you get home."

Ren flinched. "Maybe."

"Oh," Eve said. "I almost forgot this." She held up her left hand and started to pull off the diamond ring he'd given her.

Ren clasped her hand in his and shook his head. "It's your ring, Eve. You picked it out. You said it was a brilliant stone for a brilliant future. That hasn't changed."

She blinked rapidly and raised up on her toes to kiss him. "I love you, Ren Bishop. You're a good man, and you've been a good friend to me. I'll really miss you."

"I'll miss you, too." He hugged her once more, then left.

Just as he reached the curb he heard her door open. Eve walked to the top of the stoop and called out, "I hope you get your son, Ren. Don't give up trying. Sara won't be able to hold out forever."

He smiled and called back, "How do you know?"

"Because you're you."

CHAPTER NINE

KEEPING HER EYES CLOSED, Sara held on to the pictures in her mind, reluctant to reenter the real world. *Another Ren dream,* she thought, savoring the breathless passion that lingered in her memory. She'd given up trying to control her subconscious—refused to feel guilty about something she had no control over. Besides, these dreams were a very nice part of her day.

"Up and at it, sex fiend," she muttered under her breath. "This is Saturday. Bo's coming to help prep the gutters."

As she started to move, Sara realized she felt thoroughly rested, such a rare sensation that she barely recognized it. She glanced at her alarm clock and saw a flashing number twelve. Power failure, she thought—not an uncommon occurrence in the country. Did I oversleep?

Not bothering with a robe, she sprinted down the hallway to check the clock in the kitchen. As she passed Brady's room, she glanced in. Her heart stopped at the sight of his empty crib. "Brady?" she cried, clutching the door frame.

A movement just to the side of her line of vision made her jump back; the doorknob collided with her lower back, making her cry out. A large form started to rise from the floor in the vicinity of Brady's frog-shaped toy box.

"Good morning," the creature said, straightening to its full height. "Did we wake you?"

Sara's heart seemed to jump sideways. Pinpricks flooded her fingers and perspiration tingled under her arms. "Ren," she croaked.

Brady, who was draped over Ren's left shoulder in some kind of wrestling move, waved from his upside-down position. "Hi, Mommy. Ren here."

Sara tried to smile back but wasn't sure she could do it without crying. Her initial fear had robbed her of any equilibrium. Her knees felt wobbly.

"Did I scare you?" Ren asked, his concern obvious. "Bo and I were scraping the eaves outside the window, and Brady saw me. I figured you were still asleep, so I used the key you gave Bo and let myself in. I thought I'd keep him entertained until you woke up."

Ren bent low and set Brady on the floor. The boy dashed to Sara, who pulled him into a tight hug. Over Brady's shoulder she looked at Ren, who was wearing broken-in jeans and a loose denim shirt speckled with brown paint.

"You're scraping my eaves? Why?"

His gaze shifted downward. "It has its rewards."

Sara looked down and realized she was wearing her oldest nightie. She felt herself blush. "Stay here, honey. I'll be right back."

"Can I make some coffee?" Ren called after her, his voice rich with amusement. "The hired help is threatening to walk."

"Sure. Of course. Whatever."

When she entered the kitchen a few minutes later,

it was to the smell of coffee brewing. Brady was sitting in his high chair, banana smeared in his hair and brows.

"He's not real neat, is he," Ren said, humor masking any criticism.

"Were you, at this age?"

"Actually, I was considered a holy terror until I was four."

Sara took a carton of milk from the refrigerator. "Really?" she said wryly. "What happened at four?"

He didn't answer right away, then said, "My older sister drowned. Everything changed after that, including me."

His tone was flat. He wasn't looking for sympathy, just stating a fact—but Sara's heart ached for him just the same. "How terrible! I'm so sorry for your family's loss."

The toast popped up, and he dutifully applied butter. "Her name was Sandra, but everybody called her Sunny," he said, handing Brady a toasted triangle. "Dad always said that described her personality, too—bright, smart, happy. She was the perfect one actually."

Sara couldn't stop herself. She reached out and touched his arm where bare skin was exposed below the turned-back cuff of his shirt. "And after she was gone, you became perfect to take her place."

He looked at her, his face composed. "It wasn't a conscious decision—I was only four. But things changed. There was sadness and tension in our home that wasn't there before. I'm sure it affected me."

She squeezed his arm. "Only if you were human."

He smiled, but his eyes had a faraway look. "My father quit his job at the district attorney's office to stay home and take care of me. Mother was pretty shook up—it took her a long time to..." He didn't complete the thought.

Babe never fully recovered from the loss, Sara guessed. "Grief and guilt go hand in hand," she said. "Hulger's parents were in Denmark at the time of the accident, but they blamed themselves, just the same."

He moved to the opposite counter and poured two mugs of coffee. He added sugar to one and set it aside. "It happened at our family's cabin at Lake Almanor. My uncle Frank and his family were there, too. His twin daughters were Sunny's age. The men were fishing from the shore, the girls playing in the water out front of the cabin."

He took a drink of coffee. Sara gave Brady his milk in a spill-proof cup and sat down at the table. "How did it happen?"

"The three girls were messing around with a raft they'd made out of driftwood. Sunny dove underneath the raft to fix something. Apparently she got tangled in a rope. By the time the other girls figured out she was in trouble, it was too late."

"Where were you?" Sara asked, forcing herself to swallow a bite of toast.

His sad, strangled laugh broke her heart. "I was being a brat, and Mother was trying to get me to lie down for a nap."

"Surely nobody blamed you for what happened?"

"No. But the loss of a child affects everyone."

He picked up the mug of sugared coffee. "I'd better get this out to Bo before he goes on strike."

Sara leaned back. *Why did he tell me that?* Was he looking for sympathy, or was he trying to tell her he'd understand how she'd feel if he tried to take Brady from her? She suspected the latter, and it touched her deeply. She could fall in love with a man that sensitive.

"HEY, MAN, TAKE IT EASY. You're gonna scrape a hole in that downspout," Bo said, looking down at Ren from his vantage point on the ladder.

Ren glanced up. Frustration made him growl, "I'd like to strangle the person who originally primed this piece of shit."

"Are you sure that's who you're mad at?"

Ren rocked back on his haunches. "Who else would I be mad at?"

Bo wore his Raiders cap backwards. Brown paint chips made his hair and skin appear diseased. Ren was certain he didn't look any better. Talk about a detestable job! What had seemed a gallant gesture had turned into the job from hell.

"Maybe *mad* is the wrong word. How about *frustrated?*"

Ren sighed. He was frustrated—in more ways than one. The more time he spent with Brady, the more anxious he became to prove the little boy was his son. The more time he spent around Sara—especially when she showed up wearing a gossamer nightgown—the more... He put the thought aside and growled, "I'm fine. I'm still a little pissed about the way that estate lawyer blew Sara off, but she told me she has an appointment with the jerk next week, so maybe we can get the ball rolling—one way or the other.''

He looked up at his friend. ''By the way, what's going on with you and Claudie? You never mentioned your evening visit to the bookstore.''

The ladder skidded to the left. Bo cursed fluently. ''Nothing. She called the boat to tell me that Eve was looking for you. Why she felt the need to warn you, I haven't a clue, but she sounded kinda down, so I went over. We talked. I went home. End of story.'' He glared at Ren, challenging him to say more.

''Are you boys fighting again?'' an amused voice interrupted. ''Maybe you need naps, too.''

Ren looked over his shoulder to find Sara standing a few feet away, hands on her hips, a smile on her lips. In frayed shorts and a baggy gray T-shirt, she looked fresh and appealing.

''I just got Brady down. How about a break? Sandwiches and iced tea on the patio.''

They followed her to the rear of the house, where a plate of fruit and thick sandwiches on French rolls awaited on a picnic table shaded by a large green umbrella.

''I hope you're hungry, Ren,'' Sara said, smiling. He smiled back.

''Would you prefer cola, Bo?'' she asked, dropping her gaze from Ren's.

''That would be great, if you have it.''

''No problem.'' She pivoted on one heel and dashed to the house.

Bo made a gagging sound. ''What?'' Ren asked.

''She's falling for you, big time.''

Ren's heart did a little spin. ''Do you think so?''

"I'm gonna barf."

"Why?" Ren asked, exasperated.

"It hasn't even been a week since you and Eve broke up, and you're already hitting—" He wasn't able to complete the thought because Sara returned.

"You and Eve broke up? Really?"

Ren heard the concern in her tone. "Yes. She took a job in New York. Her dream job. I'm truly happy for her," Ren said, trying for a casual note.

Sara handed Bo his can of soda, then sat down woodenly. "Wow."

Ren wished he had a clue what she was thinking.

"Why are you here?" she asked suddenly. "Shouldn't you be more upset or something?"

"He's taking out his anguish on your eaves," Bo said, his tone amused. He grabbed Ren's hand and held it out for her to see. "Look at those blisters."

"Oh, my gosh!" she exclaimed, frowning. "They're starting to bleed. I'll get the first-aid kit."

She disappeared into the house.

"Cretin," Ren said, noting Bo's satisfied smirk.

Bo took a sandwich off the plate. "It was your idea to come here today."

A few minutes later, Sara returned out of breath. "I hate this house. Any time you want something, it's like running a marathon." She drew her chair close to Ren's and took his hand in hers. With a frown on her brow and bottom lip clamped between her teeth, she tenderly cleaned the raw-looking blisters on his fingers and palm with a cotton ball soaked in peroxide.

Ren tried to inhale her scent, but his nostrils crinkled from the odor of the astringent. Bending lower, he tried again. Fresh air and mustard. When she glanced up, he spotted a dab at the corner of her lips. He also had a clear view down the neckline of her shirt. No bra. Perfect, compact breasts that made his throat constrict and other parts of his anatomy swell.

Forcing himself to look away, Ren glanced at Bo, whose knowing smirk made Ren glower.

"You could try magnets," Sara said, pulling an adhesive strip out of the first-aid box. "Keneesha said she tried them on a burn once, and they worked great."

"I'll be fine," Ren said, hoping that was true. He was lusting after a woman who probably shouldn't even be talking to him. Surely her asshole lawyer had told her that.

She finished her task, then scooted back, looking from Ren to Bo. "That does it. You're both fired."

Ren, who'd just downed a gulp of tea, sputtered, "I beg your pardon?"

She ran a hand impatiently through her hair. "This is a stupid job. An endless job. It's too much for three people. I should have known that."

Ren pulled out a chair at the table and pointed to it. "Sit down. Have a drink. It won't look quite so daunting after you eat something," he promised, although he knew she was right. The entire house needed work, and neither he nor Bo was a carpenter.

"You shouldn't have to pay for any of this out of pocket, Sara," Bo said. "The house is part of your sister's estate. Let the estate pay for the repairs."

She sighed. "It's so frustrating dealing with the attorney who handles this case. He never returns my calls. He was a friend of Hulger's, and I don't think he ever liked Julia. I know he doesn't like me." She frowned. "Someone from his office called me at work yesterday to change my appointment—again. When I told him it was urgent, do you know what he said?"

Bo shook his head.

Ren tried to stop her from saying more, but she blurted out, "He said to stall Ren, so they could do a little investigating. He made it sound like I should ask for a healthy sum up front—something about *quid pro quo,* then worry about the custody battle later."

Ren exchanged a look with Bo.

Bo said, "I smell a feeding frenzy."

Ren nodded. He didn't know the attorney but obviously the man had heard the Bishop name and saw dollar signs—and the opportunity for a little legal extortion.

Bo chewed for a minute, then said, "You know, Sara, I have a friend who's a remodeling contractor. He's good, reliable and cost-effective. He owes me a favor. Want me to give him a call?"

Sara's face lit up. "I'd love it, but…I'm not sure I can afford it. The painter's bid will take most of my savings." She looked down as if embarrassed to be discussing her finances.

"I could pay for it," Ren said. Seeing her frown, he added, "If you take your lawyer's advice, I'll be paying up front just to have you *consider* letting Brady take the DNA test. This way, the money would directly benefit you and Brady, not the estate."

Sara sat back, looking dumbfounded. She turned

to Bo, who nodded. "Sounds like a good deal to me."

She took a deep breath and slowly let it out, then stuck out her hand. "You don't have to pay. I should have agreed to the test before. It's the right thing to do." Her eyes filled with moisture. "It always was. I was just afraid of losing him."

Ren's mouth dropped open. "No. That's not what I meant. You don't have to decide right now. Talk to your lawyer—"

She interrupted. "He's not my lawyer. He doesn't care what happens to Brady or me as long as the estate looks good on paper. I don't care what he says."

A pain sliced open Ren's heart. "I promise you that you won't be sorry. You'll never lose Brady. And I *am* going to pay for the painting."

She ducked her head and put on a false smile. "If you could save me from the Rancho Carmel lynch mob…"

She rose abruptly and dashed into the house. Ren looked at Bo. "Wow, I didn't see that coming."

Bo nodded. "Gutsy lady. I know I don't have to ask this, but you will treat her fair, right?"

"You know I will," Ren snapped. The two glared at each other in silence until Sara returned—the portable phone in her hand.

"It's Claudie," she said. "There's something wrong with the espresso machine, and she thought you might be able to help, Bo."

Bo put the phone to his ear. His look of surprise changed to a smile as he listened. "Jiggle it a little harder," he said. "That worked for me the other night."

Sara let out a small giggle, and Ren grinned as he saw Bo's face flood with color.

Bo rose and turned his back. "Listen, we're winding things up here, so I'll stop by on my way home. Okay?"

Sara looked at Ren questioningly. He answered her with a shrug.

Bo mumbled something else, then passed the phone to Sara, who listened for a minute before saying, "I'm sorry. I wish I'd known. I'll be down as soon as Brady wakes up from his nap."

She pushed a button on the receiver and placed the phone on the table. "Keneesha didn't come in this morning. She sent a kid over to tell Claudie she wasn't feeling good. She's been like this for over a week, but won't see a doctor. Claudie thinks it might be diabetes. We're really worried about her."

Ren suddenly felt a little sheepish about his offhand attitude toward her friends. "Would she go to a doctor if you and Claudie took her?" he asked. "There's a clinic near the hospital that deals with non-emergencies."

Sara sighed. "Maybe, but I don't want to expose Brady to any germs if I don't absolutely have to. Maybe I—"

Ren didn't let her finish. "Diabetes can be life-threatening. It's not something you treat lightly. Bo and I could look after Brady and the bookstore this afternoon, while you and Claudie take Keneesha to the doctor."

Sara seemed stunned, as did Bo.

Even Ren wasn't really sure why he'd made the offer. A part of him wanted to do something for Sara after she'd agreed to the DNA test. Another part didn't want to spend a long afternoon in an empty house.

REN'S GOOD MOOD was put to the test the minute he walked into the bookstore.

"Sara told me about the deal," Claudie said, meeting him before he took a step inside. "I don't like it. You may not be the scum I thought you were, but I ain't completely convinced you're not up to something. Just don't forget—I'm here, and I'm watching you."

Ren politely replied, "Good afternoon, Claudie. Beautiful weather we're having, isn't it?"

She snorted and backed up a step so he could walk past her to the coffee bar. He noticed a hand-inscribed sign on the brass espresso machine that read, Out Of Survice." The misspelled word touched his heart. He glanced over his shoulder. "The jiggling didn't work, huh?"

Her usually impassive face turned red. "I gotta get something out back. Don't steal nothin'."

He watched her stride confidently away, noting her outfit—jeans and a white Henley buttoned to the throat. Quite a change from the woman he'd first met that night in the bar with Bo. He speculated about what—or possibly who—had inspired the transformation.

His musings ended when a door opened at the rear of the store, and Sara walked in with Brady. The little boy's arms were filled with stuffed animals, which he dropped the instant he saw Ren. With a howling cry of joy, Brady raced across the room.

Ren dropped to one knee and opened up his arms

to catch him. "Hi, big guy. Did you have a nice nap?"

Brady began chattering away. Ren was beginning to be able to catch a few recognizable words. He listened closely, but saw the amused look Sara gave Claudie.

"We should hurry, Claudie, before Kee changes her mind. She wasn't wild about this idea, but I begged. Do you want us to wait until Bo comes?" Sara asked Ren.

Feeling confident, Ren shook his head. "How hard can it be?"

An hour later, when Bo sashayed in, Ren was looking for blood. "You dirty rotten coward," he cried. "I can't believe you did that."

Bo blinked with mock innocence. "Did what? I fell asleep. So, sue me."

"We had a rush, for Christ's sake. Nine customers, and Brady!" he exclaimed. "I don't know how Sara does it."

"Hey, this wasn't my idea," Bo challenged.

"I helped you scrape paint."

"Well, now we're even. I'm here, aren't I?"

"Yes, but you're too late. The rush is over, and Brady's settled down with a book." He gave Bo a steely look. "You owe me, Lester. Tonight. You baby-sit while I take Sara out to dinner."

"Maybe I have a hot date tonight. Did you think about that?" Bo asked.

"Does Claudie know?"

Bo turned away and headed to the coffee bar. "Okay. I'll do it." He twirled a small screwdriver and asked, "Isn't it a little premature to celebrate? You haven't even taken the test."

Ren's stomach turned over. He'd ordered the test kit online when he'd gone home to change. With express delivery, it would arrive Monday. Then, it would be a four-to-six week wait. A lot could happen in that time.

"This isn't about celebrating. It's about spending quality time with the woman who might be the aunt of my child."

Bo looked up from his work. "Might not be, too."

Ren didn't want to consider that possibility. Fortunately, the jingle of the bell over the door offered him a diversion.

SARA CLOSED HER EYES and took a deep breath, then added a spritz of cologne. *A date.* She was going out to dinner with Ren Bishop.

In the distance she could hear Bo and Brady jabbering about something. She'd already prepared a self-rising pizza for the two of them. Nerves and awkward embarrassment kept her from lingering in the kitchen, so she'd hurried back to her room to fuss with her dress.

She turned sideways to study her image in the cheval mirror. The twisted silk fabric was sculpted in a baby-doll style that made her legs look longer than they were. The low-heeled sandals helped, too.

"Sara?" Bo called from the hallway.

"I'm dressed. Come on in."

Brady tumbled in, tripping over his feet. He sprawled face-first on the carpet, but before Sara could go to him, he bounced back to his feet, laughing.

"Man, the ability to do that would have come in handy in my drinkin' days," Bo said, chuckling.

Brady crawled up on her bed and started bouncing. "Hey, monkey, that's a no-no," Sara said, reaching for him. He bounced away in glee.

Bo chased him down amid shrieks of feigned terror.

Sara withdrew a light sweater from the drawer and turned to look at the two "boys" wrestling on her bed. "I know somebody who's going to sleep like a rock tonight."

Bo sat up looking winded. "Yeah, me."

He tilted his head and gave Sara a thorough look. "Very nice."

"I haven't been on a date in so long, I'll probably try eating my soup with a salad fork."

Brady tackled Bo from behind. Bo leaned forward, drawing the child over his head but catching him before he hit the floor. "Let's go eat, wild man. Pizza?"

"Pissa," Brady exclaimed and dashed away.

Sara stopped Bo from following. "I probably shouldn't be doing this, but I couldn't resist the chance to play grown-up. Sometimes, I think my mind is turning into two-year-old mush."

Bo clapped his big hand on her shoulder in a supportive manner. "Go out. Have fun. Forget about the rest and don't worry about Brady. I'm no wimp like Ren. I can take it."

Wimp? She'd have asked for an explanation, but the doorbell took away her breath. She was going out on a date. A real live date.

"Wow!" Ren said, handing her a lush bouquet.

"Thank you!" she exclaimed. "They're beautiful. Look, Brady, pretty flowers."

Brady grabbed the hem of her dress and yanked hard, trying to reach the flowers. Ren gently removed the material from the little fist, then picked him up. Together they leaned toward the roses. "They smell nice, don't they? But women are like flowers, Brady—they don't appreciate it when you grab them. You need to treat flowers and girls very gently."

His serious tone seemed to make an impression, because Brady sniffed but didn't touch. "That was pretty sexist," Bo muttered. "I could never get away with that."

Sara laughed. "You guys are really something."

Ren seemed oddly shaken by her happy reception. He looked at Bo and said, "Can you handle the flowers, too? I don't want to miss our reservation."

Bo accepted the bouquet with a curtsy.

Giggling, Sara kissed his cheek, then knelt to hug Brady. "You be good for Bo. I love you."

Brady waved from the door, as Sara and Ren pulled away. Sara looked over her shoulder, feeling a trifle let down. "I expected that to be more traumatic. I've never left him at night before."

Ren glanced at her but didn't reply. She made small talk on the drive to the restaurant, but it seemed oddly one-sided.

Once seated at a table overlooking the river, she asked Ren, "Is something wrong?"

There was a pause before he spoke. "Bo said something to me earlier about this being a celebration...because you'd agreed to the test." His eyes were dark with emotion. "That's not what this is.

I...I don't want you to think I'm trivializing your feelings, your fears. I asked you out because I'm attracted to you and I like spending time with you,'' he said somberly.

Sara couldn't repress the smile that bubbled up from her heart. ''Ren, I had my doubts about this, too, but Claudie helped me put it in perspective.''

''She did?''

''She said, 'A free dinner's a free dinner. Go for it.'''

He seemed momentarily nonplussed, then laughed. ''She gave me some advice, too,'' he said, his lips twitching in mischief.

The look was so Brady, Sara's heart almost stopped.

He leaned forward as if to impart a secret. ''She said, 'No kissing, no touching and, above all, no oysters.'''

Now Sara was also laughing. ''Good. I don't like oysters. I don't know what I'd do if you made me eat them.''

He studied her for a moment, then said, ''You're far more beautiful than I realized.''

Her pulse quickened. ''I am?''

He nodded. ''Yes, and normally that wouldn't be a problem. But I just figured out I'm very attracted to you—and that *is* a problem.''

Her heart fluttered wildly at the word *attracted*. ''Because of the paternity issue.''

''No, actually. Because of me.''

''I don't understand.''

He sighed. ''As Bo would so eloquently put it— my social life sucks. Eve called off our engagement less than a week ago, and here I am drooling over you. Don't you think that's just a little emotionally immature?''

Sara perked up as if someone had given her a shot of adrenaline. "You're far too sophisticated to drool, Ren. But I appreciate the compliment."

"You do? You're not appalled?"

She grinned and made her brows waggle suggestively. "Actually, I'm flattered. I haven't had time for a lot of dates, so this one is kind of special. It doesn't have to be anything more than that."

Ren seemed surprised by her candor. "You never cease to surprise me," he said.

"Give it time. You haven't known me very long." She opened the menu, aware of his gaze on her. "What's good here? I've seen this place from the road."

"I haven't been here in a long time, but I understand the food's great. I think I'll have the pasta primavera."

When the waiter returned, she ordered the steak and shrimp, and Ren ordered a bottle of wine.

"How'd it go at the clinic today?" he asked, after the waiter had left.

Sara focused on buttering a piece of sourdough bread. It was one thing to talk flirtatiously, quite another to pull it off. She decided it would be best if she treated Ren as she did Bo—like a big brother.

"Kee was a wreck. Claudie gave her a hard time to keep her focused."

"Big stretch there," he said drolly.

Sara took a sip of water. "Claudie isn't as brave as she acts. When the technician put a needle in Kee's arm to get a blood sample, she almost lost it. She once told me she saw a girl OD on heroin. That might be why she's trying so hard to turn her life around.''

The wine arrived. Ren tasted it, then nodded his approval. When both glasses were filled, he lifted his glass to hers and smiled. "To good company."

Sara took a sip. Buttery and delicious.

"Bo told me Claudie's working on her high-school equivalency exam. That's a good start."

Before she could reply, an older couple stopped at their table. The man's silver hair added to his aura of power and wealth. He shook Ren's hand. "Lawrence, good to see you. Your mother tells me you're thinking of running for office in the near future. I'm glad to hear it."

"Actually," Ren said, "politics is Babe's forte, not mine. I tried to convince her to run for office, but at the time, Senator, your seat was the only one up for vote."

The man guffawed, then looked at Sara. She thought she read speculation and curiosity as Ren introduced her. "Sara owns a bookstore. We share an interest in literacy," he told them. Under his breath, he added, "Among other things."

The older couple asked a few questions about mutual acquaintances, then wished them a good evening and left. Ren looked at Sara over the rim of his glass. "What?" he asked, cocking his head.

"Nothing. It's just…they didn't seem overly surprised to see you with someone other than Eve."

He shrugged. "Yesterday's news. And, frankly, I doubt if our breakup was a big surprise to anyone other than my mother."

Before Sara could say anything, the waiter arrived with their meals. He added a bit more wine to both glasses, then tactfully disappeared. Ren lifted his glass, "To new beginnings."

Sara touched her glass to his, but found it hard to swallow over the lump in her throat. Fortunately, Ren steered the conversation to more light-hearted subjects, and Sara relaxed. Between his dry wit and the best meal she could ever remember eating, the evening flew by.

On her front porch later, she found herself wishing Claudie hadn't been quite so specific about what *not* to do.

"I had a great time. Thanks," she said, meaning it.

Ren kept his distance. "So did I. Maybe we could—" His words were cut short by Bo, who stumbled outside like a just-released hostage.

"You're back," he cried. "Thank God."

Sara frowned. "What happened?"

"You didn't tell me he likes to hide, but I only lost him twice," he boasted.

"Lost him?" Ren repeated, his tone tense.

"Hey, it's a big house, and he's fast. But Claudie called, and when I told her what happened, she suggested I tie a bell around his ankle."

"Like a cow?" Ren snarled.

Bo bristled. "I'd like to see you do any better."

Laughing, Sara stepped between them. "Thank you for baby-sitting, Bo. I'm sure the bell delighted Brady. Claudie and I put little bells on his shoes when he first started walking, because he'd take off in a blink. I should have warned you."

He gave Ren a smug look, then told Sara, "Actually, I had a pretty good time, but he wore me out. I'm taking off, if that's okay with you."

She gave him a friendly hug. Then Bo and Ren exchanged nonverbal grunts that made her repress a giggle.

Once the Mazda disappeared into the night, Sara took a deep breath and looked at Ren. He was studying her face for some reason. "Thank you for the wonderful meal and great company," she said, pleased by how calm she sounded. Memories of that first kiss were never far from her mind—a teasing hint that made her crave more. "I felt like a real grown-up."

Ren took a step closer. "A grown-up? Was that ever in doubt?"

Sara's breath caught in her throat. "All the time. Right now I feel like a teenager on her first date."

"Really?" He smiled wolfishly, his fingertip tracing the scalloped trim at her shoulder. "In that dress you look young enough to get me in trouble."

Leaning down, he narrowed the gap between them. Sara's heartbeat sped up; her lips parted on their own accord. *Kiss me.*

But at the last second he veered slightly, his lips brushing her cheek. "I have a feeling where Claudie's concerned it wouldn't take much to get me in trouble. I should leave while I'm still ahead."

Sara dropped her chin to keep her disappointment from showing. "I'll tell her you were a perfect gentleman," she said softly.

Ren didn't move. When Sara looked up, she saw something that took her breath away. Desire.

"Good night, Sara," he said, his voice low and husky. "I'll call you tomorrow. Sleep well." When he turned and walked away, Sara thought she heard him add, "Lord knows *I* won't."

CHAPTER TEN

REN STOPPED PACING the moment Rafael Justis poked his head around the door between their offices, his brows knit with concern. "Are you okay?" he asked.

"Fine," Ren said, and to prove he meant it, he walked to his desk and sat down. The young man didn't look thoroughly convinced, but he backed out and closed the door.

With a weighty sigh, he pulled his calendar into his line of vision. Six weeks...the results of the DNA test wouldn't be back for at least six weeks. It wasn't a lifetime, but it sure felt like one.

All parties had met at Armory's office earlier that morning. Sara hadn't wasted any time living up to her part of the bargain. "If it's as easy as you say it is, we can stop by on our way to the bookstore," she'd told Ren on the phone last night. He was certain he detected a nervous tremble in her voice, but she didn't hesitate when he suggested meeting at his attorney's.

"He's old school, Sara, a friend of my father's. He wants to oversee everything to ensure there are no problems farther down the road," he'd explained.

She didn't quibble. "Tomorrow morning at nine? We'll be there."

When Ren called Armory at home to confirm this

morning's meeting, the older man had expressed curiosity about why Sara had agreed to the test. "You're not in any way coercing her or taking advantage of her circumstances, are you?"

Ren smiled, pleased that Armory had the strength of character to care about Sara's welfare, too. "I'm paying to have her eaves scraped," he said.

"I beg your pardon? That's not some kind of kinky body surgery, is it?"

Ren was well acquainted with Armory's sense of humor, so he'd let the question slide. "I'm helping her finish some repairs that should have been done long ago through the estate. As a matter of fact, I'd like you to check up on the lawyer handling those matters. I'll give you the details when I see you tomorrow."

The actual test had gone smoothly. Both Sara and Brady seemed to relax, thanks to Armory's gentle charm and obvious goodwill. His grandfatherly white hair had thoroughly entranced Brady, and Ren's heart had clutched for a moment as he wished his own father were there.

To get the ball rolling, Ren began by reading the instructions aloud. Brady had been intrigued for about one minute, then wanted off his mother's lap.

"It can't be all that complicated," Armory said, pulling his chair out into the middle of the room adjacent to Ren's and Sara's. "You've got some extra stick-things there. Let's all do one, so Brady can see how easy it is. If you don't mind, young lady, I'll do yours," he said to Sara.

She giggled when the swab touched her inner cheek, and Brady immediately wanted in on the action. "Me?"

"Why don't you try Ren, Brady?" Sara suggested. "Be very gentle, sweetie. You don't want to hurt him."

Ren added extra sound effects that made Brady chortle. "Me?" he asked.

"Okay. Your turn. Open wide." Just to be safe, Ren collected two samples from Brady, then two from himself.

Armory produced four lollipops. "Sugarless," he told Sara with a wink.

And that had been the end of it. Armory had assured Ren that he would have the samples sent by courier to the company that afternoon.

Flawless. Simple. It was just a matter of waiting, Ren thought now, penciling out the weeks on his calendar. Could he wait that long? What choice did he have?

"Sir?" Rafael asked, opening the door. "You wanted to finish up the defense witnesses before lunch."

Ren rose and reached for his judge's robe. "I know. Would you please do me a favor? Call Sara Carsten at No Page Unturned and ask her to meet me in Capitol Park by the Vietnam Veterans Memorial. Twelve-thirty."

SARA HUNG UP THE PHONE—for once grateful the store wasn't busy. Her stomach felt queasy. The test this morning had been painless and she'd liked Ren's attorney, but she hadn't slept well the night before, thanks to her talk with Daniel. His concern about the test had made her begin to second-guess her decision. Was her attraction to Ren getting in the way of common sense?

"Are you sure you can trust Ren Bishop?" Daniel asked. "I'm not saying he's a low-life bum like Jeff, but he could be using you for his own purposes."

Daniel's words had haunted her sleep. Could Ren be believed, or did he plan to take Brady away from her once his paternity was established? What would keep him from seeking sole custody if he was Brady's biological father? Even Julia's wishes would take second place to that kind of leverage, wouldn't they?

Sara rubbed her temple, cocking her head to listen for Brady's quiet chatter in the story area. One of her regular customers had popped in a few minutes earlier, asking Sara to keep an eye on her little girl while she ran to the bank. Brady and the little girl had spent five minutes staring at each other before finally deciding it was safe to engage in play. Sara had felt saddened, realizing how much Brady needed to be around children his own age and how rarely the opportunity arose.

Then Ren's clerk had called, shaking her even further. The procedure that morning had gone smoothly—almost too smoothly. Why did Ren want to see her? Was something wrong?

The bell over the door tinkled, making Sara start. Her tension eased a bit when she saw Keneesha and Claudie enter. "Hello, ladies," she called. "Aren't you looking chipper today, Kee. That medicine must be working."

"I not only look good, I feel good," her friend replied, helping herself to a cup of coffee from the air pot. Instead of her usual sweet roll, however, she took a banana from the bowl and carried her snack to Sara's desk. "See this. I'm watching what I eat.

Natural sugars from fruit are better for you than refined sugars."

Sara blinked. "Wow. You've been reading all that literature the doctor sent home, haven't you?"

Keneesha gave her a sober look. "A visiting nurse came to see me this morning. She told me if I didn't take care of myself I could wind up losing a leg or going blind."

Claudie joined them. "There's an image. How much money do you think a one-legged, blind hooker could make on the street?"

The blunt question made Sara cringe, but Keneesha and Claudie looked at each other and burst out laughing. Sara shook her head. "You guys are bad."

"Not for long," Keneesha said.

Sara could tell by her serious tone that something was up. She waited for the woman to continue.

"I called back home last night. My mama lives in Georgia. She's got my kid."

"You have a child?" Sara asked, astounded by the news. "And you never told me?"

"A boy. He's fourteen. I haven't seen him since he was three. My mama told me if I left, he was as good as dead to me, so I tried to pretend he was." She was quiet a minute, then said, "Mama says he's doin' real good. Plays sports in school. She told me I could come home if I wanted to."

"So when ya leavin'?" Claudie asked, her face stony.

Keneesha gave her a look that said she understood her friend's attitude. "It'll take me a couple of weeks to get all my shi—stuff together. I gotta get my blood sugar level and my medication stable, too.''

"You're moving to Georgia?" Sara exclaimed. "Really?"

Keneesha nodded. "My mama's got diabetes, too. I figure we can watch out after each other. And being around Brady so much has made me kind of miss my kid."

Impulsively, Sara hugged her friend, tears coming to her eyes. "I will really miss you, but I think it's wonderful you're reuniting with your family. How can I help? Do you need boxes? There are a million out back."

Planning Keneesha's move helped take Sara's mind off her upcoming talk with Ren, but Claudie seemed to sense something was amiss. When they walked into the storeroom, she asked, "So what's going on with the judge? How was the big date?"

Sara sat down on a wobbly stool. "The date was fabulous. Beautiful restaurant. Wonderful food. Ren was a perfect gentleman. He even brought me flowers."

Claudie didn't look impressed.

Sara took a breath, then said, "We did the DNA test this morning."

"Bo told me." Claudie shrugged. "It was gonna happen, anyway. Are you sorry you did it?"

"No, but Daniel's worried that Ren is only being nice to me because of some ulterior motive."

"Like what?"

"Like he wants to lull me into a false sense of security so he can get close to Brady, then sue for sole custody." Sara couldn't stop her voice from squeaking as she spoke.

"Sounds like something a lawyer would do," Claudie said under her breath.

"Ren's clerk called a little while ago and said Ren wanted to see me at the park at twelve-thirty."

Claudie scratched her chin thoughtfully. "I haven't quite figured the guy out. My gut says he's dangerous, but so far he's been okay. I think I should go with you. Kee's ready to kiss the ground he walks on for insisting we take her to the clinic, so she wouldn't be much help if he tries something shady."

"Good idea," Sara said, feeling a little less troubled.

Claudie, who was neither naive nor gullible, had killer instincts when it came to men. She'd help Sara guard against her unreliable response to Ren Bishop's sex appeal.

REN SHIFTED against the wooden slats of the bench. At an adjacent bench, a homeless man slept curled in a tight ball as if trying to ward off society. Ren could sympathize with him. All morning he had been bombarded—defense lawyers, prosecutors, the District Attorney, his mother.

Somehow Babe had managed to weasel Sara's name out of Eve, and now seemed convinced Sara was a shakedown artist trying to extort money from him to support her child. Exasperated, Ren told Babe she was wrong. If anything, just the opposite was true: he was trying to extort shared custody from Sara. He'd managed to hang up without blowing up, but his patience with his mother's interference in his life was diminishing.

"Ren!" a gleeful voice cried.

Ren looked up to see Brady racing toward him. A prickly sensation attacked his sinuses, and he swallowed against the emotion that constricted his heart. If anyone had told him a child could affect him this way so quickly, he'd have laughed out loud. Actually, the strength of the bond he felt for Brady helped convince Ren of their biological connection.

He sank to one knee, and when Brady hurled himself into his open arms, Ren hugged him fiercely. "Hi, big guy, how's it going?"

Brady returned the hug, then squirmed to be free. "'Quiddels,'" he said, pointing toward a skinny creature with a moth-eaten tail.

Ren released him, and the boy took off, chasing the animal, which raced up a tree and then scolded raucously.

"Hi," Sara said, walking up to Ren.

Something's up, Ren thought, rising. If they were at a different place in their relationship, he'd take her in his arms to reassure her that whatever the problem, they could handle it together. But they were a long way from that point, which was probably why she'd brought along reinforcements.

"Hi, Sara. Hello, Claudie."

Claudie acknowledged him with a nod, then set about putting out their picnic lunch. She unfurled a blanket in the shade of a leafy buckeye tree and withdrew a soft-sided cooler from the stroller.

"I brought an extra peanut-butter-and-jelly sandwich, if you're hungry," Sara told him.

Ren knew he wouldn't be able to relax until he'd gotten his proposition out of the way. "Maybe we should talk first," he said, nodding toward the park bench.

She exchanged looks with Claudie, then walked to the bench. Her tan cotton slacks showed grape jelly smudges that almost matched her lavender pullover. A pair of dark glasses held her hair off her face. Her eyes looked worried.

He didn't know how to begin.

Sara watched his face intently as if sensing his nervousness. Claudie broke the silence by calling Brady to come eat his sandwich. Ren watched the boy swerve from his pursuit of another squirrel and run to the blanket. Brady dropped flat, wiggling in protest when Claudie wiped his hands and face with a cloth she produced from a plastic bag.

"I really appreciate what you did today," Ren started. "I just wish there were some way to expedite matters. Six weeks is a long time to wait." He scooted forward to face Sara. His heart pounded in his chest. "But I have a suggestion for the interim that I'd like you to consider. I thought about it all day yesterday. I realize it may sound a little radical, but..."

Her eyes widened. "What?"

"I'd like you and Brady to move in with me. Into my house, I mean. It's a big house—five bedrooms, four baths. I have a housekeeper who comes twice a week."

Sara appeared dumbfounded, as if that were the last thing in the world she expected to hear him say.

"If you think about it, it makes sense...in a way. My place is closer to town. You wouldn't have that long commute. And you mentioned at dinner you were thinking about selling Hulger's house. This way a Realtor could show it without your having to worry about keeping it spotless."

Sara looked at Claudie, who suddenly shot to her feet and stomped over to the bench. "Are you freakin' nuts or what?" Claudie shouted at Ren.

"Claudie," Sara said reprovingly. Ren followed her gaze to Brady, who sat cross-legged on the blanket, watching with big eyes.

"Well, excuse me, but that's the lamest proposition I've ever heard. He must think you're stupid, Sara. That's all some family court judge would need to decide in his favor if he wanted to press for custody."

Ren watched Sara's expression turn anguished. Inwardly he groaned, cursing himself for being so stupid, cursing Claudie for being so smart.

"That was never my intention."

"Yeah, right. Then why suggest it? Out of the goodness of your heart?"

Oh, his heart was involved, but Ren couldn't claim altruistic motives. Purely selfish was more like it, since this arrangement would give him a chance to be around the child he was coming to adore and the woman he desired.

"It seemed like a practical solution. Sara hates her house, and it's a long, unpleasant commute."

Claudie snorted. "If she wants to move, she doesn't need your help."

Ren recognized the truth in her words. His perfect scenario was flawed, seriously flawed. "You're right," he said quietly.

He rose, hoping to salvage some pride. He looked at Sara and said, "It seemed like a good idea at the time." He gave her an apologetic smile and started to leave.

"Nooo," a voice cried.

Ren glanced over his shoulder and saw Brady scramble to his feet and charge after him. Sara caught the little boy in her arms. She fought his struggles, then comforted him when he started to cry. Over Brady's sobbing shoulder, she looked at Ren. He was too far away to read her eyes, but he thought he saw tears. He cursed himself for causing her more anguish. *Damn*. He turned away and kept walking.

SARA AND CLAUDIE didn't speak the whole way back to the store. Both seemed to share some kind of emotional ennui. Sara still felt stunned by Ren's offer. Why would a man like Ren Bishop open his home to a stranger? Could he really be trying to compromise Sara's custody? Somehow Claudie's explanation seemed too cold-blooded for a person as kind and generous as Ren.

It was with a sense of relief that she greeted Bo when she found him arguing with Keneesha above an atlas. "This boy ain't never been to Georgia, but he thinks he knows the quickest way to go."

"It was just a suggestion," Bo said testily.

"Bo, I need your help," Sara said quietly.

He turned to her. "What happened?"

Claudie extracted a grumpy Brady from the stroller and passed him to Sara. "You rock. I'll tell him all about it," she said.

Sara nodded and moved to the rocking chair a short distance away. Once seated, she closed her eyes and listened to the retelling of Ren's strange offer. She couldn't help picturing the look of pain on his face when he heard Claudie's accusation.

"What do you think he had in mind?" Sara asked

in a low voice. She could tell by Brady's breathing that he was almost asleep.

Bo paced back and forth a few steps. "I know Ren is lonely—who wouldn't be, living in that big house? And things were never really all that great with him and Eve. They hung out and went through the motions more because it was expected of them than because they really loved each other. I knew that from the beginning. But this is kinda scary."

"You mean, he was for real?" Claudie asked, her tone shocked. "He wasn't just using Sara to get hold of Brady?"

Bo gave her a stony look. "Ren wouldn't do that. He may be a forty-year-old guy who's starting to think life is passing him by, but he's not cruel and calculating. If he asked Sara to move in with him, it's because he wanted her and Brady around."

Before Sara could ask about the risk to her custody claim if she did consider Ren's offer, the bookstore bell chimed. All watched as an older woman stepped inside, then paused to look around. When she zeroed in on the group huddled around Sara's desk, Bo groaned, "Uh-oh."

Sara's stomach rose and fell. Instinctively she tightened her hold on Brady, who was deadweight in her arms.

"I wish to speak with Sara Carstairs," the woman said, her voice strong and cultured.

Sara recognized the voice from Ren's answering machine. *Ren's mother.*

Sara rocked forward and stood. "I'm Sara *Carsten,*" she said, emphasizing her last name. "If you'll give me a moment..." She bent down to place Brady in his playpen. She positioned one of his stuffed animals beside him, then rose and turned to face Ren's mother.

"You must be Mrs. Bishop," she said. Stepping forward, she put out her hand.

Babe took Sara's offered hand with discernible reluctance; she shook hands using two fingers and her thumb.

"These are my friends," Sara said. She started to introduce them, but Babe made a dismissive motion with her hand.

"Yes, I know Bo. Haven't you got work to do somewhere?" she asked, giving him a steely look.

"Oh, yes, most definitely. See you later, Sara." *Sorry,* he mouthed before hurrying away.

"Coward," Claudie whispered.

Mrs. Bishop gave her a quelling look that caused Claudie to edge closer to Keneesha. "I wish to speak with you alone," Babe demanded.

Sara walked to her desk, but motioned for Keneesha to stay sitting. "I'd prefer my friends to stay."

Babe's lips narrowed. She gave Sara a chilly look. If she weren't so cold, Sara thought, she'd be beautiful. Several inches shorter than Sara, Babe Bishop carried herself like a queen. Her exquisite suit of light pink wool dramatized her slim, athletic figure.

"Very well, if you insist," Babe said disapprovingly.

Reaching into the large leather purse she carried, Babe produced a plain manila file folder and laid it on Sara's desk. The cover flipped open, revealing a glossy photograph obviously torn from a men's magazine. The idea of Ren's mother toting that around almost made Sara laugh—until she zeroed in on the face in the photo.

"Julia?"

Sara grabbed the thick dossier.

"You didn't know your sister posed for *Playboy* magazine?" Babe asked, her tone showing surprise.

Sara shook her head, blood pounding in her temples. *When? Why didn't she tell me?* In the photo, Julia—in thigh-high white stockings and with a nurse's cap tilted at a rakish angle—posed beside a gurney. Her temptress smile was one Sara had seen her use many times when teasing men.

"She lost her job at the hospital because of it," Babe said.

Sara vaguely recalled some kind of fracas around the time of her own trouble with the law. Julia had downplayed her firing as political nonsense, and consequently Sara hadn't given it much thought.

"She wasn't unemployed long, however," Babe added, her tone steeped in innuendo. "Her future husband hired her. A short time later, she married the boss. I believe they call that 'job security.'"

Sara scanned the report from Babe's private investigators. She noticed neither Ren's nor Bo's name appeared in the report, so she reckoned Babe had acquired it independently.

"Why did you do this?" Sara asked.

"My son has a big heart. He doesn't see things in black and white, but I do. Right now, he's only thinking about doing the right thing for the child— but somebody has to look to the future. If the boy is going to be a Bishop, we have to know everything there is about his mother so we can be prepared."

"Prepared for what?"

"When a person enters the political arena, the press has been known to dig. It's best to know in advance what they'll find so one can put the proper spin on it."

Sara had no problem picturing the spin they'd put on Julia—a tramp who posed in the nude seducing a judge, then hiding his child from him. Sara looked at Brady, sleeping so peacefully, and knew she'd do anything to keep him from having to hear those kinds of lies about his mother.

"What do you want from me?" Sara asked.

Babe seemed momentarily taken aback by Sara's frankness. "I want the same thing my son wants."

Sara looked at Claudie, who slowly shook her head, warning Sara not to do anything impulsive. Sara shrugged as if to say, *What choice do I have?*

Turning to Babe, Sara said, "An hour ago, your son asked me for something that I feared would compromise my claim for custody if this went to court. I told him no. I'll change my answer to yes if you agree to destroy this file—" she dropped the folder to the desk "—and give me your word that Brady will never be exposed to its contents. My sister was a good person. She may have made mistakes in her life, but she loved her son with all her heart, and I won't have him believing any differently."

Babe gestured dismissively again. "I can't speak for the press but I can't imagine any of this will come up as long as the child is under Lawrence's protection."

Protection. The word, which sounded so feudal, continued to skip through Sara's brain long after Babe left. Ren might be able to protect Brady from the past, but who would protect Sara from falling in love with a man whose main goal was acquiring a son? Or was it already too late?

Sara knew if she were honest she'd have to admit that Ren's offer initially thrilled her, for no other reason than that it would give her a chance to spend more time with him. But Ren wasn't looking for a girlfriend—he just ended a relationship, and Sara had heard enough rebound horror stories from other women. *Unfortunately,* Sara thought, *that doesn't mean I can keep my heart from going crazy whenever he looks at me.*

"Whatcha thinkin', Sara J?" Keneesha asked.

Sinking back into the rocking chair, Sara regarded her friends and sighed. She couldn't tell them the truth. "I was thinking, 'So this is what it's like when you sell your soul to the devil.'"

Claudie snickered. "A witch is more like it."

Sara groaned. It was one thing to make a pact with the devil but quite another to see it through. "Well, right or wrong, it looks like we're going to need more boxes."

Bo SHADOWED REN from the courthouse. It wasn't hard since Ren seemed oblivious to the world around him. In the dozen or so blocks to his house, he'd only just missed running over a dog, then sat through a green light until another driver angrily leaned on the horn.

When they reached Ren's house, Bo waited a few minutes before entering through the back door, which his friend had failed to lock. Apparently lost in thought, Ren stood at the base of the stairs. Bo grabbed his elbow from behind, and with a twist of his wrist slammed Ren up against the wall. An *oof* of air left Ren's lungs, and he drew his arms up defensively, crying, "Jesus, Bo. What the hell are you doing?"

"Beating the shit out of you," Bo snarled, needing to release the tension that had been building ever since Babe Bishop had showed up at the bookstore. Not only did Ren's mother always manage to make Bo feel eight years old and worthless, but the more Bo stewed over Babe's attitude, the more upset he became about Ren's outrageous proposition. Like mother, like son—always trying to control other people's lives.

"Could you at least tell me why?" Ren asked, moving slightly out of the line of fire. His briefcase clattered to the tile floor.

"Why'd you ask Sara to move in with you?"

Ren didn't seem surprised that Bo knew of his suggestion. His shoulders slumped in defeat, and he sank downward, his shoes making a hissing sound against the tile. "Because I'm an idiot, okay?"

Bo folded his arms across his chest. "That's a start."

Ren dropped his head in his hands. "I think I'm in love with her, Bo. I know it's crazy and I shouldn't be feeling this way."

"So this moving-in thing wasn't some ploy to get leverage in a custody suit?"

Ren groaned. "That's what she thinks, isn't it. Claudie pounced on that, but I didn't think Sara would believe it. Does she hate me?"

Before Bo could answer, the doorbell chimed.

"Did you order a pizza to go with my beating?" Ren asked sarcastically as he got to his feet. He yanked open the door without checking the peep-hole.

"Sara," he croaked.

Bo hurried into the foyer. His mouth dropped open at the sight of Sara, Brady and Claudie standing on the stoop. A diaper bag, two oversize totes and one small old-fashioned suitcase rested between them.

Sara stepped inside. Claudie, who held Brady's hand, crowded behind her.

"All right," Sara said, glancing first at Bo, then back at Ren. "This is the way it is. I cut a deal with your mother this afternoon. Has she talked to you?"

Ren shook his head. "Not since this morning. I told her to stay out of this. What did she do to you?"

"We can go into that later. The bottom line is I've agreed to move in here."

"My *mother* asked you to move in with me?"

"Not exactly. In return for her destroying some very mean-spirited information about Julia—" She looked at Bo, her eyes narrowing. "Did you know Julia posed for a magazine?"

He gulped. "Yes."

"Did you know?" she asked Ren.

He nodded. "It was in Bo's report. It didn't seem like a big deal to me."

Some of the stiffness went out of her posture. Claudie coughed, and Sara went on. "Anyway, your mother agreed to destroy the file if I did whatever you wanted. You asked us to move in with you, so here we are. I don't think this is exactly what she meant, but this is what she's getting."

Bo almost choked on his howl of laugher. "I bet

the old bat shits green when she finds out,'' he said, ignoring Ren's brusque shove.

Sara frowned. "But there's one condition," she said, her tone formidable.

Bo sobered. He glanced at Ren, who seemed to be holding his breath.

"What kind of condition?" Ren asked.

"Claudie moves in, too. This is purely a business arrangement. We're here until the DNA test results come back and we know whether or not you're Brady's father. If you are, I want your word we'll work out a fair and equitable joint-custody arrangement. If you're not Brady's father, I should have my house sold by then, and Brady and Claudie and I can find a place closer to work. Agreed?"

Ren didn't hesitate. "Yes."

"I'll start bringing in your stuff," Bo said, scooting past Claudie, who gave him an evil look. He hurried to the Toyota wagon. With his back to the house, he didn't care who saw his grin. Who but Sara could have turned the tables so neatly on Babe Bishop? he thought.

The poetry of it almost made him weep with laughter.

CHAPTER ELEVEN

SARA SHIFTED BRADY to her left hip and walked through the dining room to the kitchen. She'd been through every room the previous evening moving breakable objects out of Brady's reach. Overall, Sara liked the house, but she didn't care for the dining room, which struck her as gloomy and ostentatious. Ren said it was next on his remodeling list.

Her hand was poised to push open the door, when Sara caught the sound of voices—angry voices. She started to turn around, but Brady yodeled, "'Nana"—the word for his favorite fruit.

The door swung inward, and Ren looked at them. "Good morning," he said. "Come in."

Sara cautiously stepped into the sunny kitchen. Dressed in baggy sweatpants and a tank top that showed a dark trail from jogging, it was apparent from the screwdriver in Ren's hand that he'd been in the process of assembling Brady's high chair when an unexpected guest had arrived.

His mother stood beside the counter, arms folded across her chest. Her three-piece ivory slack outfit made Sara regret throwing on yesterday's shorts and T-shirt.

"Sit down. I'll have this together in half a minute," Ren said, squatting beside the pieces of molded plastic. "Mother, you remember Sara, the woman you tried to blackmail."

Babe sputtered. "I did nothing of the sort. Did she tell you that?"

Sara clutched Brady tighter. The little boy stared at Babe with big eyes. Sara figured he was either drawn to her impressive gold necklace or fascinated by her bristling outrage.

Screwing up her courage, she stepped forward. "I told him the truth, Mrs. Bishop. That you had photos of Julia that you threatened to use if I didn't cooperate. Moving here was your son's idea, not mine."

Babe seemed to shrink slightly, although her chin remained high. "It's not as though I planned to give those photographs to the press—they could damage Lawrence's reputation as well, since he was associated with her."

Ren shot to his feet. "Her name was Julia, Mother. She was a beautiful, exciting, dynamic woman. I wasn't associated with her. I made love to her, and I don't regret it—especially not if the DNA test proves I'm Brady's father. This child—" he stepped beside Sara and put his hand on Brady's head "—is a blessing. He's already brought more light and happiness into my life in a few short weeks than I can remember feeling in a long, long time."

Babe started to speak, but Ren added, "I want those pictures, Mother. In fact, I want your entire file on Sara, Brady and Julia. We'll have a little bonfire tonight and toast marshmallows."

His mother, who was staring at Brady, turned abruptly to pick her purse off the counter. "If that's the way you feel about it. I was only trying to help."

She left without saying goodbye, and Sara

doubted Babe would be around much during the next six weeks.

"Well, that was fun," Ren said dryly. "I always like to start my day with a little family drama."

Sara tried not to laugh, but the relief she felt was too great. She tickled Brady under his arm, and he giggled, too, until he spotted a familiar yellow fruit. "'Nana," he cried triumphantly.

Sara peeled the banana and sat down on one of the stools, positioning Brady on her lap. "Thanks," she said softly.

Ren tightened the last of the screws, then turned the chair upright. "For putting this together? No problem. Having familiar stuff around will make everything a little less confusing for Brady. Don't you think?"

Sara nodded. "Yes. But I meant thank you for defending Julia."

Ren held out his arms to Brady, who went without hesitation. He carried him to the high chair, then helped Brady wiggle his chubby little legs through the opening. Once Ren had secured the strap around Brady's waist, he looked at Sara. "My mother is a complex person. I'm sure she has my best interests in mind. The only problem is, we don't always agree on what those are."

"Is this going to cause problems between you? Maybe I shouldn't have—"

He didn't let her finish the thought. "I made it clear to Mother before you came in that you and Brady and Claudie are off-limits to her. She's welcome here anytime as long as she's prepared to treat you civilly."

Sara didn't say anything. She knew all about difficult mothers, and only hoped he wouldn't have to cope with long-term repercussions after she and Brady were gone.

"Believe me, Sara, I know my mother. She's a born politician. Give her a little time, and she'll find a way to blame this on someone else, but I guarantee it won't be you or Brady." He grinned. "I think Armory's her new target. She's mad because he left her out of the loop."

Sara smiled. She didn't believe him, but his joking helped ease some of the weight on her shoulders.

"How'd you sleep?" Ren asked, walking to the counter where the coffeepot sat.

"I slept fine," she lied. Despite an exhaustion so complete she'd expected to sink into oblivion, Sara had tossed and turned, rehashing her decision. She kept asking herself if her true reason for giving in had more to do with the attraction she felt toward Ren than her need to protect Julia's memory.

When she looked at Ren, she found him staring at her. His facial expression remained neutral, but the look in his eyes set her heart racing.

"Coffee?" he asked.

He poured her a cup and carried it to her. Sitting on the high stool, she was just about eye level with him. He smelled of maleness and fresh air. Was it that or the aroma of the coffee that made her mouth water? She could easily reach out and touch his chest, where a few errant dark hairs curled above the neckline of his tank top.

"*O*'s, Mommy," Brady hollered, breaking the spell. "*O*'s."

Ren set the cup on the table and spun around. "*O*-what?"

Sara moved past him in search of the box of cereal she'd brought from home the night before. "Cheerios," she explained, retrieving it from a lower cabinet.

Ren took a carton of milk from the refrigerator and was reaching for a bowl, when Sara told him, "Brady likes his cereal dry. I pile it right on the tray—one less bowl to wash. Let me find his spill-proof cup."

"It's in the dishwasher," Ren said, opening the appliance door. He pulled out the cup and wiped it with a towel before handing it to Sara. "Dry cereal? Why dry cereal?"

"Tell Ren why you like your cereal dry, Brady," she said, pouring milk into the *Lion King* mug.

Brady chewed a bite of banana, then said in Brady-talk, "It goes *crunch-crunch* on my teeth better."

Ren's face screwed up in concentration. "He likes crunchy peanut butter?" he asked Sara.

She laughed. "Pretty close. You're getting better at understanding him." She set the mug in front of Brady. "He said he likes it crunching on his teeth."

"Oh."

"Brady knows his teeth are very important. That's why he drinks milk and brushes after every meal. Right Brady?"

Brady looked at Ren and gave him a toothy grin, complete with half-eaten cereal.

The swinging door opened inward, and Claudie walked hesitantly into the room. Ren did a double-take at seeing her with hair sticking up and no makeup. Sara thought Claudie looked about twelve in her baggy boxer shorts and wrinkled T-shirt.

"Can I use the pool?" she asked in a shy voice.

Ren reached for the key, which he'd placed on the top shelf of the brass baker's rack the night before. They'd all shared pizza on the patio last night after Bo and Sara had returned from a second run to her house. Brady had headed straight for the pool—a move that had alarmed Ren despite the presence of a fence. After some searching, he'd managed to locate a padlock and key. He hadn't returned to his cold pizza until the lock was safely on the gate, the key hanging where only adults could reach it.

"My mother fought long and hard to keep this pool from being built," he'd told them. "In the end, my dad twisted her arm by convincing her it would be good for his heart. But she insisted on the tallest, safest fence on the market. I've been lax about locking the gate because I was the only one using it, but from now on, we use the lock."

Handing the key to Claudie, he said, "There are beach towels in the cabana. You can swim, can't you?"

She gave him a black look. "I once lived six blocks from Lake Michigan. I can swim." She exited through the sunroom's sliding glass door, pulling the screen closed behind her.

The morning breeze filtered into the room. Mature trees and well-groomed bushes kept the yard shady and cool. Sara moved to the window and watched her friend execute a clean dive into the water.

"I want you to know I appreciate your doing this, Sara," Ren said.

Sara looked over her shoulder. "It was probably a mistake."

He didn't dispute that but said, "I'll do my best to make sure you don't regret it. If I can help you get your house on the market or anything else, just let me know."

He is a good man, Sara thought. *It's not his fault I'm falling in love with him.*

"I'm going to run upstairs and take a shower," he said, swallowing a last gulp of coffee. "When I get back down, I'll fix you and Claudie breakfast."

"You don't have to do that."

He flashed a smile that made Sara's heart stop. "I know, but I want to. This is our first morning together. I'd like to do something special. I make a great omelette. Wait'n see." He gave her a nod, fluffed Brady's curls on his way past, and then disappeared out the swinging door.

Sara was idly squishing *Cheerios* with her thumb, when Claudie returned a short while later. Wrapped in a huge yellow towel, she padded barefoot to the coffeepot and poured herself a cup. "Where's the judge?"

"Showering, but when he returns he's going to fix us a big, beautiful breakfast."

Claudie's brows shot up. "Cool." She studied her friend. "My room is as pretty as one of those bed-and-breakfast places you see in fancy travel magazines. I slept like a princess last night, Sara. How 'bout you?"

Sara looked at her. "You know that story about the Princess and the Pea?"

Claudie nodded.

"The pea was under my mattress."

Claudie, who seldom touched anyone other than Brady in a casual manner, walked to where Sara was sitting and placed her hand on Sara's shoulder. "Don't keep beating yourself up about this, Sara. You're doing the best you can. Remember? That's what you always tell me."

Sara swallowed the lump in her throat.

"Besides," Claudie continued, "it's like I told you last night. If Brady is the judge's kid, you'll have firsthand knowledge of how he lives so it'll be easier for you to share custody. Most women who give up their babies never know if they're being treated good or not."

Sara heard something very telling in Claudie's tone but didn't pry. "You're right," she said. "Getting an ulcer over this isn't going to help matters. Besides, I still have to deal with that damn estate lawyer. I wonder what he'll say when I tell him I moved out and want to sell the house."

Ren walked in at that moment. Sara had no idea a man could shower and dress so rapidly, but except for damp curls where usually there were tidy waves frozen in place by mousse, Ren looked ready for the courtroom. He moved about the kitchen with economic motions honed by practice.

"I'd offer to help, but somehow I think I'd only be in your way," Sara told him.

"You can man the toaster, if you want to help," he said. "Claudie, you're in charge of juice. There should be orange and cranberry in the fridge."

The three worked in harmony to the background chatter of Brady, who, growing restless, began spinning Cheerios across his tray like hockey pucks. A dozen or so casualties fell to the floor. Sara planned to release him from his chair as soon as she finished buttering toast, but Ren beat her to it. Ignoring the threat to his spotless gray flannel suit, he jerked the tray free, dumped it in the sink and hoisted Brady into his arms.

"You look ready for some fresh air, young man," he said, carrying Brady to the door. He nudged the screen open with his foot and set him down outside. "Go see if there are any squirrels in the yard."

"'Quiddels?" Brady asked brightly. With that, he shot away.

Sara saw the look on Ren's face as the little boy raced about, enjoying his new world. It was the same expression that might have sent her to her knees last night if she hadn't already been kneeling beside the huge tub. Her room and Brady's were connected by a spacious blue-and-white tiled bath, and she'd been dodging Brady's happy splashes when she'd looked up to find Ren watching the scene. His face had seemed poignantly expressive, as if he were glimpsing something painfully dear to his heart.

After the bath, Sara had dressed Brady in his summer-weight jammies and an overnight diaper. She had been thinking about which book to read him, when Ren poked his head in the doorway. She motioned him over and arbitrarily grabbed one of the books she'd brought from home.

"Would you read him a story?" she asked. "I want to check on Claudie."

Although surprised, he'd risen to the occasion by snuggling Brady on his lap in the chintz-covered armchair and plunging into a rousing rendition of "The Three Little Pigs." Sara had watched from the doorway. Ren's obvious joy at Brady's pleasure touched her deeply.

Now she felt Claudie looking at her. Embarrassed, she asked Ren, "Will he be safe outside alone?" Her tone sounded stiff and overprotective.

"I think so. I'll call the gardener later to make sure none of the plants are poisonous," Ren told her.

Sara shook her head. "Brady doesn't eat plants. I meant, will he be safe from getting out or wandering away? I couldn't let him out alone at Hulger's house."

"Yeah, a mountain lion might have come down and got him," Claudie teased.

"Well, we do have a neighborhood cat that digs up the flower beds, but I don't think he's ever attacked anyone," Ren said lightly. He glanced outside before returning to his egg preparations. After a minute, he said to Sara, "I overheard what you said to Claudie about your house when I came in. I'd like to suggest either Armory or I go with you when you talk to the estate lawyer. I don't like the way the man's been treating you. Would that be okay?"

"Are you kidding? It would be great. He intimidates the heck out of me."

"That's because you've never seen him naked," Claudie said.

Both Sara and Ren turned to look at her. She blinked coquettishly, causing Ren to burst out laughing. "Remind me never to get on your bad side, Claudie," he said, chuckling as he slid a steaming omelette on a plate and carried it to the table.

"Bon appétit," he said. "Sara, you're next."

Sara took the plate of toast to the table, then sat down on the stool opposite Claudie. A girl could get used to this, she thought dreamily, until a sober voice in her head reminded her this arrangement was only temporary.

After serving Sara, Ren rinsed the pan and bowl and placed them on a wooden rack beside the sink, then walked to the little white box near the door to the garage. "Let's go over this one more time," he said, and proceeded to point out the mechanics of the alarm system. He'd explained the whole thing the night before when he'd issued Sara and Claudie house keys. "I've left a note on my desk for Revelda, in case you leave before she gets here. She's terrific—you'll like her, and she will go nuts over Brady." He picked up a well-used leather briefcase from beside the counter and started to leave. "Well, have a good day. I'll see you tonight."

"Wait," Sara said. "Aren't you eating breakfast?"

"Already did. I'm an early riser. Sorry to run. If you need to reach me, get a message to my clerk, Rafael Justis. 'Bye."

The door closed, and Sara cocked her head to listen for the sound of Ren's car starting. When she was sure he was gone, she dropped her chin in her palm and sighed. "This is very strange."

Claudie nodded sagely. "We're not in Kansas anymore, are we?"

"Nope," Sara said, taking another bite of the most delicious omelette she'd ever eaten. "I'm not even sure we're still in California."

REN'S MIND RACED as he dashed up the steps to the third floor of the courthouse. He couldn't quite believe how things had worked out. Sara and Brady were living under his roof—and he had Babe to thank for it. The improbability of that fact made him grin.

He flashed back to his conversation with his mother prior to Sara showing up. Babe had been mortified to learn that her machinations had resulted in Sara and Brady moving in with him. "That's preposterous!" she'd stewed. "That was never my intention."

Ren hadn't cut her any slack. "I'm sure it wasn't, but they're here, along with Sara's friend Claudine. And as long as they are my guests, Mother, I expect you to treat them with respect. This is a complicated matter. Until we have proof that Brady is my son—"

"You just have to look at him to know, Lawrence," Babe had interrupted. "He has the Bishop eyes."

Ren hadn't been able to prevent the little surge of hope that followed her words. "Blue eyes are a dime a dozen, Mother. We need biological proof, and that won't be back for another six weeks."

"I understand that, which is why I have not allowed myself to regard him as my grandson. But why do they have to stay *here?*"

"Because I want Brady to get to know me, and I want Sara to feel comfortable with my parenting skills if it turns out I'll be sharing custody with her—which will only happen if Brady's my son. If he isn't, then you and I are to blame for turning Sara's life upside down, and we'll be lucky if she doesn't sue us."

As he passed through the outer office area, Ren paused at his clerk's desk. "I know I'm late, but could I have a few moments of your time?"

An idea had blossomed during the drive to work—given the short distance, it wasn't fully formed, but Ren hoped Rafael could help shape it. Ren had met Rafael's wife on several occasions and he knew the couple had two small children. He figured Rafael would be the perfect resource.

As Ren hung up his suit coat and adjusted his tie, Rafael entered the room, walking to the desk. "What's up? You seem pretty energized."

"I am. I had a great run this morning. Plus, I have some guests staying at my house. That's what I wanted to talk to you about. Sara Carsten and her eighteen-month-old son are staying with me for a few weeks. I think Brady—that's Sara's little boy— might benefit from mixing with other children. How did you and Daria decide on which day-care center to use?"

Rafael, who seldom showed surprise at anything that happened within the hall of justice, was slow to answer. "Constancia is six now. She's in first grade. Paulo's four—he goes to a Montessori preschool. It's a very nice place, but it doesn't take toddlers. The kids have to be potty trained."

"Is there any place in this area that takes babies?"

"I think Bright Stars does, but I'll check with Daria. She researched all the local day-care providers and preschool programs for a paper she did recently. Her major is early childhood education."

Ren fastened his robe and took the sheaf of papers Rafael handed him. "Thanks. Tell her I'd really appreciate the help."

Ren sensed the other man's curiosity. "If she

could give me a couple of names this morning, I might try to visit them during the lunch break.''

"No problem.''

Once Ren sat down behind his raised dais, he drew on years of practice and his law school training to stay focused for the next three hours.

When his hour and a half lunch break arrived, Ren visited the first of four facilities on Daria Justis's list: Bright Stars. According to Daria's synopsis, the place offered something called "layered structuring" with emphasis on Montessori teaching aids. The director greeted him at the door.

"I'm so pleased you're considering us, Judge Bishop. Won't Mrs. Bishop be joining you?"

Ren hadn't been expecting the question. His pulse spiked. "Not today. I'm doing the preliminary legwork," he said, realizing how public his and Sara's living arrangements would become if they enrolled Brady in day care. Maybe he'd be smarter to wait until they had a formal custody arrangement.

He almost turned around, but the director, an enthusiastic woman with a beaming smile, took his arm and led him into the facility, which had been converted from a home built in the same era as Ren's. The high, cove ceilings and big windows gave the rooms a light and airy feeling. Squeals of laughter and children's voices made Ren smile. Before he left, Ren had acquired a new best friend—a toddler named Michael who melted Ren's heart with his slightly crossed eyes and thick glasses.

He gave the boy a hug before leaving. On the outer stoop, Ren asked the director about the child. "He's from a single-parent home. His mother works in the Building. He's very bright and loving but craves male attention. He latches on to every adult male who comes to visit. You should have seen him with the firefighters who gave us our annual fire-safety talk. You'd have thought they were gods.''

Ren found he didn't have time to visit the second address on his list, but he liked Bright Stars. If Sara liked the place—and the idea of putting Brady into daycare—he planned to offer to pay for Brady to attend the morning program a couple of days a week.

A quick stop at the hardware store nearly made him late for court.

"Sir, do you mind me asking? Does this day-care thing have anything to do with Mr. Lester's inquiry?" Rafael asked, as they hurried toward Ren's courtroom.

"What inquiry?"

"He called right after you left and said to ask you if he could officially close your missing persons case? He said he's tying up loose ends because he has a new case starting and may be out of town for the next few weeks."

"Damn," Ren muttered. Not only would Ren miss his friend on a personal level, he'd come to rely on Bo as a sort of mediator. Ren knew Sara liked and trusted Bo and valued his opinion. And Claudie seemed less hostile to Ren when Bo was around. Although he and Claudie bickered like siblings, Ren knew Bo liked the young woman and was hoping she'd make the transition to a better life.

"Please call him back and ask him to come by after work. I need to talk to him." Ren saw Rafael make a note on his pad. He decided the young man deserved to know some of what was going on. "In answer to your question, yes, this all pertains to the search I hired Bo to conduct. He found that the woman in question was killed in an accident last summer, leaving behind a young child. Sara is the boy's legal guardian. They're living at my house until she can find suitable housing closer to town.''

If Rafael was shocked, he didn't show it. ''My sister and her husband just moved into one of those new town houses on the other side of the river. I could get her some information if you want.''

Ren didn't, but he nodded. ''Thank you. That would be nice. Don't forget about Bo. I need to see him today.''

BO DIDN'T WANT to talk to Ren. He'd vacillated all night about the wisdom of Sara's move. When she'd showed up on Ren's doorstep, Bo had worried his friend might stroke out, but with that inborn Bishop poise, Ren had handled the whole transition with grace. He'd sent Bo and Sara back to Sara's for another load of belongings, while he and Claudie and Brady disassembled the double bed in what would serve as Brady's room.

Sara had been in a somber mood during the drive, but Bo did his best to buoy her spirits by congratulating her on her amazing coup. ''You are my new hero,'' he'd told her. ''For some reason Babe Bishop has my number. You saw how she acted at the bookstore. I can't explain it, but she gives me that haughty look of hers and my blood turns to water. When we were in college, Ren would drag me home for the holidays because my family lived on the East Coast. I'd try real hard to be on my best behavior, but Babe seemed to consider me a bad influence on her son.''

''How about Ren's father?''

''Larry? He was a peach. Everybody adored him. So easygoing and likable. Once in a while he and I would slip away to go boating on the river. I think that's when I decided I'd one day live on a houseboat. Larry loved the water and he made me appreciate its serenity.'' Picturing that particular time in his life—when most days were spent recuperating from a hangover—Bo couldn't help marveling at Larry's insight and kindness.

''Ren is a lot like his dad. Thank God. I'd have killed him years ago if he was like Babe. She's sort of a female version of *my* dad, which explains why I haven't been home in ten years. Those kind of people need a little comeuppance now and then. So my hat's off to you, Sara.''

Sara had groaned and sunk lower in the passenger seat of her station wagon, which Bo was driving. ''You don't understand, Bo. I think I overreacted. Julia used to tell me, 'Act, don't react. You'll live to regret it.' I have a feeling I'm definitely going to regret this move.''

''I disagree, Sara. I think this is a good first step— a transition. Ren can provide a sort of way station for you and Brady until you get your bearings.''

''That makes it sound as though I'm using Ren,'' she'd said, and Bo had sensed her true feelings toward Ren. She, of course, didn't know Ren had admitted to Bo his love for her. If Sara felt the same for Ren, things might either work out great or blow up something fierce. That was why Bo distrusted love. He'd had a few romantic attachments over the years, but had always managed to keep them friendly. The one time the word *love* had entered the picture, things had immediately gone sour. No, Bo Lester didn't have much faith in love.

Now, stifling a sigh, he knocked on Ren's door.

"Come in, Bo."

Bo shuffled in. He walked to the window, not meeting Ren's eyes.

"Rafael told me you might be out of town for a few weeks. Is that true?"

Bo shrugged. "A guy from Security West called me this morning. They're hardwiring some new condos in Placerville. They need a supervisor."

"I thought you'd given up that side of the business."

"The money's good."

"I'll match it if you stay."

Surprised by the offer, Bo turned. He rested his shoulder against the window and studied his friend. "Why? I've done everything you asked. I found Julia. I hooked you up with Sara. The rest is up to your DNA guys. What do you need me for?"

Ren made a few squiggles on a piece of paper. "I'm so far over my head here, I don't know which end is up." He looked at Bo. "I really care for Sara, and I know she feels a certain attraction toward me, but this is all moving too fast." He held up his hand when Bo started to point out the speed of the situation could be attributed to Ren. "I know, I'm to blame for that fact. But the bottom line is, I'm afraid I'll blow it."

"And you think I can help?"

"Yes. Sara likes you and trusts your advice."

Bo's hackles started to rise. "What are you suggesting I do? Manipulate her?"

"Of course not. I'd just like you to be around to help make sure things go smoothly. Sara has Claudie for the same reason."

Bo snickered softly. "I thought Claudie was a chaperone. Do you need two chaperones, Mr. Stud Muffin?"

Ren shot him a dark look. "I'm talking moral support."

To his surprise, Bo found himself sympathetic to Ren's cause. He pushed off from the window and walked to the door. "I'll stick around for a couple of weeks, but no more baby-sitting. Not alone, anyway. Brady's too damn fast for an old man like me." He paused, his hand on the doorknob. "If you tell anyone I said that, however, I will amputate your left nut." With that, he left.

At his car, Bo paused. He'd never admit it, but in a way he envied Ren. Brady was a great kid, and Bo had lied when he'd said he wouldn't baby-sit. He didn't blame Ren for wanting to make sure things went smoothly—a lot was riding on what happened in the next few weeks.

SARA WAS STARTING TO THINK about locking up the store, when Ren walked in the front door. The sight of him made her heart shift gears.

"Hi. What are you doing here?" she asked, hoping she didn't sound as giddy as she felt.

"I know I should have called first," he said, bending low to pick up Brady, who'd hurled himself at Ren's kneecaps. "But I was hoping I might persuade you and Brady to have dinner with me. I thought I heard Claudie tell Bo last night that she was planning to study at the library tonight, and this way you could ride home with me and she could have your car."

"That's incredibly thoughtful."

He lifted Brady up and nuzzled his belly, making the toddler shriek. "Not altogether altruistic, though. I have no idea what's available in the refrigerator, and I don't want to go to the grocery store." He set Brady down and gave her a serious look. "Plus, I want to talk to you about a few things."

Sara gulped. If she'd somehow convinced herself today that she and Ren would be able to cruise along like two vessels occupying the same waters without bumping into each other, she knew now she'd deluded herself. Ren seemed to have every intention of staying connected to her and Brady. What that meant exactly, she didn't know.

"Okay. I'll go tell Claudie—she's in the reading area. Here are my car keys," she said, taking the key ring from her desk drawer. "Would you mind transferring the car seat?"

A grin popped up on Ren's face. "Don't have to. I bought a new car seat today and had it installed. I figured it was a heck of a lot easier than switching yours back and forth."

Sara swallowed. Either he was very confident of the results of the DNA test or...Sara wasn't sure what other explanation might exist.

She waited until they were seated in the noisy, family-friendly atmosphere of a local Italian restaurant to ask. "The car seat is very nice, Ren. Top of the line. Wasn't it a bit extravagant for a couple of weeks? What if the test comes back negative?"

He rolled his shoulders. "It cost a hundred and forty-five dollars. That may seem wasteful for a month's use, but I value my time, and the time it takes to transfer yours back and forth seemed like a bigger waste to me."

He pulled two bread sticks from a tall glass container in the center of the table and handed one to Brady, who waved it like a wand. "As long as we're on the subject, I'd like to suggest another way to spend some of my money." His words were light, but something about his tone struck her as serious.

"How?"

"I'd like to pay for Brady to spend two or three mornings a week in a preschool. I looked at one today." He produced a slim promotional flyer from his jacket pocket. "I have the names of three others from my clerk's wife."

Sara studied the glossy paper. She was amazed that this would even cross Ren's mind. It was as if he'd read her thoughts. She'd wanted to place Brady in some kind of day-care situation so he could be around other kids his age, but she hadn't been able to afford it.

She looked up and found him watching her. "This is very generous of you."

His face lit up. "Are you okay with it? You're not upset that I didn't consult you first? It was sort of spontaneous. I thought about it on the way to work. Brady looked kind of lonely out back without any playmates, and I figured it might be hard for you to arrange day care when you're alone at the shop all day."

She swallowed against the lump in her throat.

"I'm fine with it. If you like this place, we could take Brady there and see what he thinks."

"Terrific. Maybe during lunch tomorrow." He turned to Brady in his high chair and ruffled his curly locks. "What do you think, big guy? Want to go to school?"

This time Sara missed Brady's reply—her heart was pounding too loudly. But Ren nodded and laughed as if understanding every word. Sara tried to take a mental picture of the moment, hoping to keep the image in her head forever. This might be the closest she'd come to a traditional family setting, and it was so beautiful it almost broke her heart.

CHAPTER TWELVE

SARA KEPT ONE EAR on the sounds coming from Brady's room as she answered the phone beside her bed. Since Ren had departed for the golf course only twenty minutes earlier, she didn't expect him to be calling—everyone knew his aversion to cellular phones. Hesitantly, she put the receiver to her ear, hoping the caller wasn't Ren's mother.

"Hello," Sara answered tentatively.

"Sara? This is Janice Andrews. Am I calling too early?"

Janice was the real estate agent handling her house. "It's never too early in the home of a toddler," Sara assured her. "Have you heard anything?" Janice had shown the house to a couple from Texas on Thursday.

"Yes. Are you sitting down? They called last night with an offer—a good, solid offer, Sara. Cash."

Sara couldn't believe it. The house had been on the market for three weeks, and while a dozen prospective buyers had toured it, all expressed concern over the amount of landscaping left to complete. "Really? They'll take it as is?"

"Yes. It turns out the wife is into exotic animals, and she plans to make a habitat for her pets. I didn't dare ask what kind. Let the neighbors deal with that."

Sara grinned, picturing the look on Mary Gaines's face if an emu or llama showed up next door. "That's amazing, Janice. I'm thrilled. When do they want it?"

"The sooner the better. I've got their deposit money in hand. Do you want me to run over with the paperwork? I could be there in an hour—I have to return a few calls first. Trust me, Sara, it's everything you hoped for."

Although Sara would have liked to have Ren present, she agreed to meet the woman at ten-thirty. She hung up the phone and sat down on her bed.

"If that was supposed to be good news, I sure don't want to see how you take bad," Claudie said, entering Sara's room through the bathroom that connected to Brady's room. She balanced a stack of folded clothes on one arm. This was Claudie's week for laundry.

When she and Sara had first moved into Ren's house, they'd agreed to divide up certain chores. Revelda did the general sweeping, dusting and vacuuming downstairs, and she cleaned Ren's room. Sara and Claudie looked after their rooms and Brady's. Laundry was a shared task—one that Ren had asked to be included in, as well.

Claudie set a neatly folded column of clothing on Sara's dresser. A pair of white Jockey shorts fell off the pile and dropped to the floor. Picking them up, Claudie grinned. "Nothing like dirty clothes to put everybody on the same level. He may be the judge, but I fold his shorts."

"Laundry—the great equalizer," Sara said, smiling.

To Sara's amazement, Claudie and Ren had developed a playful kind of repartee that Sara envied.

With Sara, Ren was always thoughtful and considerate, but somewhat circumspect. With Claudie, he allowed himself to cut loose a little.

"That was Janice. She sold the house."

"You're kidding! That's fantastic."

Selling Hulger's house had proved to be a valuable learning experience for Sara. Ren had accompanied her to the appointment with the estate lawyer. Sara had expected the meeting to be confrontational. To her surprise the man had been understanding, even supportive, when she informed him of her desire to sell the property.

"Wise move," he'd said. "I thought the house was a bit unwieldy for a woman alone."

"I don't think it would have been much easier for a man," Sara had returned.

"Of course not. I didn't mean it that way. I only meant—"

Ren had cut him off by laying a business card on his desk. "My lawyer's number. He's going to help Sara with some other legal matters, and I'd appreciate it if you'd send copies of the trust history to him."

"Are you suggesting some impropriety?"

"Not at all. I'm just curious why Sara has had to fight for every nickel she needed to care for Brady. I agree that it's important to save for the future, but not at the expense of the present."

Sara had never seen Ren pull rank before. Later, when she described the episode to Bo, he'd told her, "You think that was something, you should see him take on bad cops. Ren doesn't tolerate ineptitude."

"How long 'til escrow closes?" Claudie asked, bringing Sara back to the present.

"I don't know, but Janice said it was a cash deal."

"Cash? What is he? A drug czar? Maybe he's in a witness relocation program."

Sara shrugged. "All I know is they're from Texas and they have four kids. The youngest is an infant, and the wife fell in love with Brady's room."

At the sound of his name, Brady dashed into the room, his arms stuffed with toys. He dropped the load in a patch of sunlight on the floor, and began to play.

"I guess this means we should start house-hunting, huh?" Claudie asked, her tone subdued.

A flutter of trepidation danced in Sara's chest. "I guess so." She glanced at the calendar by her bed—it was already July 8. The results of the DNA test could be back any day, and she hadn't managed to make herself take a single step toward the future. Instead, she allowed the simple pleasures of living—volunteering at Brady's day care, running the book drive, spending time with Ren—to keep her from planning ahead.

"Maybe Monday," she said, trying to sound upbeat. Changing the subject, she asked, "Did Ren say what time our reservations were for tonight?" She walked to Brady and knelt beside him, picking up one of the new trucks Ren had given him.

Claudie ground her bare toes in the thick carpet. "Are you sure about this? I told Ren it's not necessary."

Sara looked up, smiling. She knew Claudie was both pleased and unnerved by Ren's reaction to the news she'd passed her equivalency test. He'd immediately called Bo and set up a dinner date. "Don't be so modest. This is a terrific accomplishment, Claudie. We are definitely going to celebrate.''

"But the Stockton Club is the most exclusive place in town. And I doubt if Brady will like it there.''

Sara tousled her son's hair. "You may not believe this, but Mrs. Bishop is coming over to stay with Brady.''

"What?'' Claudie croaked. "Are you okay with that?''

Sara sighed. "I was a little hesitant at first. But Ren says his mother is looking forward to getting to know Brady. I think she's beginning to believe he might be her grandson. Now, it's just me she doesn't approve of.''

"Wow, Brady! Grandma Mean-Lady's coming,'' Claudie said. "She'll probably serve you boiled bat tongues and lizard innards for dinner. Yum, yum.''

Fighting a smile, Sara scolded her. "You shouldn't tease him like that, Claudie. He comprehends more than you and Bo give him credit for. Just because you can't understand everything Brady says doesn't mean he can't understand you.''

Claudie gave Brady a long, serious look. "Really?''

Sara nodded. "Just the other day Brady told Ren that Uncle Bo and Aunt Claudie were getting married.''

"What?'' Claudie shrieked.

Sara tried not to smile. "Well, not in so many words. But Ren was sure that's what he meant.'' Actually, Brady, who seemed to prefer things grouped together rather than alone, used his favorite expression, "bofagator''—which Sara interpreted to mean "both together''—to describe his adopted aunt and uncle. Ren took that to mean Brady thought Bo and Claudie should get married so he could stay with them at Bo's houseboat more often.

Claudie stared at Brady as though he'd just grown horns. "Good God. He's not really that smart, is he?"

Sara hid her grin with her hand. "All I'm saying is, you'd better start thinking of him as a miniature adult, not a puppy."

Brady picked up on the word *puppy* and started barking like the neighbor's dog.

Claudie dropped to her knees and charged forward, growling. Brady's shrieks of laughter made Sara cover her ears. He jumped on Claudie's back, demanding a horsy ride. The play continued until Claudie collapsed. "You're too much, Brady boy." She pulled him into a hug. "But I love you."

Sara's eyes filled with tears. She'd never heard Claudie use those words about anyone or anything.

Claudie stood up and walked to the door. "Ren told me he made the reservations for seven, so I thought I'd open up this morning. Then you and Brady can come down after his nap. Angela's coming in to help with inventory."

Angela was Claudie's new recruit—a skinny, pimple-faced girl whom Claudie was trying to keep from a life on the streets. She hadn't been in the market for a job and didn't seem to appreciate Claudie's interference, but somehow Claudie had persuaded her to give the bookstore a chance.

"Is it okay if Bo picks you up after work?" Claudie asked. "I need to use the car to run a few errands."

Sometimes Sara couldn't help but marvel at the changes she'd witnessed in her friend over the past month. She didn't know if the impetus had been Claudie's scholastic achievement or the fact that she felt—and was—needed by Sara. The respect Bo and Ren gave her might have helped, too, Sara thought.

"Fine. I have to take Brady to his playgroup at ten, then meet with Janice. Later, I want to run a box of books over to the jail."

"Will that give you enough time for Brady's nap?" Claudie asked. "We don't want him grumpy for Grandma you-know-who."

Sara laughed and shook her head. "Ren will be back around noon. He's going to stay with Brady."

Claudie confirmed the last of their convoluted child-care and social arrangements, then left.

Sara put away her clean clothes and finished straightening up her bedroom. She loved her room. At the thought of leaving this place, a small sound of pain escaped from her lips.

Brady looked at her curiously.

She smiled to reassure him. "Which is the new truck Ren gave you, Brady?" she asked, motioning him to come to her. "Is it red? Show me the red one."

He studied the pile a moment, then snatched a bright red fire truck from the jumble and carried it to her.

Sara clapped and gave him a big hug. Claudie wasn't the only one benefiting from all the attention. Between Ren and Bo, as well as the teachers at Bright Stars, Brady was blooming. There was no denying that Ren Bishop had made a huge difference to the lives of Sara and her extended family. So why did she feel so miserable?

Absentmindedly accepting the toys Brady brought her, Sara sat on her bed and thought about her relationship with Ren. In the four weeks they'd been living under the same roof, he'd done absolutely nothing untoward or improper. He treated her with respect, yet, there was something—a heat, a tension—between them that she sensed but couldn't define.

She knew Ren felt it, too, but any time she caught him looking at her with what might be longing or desire, he turned away. Whenever they accidentally touched, Sara felt sparks reverberate through her body, but Ren would merely apologize and put more space between them.

Sara hadn't forgotten their kiss, but apparently Ren had. Sighing, she blinked back tears, silently admitting the futility of her feelings. How could she expect Ren to lust after her when he'd made love to Julia? Sara knew Ren liked her, respected her, but he didn't feel that same gut-wrenching passion that made Sara listen for his footsteps at night. That made her sneak into his room early each morning to watch him from the window as he did laps in the pool.

Sara wasn't sure she could last another two weeks, but the alternative was just as harrowing. The cliche—caught between a rock and a hard place—came to mind. How could she stay? Worse, how could she leave?

"So, HOW DO YOU PLAY this game, anyway?" Bo asked, examining a golf ball as if it might hold a clue.

Ren, who was in the process of squaring his stance in front of the first tee, looked up and frowned. "You took golf in college, Bo. I know. I lent you my clubs."

"Oh, yeah, I forgot," Bo lied. He hadn't set up this golf date to knock around little white balls. He was a man with a mission.

He waited until Ren started the downward stroke of his swing, then said, "It's time to shit or get off the pot."

The club made a dull *thunk* when it connected with the ball; a large hunk of grass flew up, too. Ren glared at him. "There is a certain etiquette to follow, Lester. Don't talk when someone is swinging."

"Oh, I thought that only applied in baseball."

Ren stuffed his club back in the bag, then moved aside.

Bo wiped his hands on his checkered double-knit pants—the most audacious he'd been able to find—and approached the finely manicured tee. "I meant it, though," he said, squinting down the fairway as though he gave a hoot.

"Meant what?"

"You've got to do something. You're killing her."

"Who?"

"Who do you think?"

Bo swung the club and felt the wooden head connect squarely with the ball. The ball arched into the air and flew straight down the green turf. "Wow. I think they call that beginner's luck."

Shoulder-to-shoulder the two men walked down the fairway. Ren didn't look at Bo when he said, "You're wrong. Sara's doing great. Brady loves his school. Claudie's a success story. Everybody's fine."

Bo knew by Ren's tone that he didn't believe what he was saying, even though it was all fact.

Everyone *was* doing great—except the two lead players, who were miserable.

Ren stalked to his ball, grabbed a club and walloped it with enough force for Bo to hear the swishing sound as the club sliced through the air. Bo watched the ball streak along the outer edge of the fairway, then drop into the rough. "Tough break," he said unsympathetically.

Ren gave him a black look and marched away. They met up again at the first putting green. "I didn't mean you were killing her on purpose," Bo said, a second before Ren's putter connected with the ball. The ball hugged the cup for a heartbeat before arcing away to stop four feet from the hole.

Ren's epithet made Bo snicker.

"I'm not killing her," Ren shouted.

The words seemed to echo in the still morning air. Ren closed his eyes and lifted his face to the sky. "Great," he muttered. "If the paternity issue doesn't screw up my reelection, a murder scandal will."

Bo putted his ball into the cup, then walked to Ren's side. He patted his friend's shoulder consolingly. "It's not like you love this job, anyway."

"How would you know?"

Bo shrugged. "I watch people, Ren. It's what I do. And I've watched you for twenty years. I know you took the judgeship for the same reason you went to law school—because it was expected of you. But you don't love it. I'm not saying you're not good at it, but it's not your thing."

Ren looked at him with a blank kind of astonishment.

"What?" Bo asked. "Did you think I was just some illiterate gumshoe?"

Ren didn't respond. He finished his putt, then packed away his equipment. "Let's go get some breakfast. We can talk there."

"What about the rest of the game? It's starting to come back to me. I must not have been bombed that entire semester."

THE COFFEE SHOP Bo picked out was not the kind of place Ren or any of his golf buddies would frequent, which probably was why Bo chose it, Ren thought, pulling into the parking lot behind the Mazda. Ren sent Bo in to pick out a table, while he used the phone.

Sara answered; her voice made an automatic smile spring to his lips. He loved the sound of it.

"Hi. It's me. Bo and I cut our game short. We're grabbing a quick cup of coffee, then I'm coming home. Do you need me to pick up anything?"

"Um…no, not that I can think of. What will your mother want for dinner? I was planning hot dogs for Brady."

"Perfect. She loves hot dogs," Ren said, grinning at his blatant lie.

"Okay." She didn't sound as though she believed him. "Oh, and guess what? Janice just called—she said the house is sold."

Ren's heart jumped skittishly. "Really? That's great news."

Sara hesitated a moment before agreeing with him. "She's going to come over in a little while with the proposal. If you're here, maybe you could look it over for me. I hate to ask, but…"

Ren bit off a curse. Didn't she know he'd do anything for her? Why did she always sound so apologetic when she asked for a favor?

"No problem. I should be there in twenty minutes. I'd better run. See you soon."

Sliding onto the booth's cracked, red plastic cushion, Ren saw Bo look at him appraisingly.

The waitress delivered two coffees. "Menus?" she asked.

"No, thank you, we can't stay," Ren said.

"We can't? Why not?" Bo asked, when she walked away.

"Sara sold the house. She wants me there when the Realtor brings the paperwork."

Bo added a packet of sugar to his mug. "Hey, that's good news. Did she sound happy?"

Ren thought a moment. "Sorta."

"'Sorta.' What does that tell you, Ren? A woman sells the biggest white elephant ever built and she's just sorta happy? What is wrong with that picture?"

"I didn't get all the details. Maybe it's not a good offer."

"Bullshit. Janice is a mercenary. She wouldn't bring in a shabby offer. I'm telling you Sara is miserable. She's sinking fast, bud."

"You make her sound like the goddamn *Titanic*."

Bo sat back, giving Ren a look his friend knew all too well. With a muffled curse, Ren gave up. He knew Bo was right. Worrying about Sara kept Ren from sleeping at night. He pushed his coffee cup away and said, "What am I supposed to do? I've tried everything I can think of. I know she's happy about Brady's school and she was jumping for joy over Claudie's exam—but you're right. Something's missing."

"Like the sparkle in her eyes," Bo said, sitting forward again. "God, I miss that little glint of humor whenever she'd look around and see one of us standing there. I haven't seen that in weeks.''

''I know,'' Ren said. ''I tried gifts. I made her go to that day spa. We've taken Brady to the zoo and the wild animal park and Discovery Zone. He's been doing great in his swim lessons, and I know she's thrilled with that. He loves school and he's getting along well with the other kids—''

Bo shook his head. ''Brady's not the problem.''

''And Claudie is doing fantastic. Ever since Sara made her assistant manager at the bookstore, you'd swear she's a different person.''

''It's not Claudie.''

''Babe hasn't—''

''Ren, it's you.''

Ren exhaled as if Bo had hit him in the gut. He ran his hand through his hair impatiently. ''I've tried to keep my distance, Bo. God, it's been killing me, too. You should see her in the morning when we're downstairs alone. She likes to get up when she hears me come in from doing my laps. There's something so fresh, so innocent about her. Damn.''

Bo was silent a minute, then he said, ''Have you talked to Sara about your feelings?''

''Hell, no. Do you want to see her head for the hills? Christ, Bo, it can't be easy living in the same house with the man who slept with your sister and could be your nephew's father. I don't know why she doesn't hate me.''

''I don't either, but you know she likes you. Maybe she likes you as much as you like her.'' Bo made a sound of disgust. ''Did I just say that? Maybe I need to go back to high school.''

Ren frowned. ''I don't know what to think, but I agree that things can't go on like they are. I was planning on talking to her tomorrow—we've got Claudie's party tonight, but maybe we can grab a few minutes alone once Janice leaves."

Ren reached in his pocket for his wallet, but Bo said, "Get out of here. Go home to Sara. Try not to blow it, okay?"

REN THOUGHT ABOUT Bo's words all the way home. As he pulled into the driveway, he noted the late-model Suburban with the real estate logo on the door parked in front of the house. He left his clubs in the trunk and hurried inside.

Sara and Janice were in his office, sitting on the sofa with a stack of papers between them. Instead of going to his desk, Ren sat down on the other side of Sara. She seemed startled by his proximity but didn't edge away. "You got here fast," she said. "We barely sat down."

"Time is money in the real estate business. How's everything, Janice? What have you got for Sara?"

The actual paperwork was a snap. Janice, a true professional, seemed perfectly comfortable walking Sara through all the steps, answering her questions with courtesy and understanding. The offer was sound, better than he'd thought possible.

Later, as he and Sara walked Janice to the door, he said, "I'm very impressed, Janice. That was not an easy house to market. You certainly earned your commission."

"Thanks, again," Sara called to Janice from the step. She watched until the Suburban was out of sight, obviously reluctant to go inside with Ren.

Screwing up his courage, he held the door open and said, "Sara, could we talk?"

She faced him, a grim look on her face. "I have to pick Brady up from his play group in fifteen minutes."

"This won't take long."

She walked inside and waited for a signal from Ren. He led the way to the back patio. He knew one of her favorite places was the gazebo. In fact, he'd added thick pads upholstered in a rich forest-green print just for her. He sat down on one side of the octagon; she sat opposite him.

She wore a simple cotton shorts set of peachy orange. Her newly acquired tan made her arms and legs look sleek and sexy. The sun had lightened her hair several shades to a warm honey color. Ren longed to reach out and pull her into his arms.

"Sara, I..." The lawyer in him had a whole speech prepared, but in the end it was the man who blurted out, "I love you."

Sara frowned as if trying to decipher a foreign word. "How do you mean that? The same way you love Brady and Bo and Claudie?"

"I don't love Claudie. She's a pain in the butt. I like her, and I respect how she's turned her life around, but I don't—" Ren shook his head to get back on track. Her question had thrown him. But he realized it was valid. "You're right. I love my friends and family. A lot. Especially Brady. But those feelings have nothing to do with the way I feel about you."

"They don't?"

Ren tapped his forehead with his fist. "I'm really bad at this. I guess I don't know how to explain love because I've never been in love before."

"Eve..."

He shook his head. "Eve and I seemed liked a

good idea at the time. That's it.'' He sat forward, closer to her. Sara didn't draw back, but she seemed wary. ''Sara, I know you're not happy here. I've tried to make everything as easy as possible because I wanted to give you time to get to know me. I hoped that maybe, if I was lucky, you'd start to feel about me the way I feel about you.''

He reached out and took her hand in both of his. ''I know it's a little crazy to think two people thrown together the way we were could actually fall in love, but that's what happened—for me, anyway.''

Her hand trembled but she didn't pull it back. She looked at him, searching his eyes. ''Are you saying you want to—'' The color in her cheeks deepened.

''You have no idea how hard it's been for me to resist you.''

''*You've* been trying to resist *me?*'' she whispered.

She sounded so dumbfounded that Ren moved back, knowing that the best way to avoid blowing this was to take it slowly and deliberately. ''Sara, I'm crazy about you. About your smell. Your smile. The way you look in your swimming suit. I fantasize about the way you'll look out of your swimming suit.''

Her blush deepened.

''You're sexiest in the morning when you're all sleepy-eyed, standing there with a cup of coffee, waiting for me when I get out of the pool. No, wait, I've changed my mind. You're even sexier when you've just tucked Brady in bed and you stand beside his door with your eyes closed listening to him. I can't tell you how many times I've thought about scooping you into my arms and carrying you to my bed.''

"That's sexy?'' she asked, tilting her head dubiously.

"To me it is. Because I know the energy and soul you put into raising that little boy, and I love you for it.''

Sara sat forward, and Ren saw tears glisten in her eyes. "Do you mean *love* love? Not just I'm-Brady's-mother love?''

Ren reached out and cupped her jaw in his palm. "I mean forever, long-after-Brady-is-grown-and-gone love. Just you and me, Sara. The whole nine yards, as Bo would say.''

She squeezed her eyes tight and moved back. She drew her knees to her chest and wrapped her arms around them. "Ren, I love you, too, but I can't make love to you.''

Ren's heart soared, then crashed. "Why not?''

She wouldn't look at him. "I couldn't stand to see the look of disappointment on your face.''

"What are you talking about?'' Ren asked, although deep inside he knew.

"I could never live up to my sister's image. Even when she was alive, I barely fit in her shadow. You've had two years to build and shape your memories of a sexual goddess, and trust me, I'm not like that. I don't even know how to pretend to be like that.''

Her confession ripped his heart out. Moving very cautiously, he slid along the gazebo seat until he was beside her. He wiped a tear that seemed poised to drop to her cheek. "I kissed you once, remember?'' She nodded. "At the time I thought it was a mistake. I thought it would complicate things between us.''

He lowered his head and kissed her cheek, the corner of her eye, the bridge of her nose. "Maybe my mistake was in stopping."

She tilted her head to meet his lips.

SARA CLOSED HER EYES and slipped into the magical world Ren provided. His lips were warm and sweet, a hypnotic blend, gentle and demanding. When his tongue entered her mouth, a spike of passion ripped through her midsection. On their own, her arms went around his shoulders.

Ren gently pushed her knees away so he could move closer. Without the impediment he pulled her to him; her bosom flattened against his chest. Sara wondered if he could feel her heart pounding. He slipped his hand beneath her top and made room between them to cup her breast. The warmth of his touch spread to every part of her body.

He pulled back and looked into her eyes. "Sara, you have beauty so rare, so perfect, no one can compare to you. You said yourself, sex without love doesn't really count, whether it's good sex or bad sex—it's only sex."

He's right. Sara realized in that instant Ren wouldn't be thinking of Julia when he made love with her.

She smiled. "Should we go to my room? Or yours?"

His grin made her heart flip. "How 'bout the Hyatt?"

"Do they have baby-sitters?" The word barely left her lips before she pushed him back and jumped to her feet. "Oh, my God! I forgot about Brady."

"Hell!" Ren exclaimed. "So did I. Go get your purse. I'll meet you at the car."

Like an Indy driver, Ren raced to the house where two harried mothers were waiting patiently at the door for parents to show up and claim their children. Ren apologized profusely, while Sara rounded up a very wired Brady.

In the car, they shared simultaneous sighs, then looked at each other, grinning. Sara couldn't name a time when her heart had felt more filled with joy.

"We're postponed till tonight, right?" he asked, reaching out to claim her hand.

"What about Claudie's party?"

"After the party." He smiled at her with a wicked gleam in his eye. "Don't worry—I promise I won't ask you to skip dessert."

She brought his hand to her cheek. Just the scent of his skin made her heart happy. "I read something once about strategically placed whipped cream," she teased. "Maybe we could make our own dessert."

His low groan made her laugh.

"Did we decide where?" he asked, glancing over his shoulder at Brady.

Sara thought a moment, picturing the kind of love that belonged in a home filled with family, children and friends. "Your room."

CHAPTER THIRTEEN

"So? WHAT DO YOU THINK'S going on?" Bo asked Claudie once they were sitting beneath the shade of the gazebo. "Is this little celebration tonight going to involve more than your personal achievement? Maybe we're going to see a little high-scoring by Judge Bishop, too, huh?"

He'd recognized a change in Sara the minute he walked in the bookstore to pick her up. His gut instinct told him it was good, but he didn't ask, choosing instead to observe.

"I don't know," Claudie said. She wore a simple, canary-yellow linen dress that gave her a young Audrey Hepburn look. "They both seem a little weird. Ren was humming when he carried out the garbage. When I asked him what was going down, he hugged me." She frowned. "What about Sara? What'd she say on the way home?"

"She said they had a long talk." He snickered. "I think perhaps there was less talk and more touch."

Claudie's eyes opened wide. "Seriously? It's about time."

"Ren and I did a little golfing this morning, and, I told him to shit or get off the pot."

Claudie made a gagging sound. "That's romantic."

"Humph. It worked. When I called him at noon,

he said things were clicking. I got the impression progress had been made.''

Claudie looked skeptical. "I hope so. For a while there, I was afraid I was going to have to be the one to kick him in the butt.'' She crossed her legs.

Bo noticed, as he had on several occasions, the shapely quality of her limbs. Claudie and Bo had spent a lot of time together thanks to Brady. This wasn't the first time Bo regretted an obvious lack of interest on her part—a friendly camaraderie seemed to be the extent of their relationship.

"Do you think he'll propose?"

Bo pictured the look on Sara's face when he'd entered the store. She'd been wearing a denim skirt and a T-shirt with the slogan I Read For The Love Of It. Bo thought she looked as radiant as an angel atop a Christmas tree. But when he mentioned the sale of her house and the changes it would bring, some of that glow had dimmed. "Maybe, but I think whatever's going down is still in the early stage.''

Claudie frowned. "I don't know. It's been like a pot ready to boil around here lately. So I wish he'd hurry up. Maybe even tonight.''

"Nah. Ren likes to take things slow and conservative.''

"Wanna bet?"

Bo couldn't resist the challenge in her eyes. "You're on." He looked at her sternly. "But there's one condition. No interference. Tonight we're just out celebrating your scholastic triumph—no matchmaking, okay?" he said. "If it's the real thing, it'll happen on its own.''

Claudie stared at him a moment, then threw her head and laughed. "God, Lester, that sounded positively poetic. You'd better be careful or someone

might mistake you for a real human being instead of a redneck hillbilly.''

He gave her his most ferocious squint. ''How'd you like to wear that pretty little dress swimming?''

With a shriek of fake terror she bolted from the gazebo. Smiling, Bo followed.

SARA HAD JUST PUT the finishing touches on her eye makeup, when she heard the sound of the doorbell. ''Can somebody get that?'' she hollered.

''I'm still working on Brady,'' Ren called back, followed by a high-pitched shriek and Ren's muffled ''Come back here, you little sneak.''

Sara had returned home from the store to find Ren up to his elbows in bubble bath, trying to wash Brady's hair. So sweet was the image that she'd watched in silence longer than she was able to afford to do. Then, realizing she was running late, she'd grabbed her clothes and dashed to Ren's bathroom. Although pressed for time, Ren's big marble shower evoked an exhilarating fantasy—just the scent of his soap was enough to make her wish the festivities were already over.

Would they make love tonight? Sara was pretty sure the answer was yes, and the thought made her jittery with anticipation, queasy with apprehension. She had no idea how she was going to get through dinner. It had been tough enough dodging Bo's and Claudie's questions earlier.

''What am I—an open book?'' she'd asked aloud after Claudie's barrage of questions that afternoon. Julia had always said Sara was too easy to read. *''You give away all your secrets every time you smile,''* she'd once said. Sara feared that was true.

Somehow she'd managed to keep her feelings about Ren a secret, but it had been difficult.

All that's changed now, Sara thought as she started down the hallway. Ren and I are going to be together. A nagging voice reminded her that she didn't know exactly what that meant—but he had used the *L* word. She was almost to Brady's door, when a flash of movement made her pause.

Shrieking with delight, a naked Brady dodged Ren's outstretched hands. "Come back here, you little streaker. I could put you in jail for indecent exposure," Ren teased.

The doorbell chimed again, making Sara tear her eyes from the scene. He said he loves me, she thought, slowly descending each step. *God, what if it's true? What if he meant it—really meant it? Could we make a family here in this beautiful home? Maybe give Brady a baby brother or sister some-day?*

Her speculation ended the moment the front door opened and a familiar head popped into sight. "Is anybody home?" Babe Bishop asked, stepping into the foyer.

Sara gulped. Even dressed in a wonderful black Yves Saint Laurent sheath—her splurge at the con-signment shop down the block from the bookstore—Sara felt inferior. To her amazement, today Babe wore sporty knee-length shorts and a loose top in a post-holiday red, white and blue pattern. Sara had never seen her dressed so casually.

"Sorry, Mrs. Bishop. Ren's upstairs with Brady, and I just finished getting ready," Sara said, closing the door behind her. Babe's expensive-smelling per-fume reminded Sara she'd forgotten to put on cologne. "Come in. We really appreciate your helping out like this."

"You're welcome."

Sara looked at Babe more closely. For some reason the older woman seemed subdued, a little sad even. "Are you all right? Are you sure this isn't too big an imposition?"

Babe straightened haughtily. "I managed to survive Lawrence, I'm sure I can handle Brady."

"Of course. I didn't mean to imply you couldn't. I just thought you seem a bit...down."

Babe stepped back as though the observation had somehow undermined her control. Her chin rose in a standard Babe Bishop gesture, but her gaze went to the top of the stairs. Sara looked, too. No one was there. All she could see was the collage of family photos.

In a halting voice, Babe said, "Today's the anniversary of my daughter's death."

Sara's heart sunk. Ren hadn't mentioned that fact. He rarely spoke of his sister, and Sara had never pressed for details of the accident.

"Oh, no," Sara cried. "I'm so sorry. We'll cancel. You don't have to do this."

"Nonsense. It was almost forty years ago. I sometimes feel a little blue, but it'll pass. I'm fine."

Sara took a step back. "Would you care for a glass of wine?" she asked, wishing Ren would appear.

"Yes. Chardonnay, please. Lawrence usually keeps a bottle chilled for me."

"I think there's some in the refrigerator," Sara said. She walked toward the kitchen, conscious of Babe following her.

They were halfway through the dining room,

when Sara heard Babe gasp. She looked over her shoulder and saw Babe standing frozen in the middle of the room, looking around in shock. Ren had hired the same contractor who'd made the repairs on Sara's house to renovate his dining room. A crew had begun stripping the walls and cabinets on Monday. The chandelier was gone—six black holes for the new recessed can fixtures made the ceiling resemble a domino. Babe's table and chairs were stored in the garage.

"Didn't Ren tell you he was remodeling?" Sara asked gently.

"He might have mentioned it, but I didn't think..." Babe walked to the wall where the windows, now relieved of their heavy venetian blinds, displayed a panoramic view of the backyard. She ran her fingers over one of the few strips of embossed wallpaper that remained. At its edge was a remnant of an earlier wall covering—pale blue, the color of a summer sky. "This was Sunny's favorite room. She would come home after school and do her homework at the dining room table."

Babe looked out the window. "We used to have a big concrete birdbath right there—" she said, pointing.

Sara could almost picture it nestled among the thick ferns and philodendrons.

"She loved to watch the birds play and splash," Babe went on. "She was such an animal person. I always imagined she'd grow up to be a veterinarian." A bemused look crossed her face. "I wonder what ever became of that fountain."

Sara had no answer. Her heart ached for the loss Babe Bishop had endured. Quietly she slipped into the kitchen and poured a glass of wine. Hurrying back, she handed the glass to Babe, as if her offering might in some way ease the pain. Ren's mother accepted it without looking at Sara, her attention focused on Bo and Claudie, who were walking across the lawn from the direction of the gazebo. They were obviously laughing and joking with each other.

"She's come a long way toward changing her life, hasn't she?" Babe asked.

"Some might say a quantum leap," Sara said. "I had good news from my friend Keneesha, too. She's back in Georgia." Keneesha's e-mail message yesterday said her health was stable and she'd reconciled with her son, who was teaching her how to work the computer. Sara couldn't have been happier for her.

"Nobody chooses the low road," Sara said quietly. "Sometimes you just find yourself there."

Babe turned to look at her.

"When you get off-track, you sometimes need a helping hand to get back on course." Screwing up her courage, she said to Babe, "After you showed me that picture of Julia, I spent a lot of time thinking about why she would have done that—it wasn't like her at all. You have to understand," Sara continued forcefully, "Julia was a very private person. With good reason. When she was twelve, our mother's boyfriend tried to molest her. He'd been living with us for over a year, and he was very sneaky about 'accidentally' catching Julia in her underwear, leaving pornography around for her to see, and touching her even though she tried to avoid him—" Her voice cracked. "Anyway, the point is, Julia *never* would have posed for that picture without a very compelling reason."

Babe remained silent.

Taking a deep breath to regain her composure, Sara said, "I think she did it to help me."

"How do you mean?" Babe asked.

Sara knew what she was about to say would probably drop her even lower in Babe's opinion, but she didn't care. "My mother died shortly after I graduated from high school. She was only forty-nine."

Sara sighed, trying to picture herself at the time—barely eighteen, scared spitless and all alone, except for Julia. "I was working at the bookstore but I didn't feel as though my life was going anywhere. Julia was dating a guy who was stationed at Travis—he made the Air Force sound exciting and glamorous. So one day I enlisted."

Babe didn't show any sign of surprise, so Sara guessed this part of her history had shown up on her background check. "At first it felt like I could make a life for myself in the military—the structure was something I'd always craved. But I was young and naive, and I made a couple of bad choices. I might have gone to jail if Julia hadn't come to my rescue. She hired a lawyer to defend me."

"I thought the Air Force had to provide you with a lawyer," Babe said.

"They did, but Julia said that wasn't good enough. She wanted the best person money could buy. She wired me the money to pay him—he wasn't cheap. She never told me where the money came from, but I think I've now figured it out." Sara bit down on her lip.

In the kitchen, Bo and Claudie's banter seeped from the backyard through the door. Babe took a sip of wine, then cocked her head as if in thought. "Lawrence has always picked up strays. One Christmas I bought him a purebred puppy—a Cardigan

Welsh corgi. I wrapped up a photograph of the breed because the dog was too young to leave its mother—but do you know what Lawrence did?''

Sara shook her head even though Babe didn't seem to be addressing her directly.

"He said, 'Thank you, Mother,' then ran to the garage where he'd been hiding the most ragtag looking mutt on the face of the earth. He told me that since I was willing to let him have a puppy, he'd prefer the one he'd found, instead.''

Momentarily, her smile seemed tinged with pride, but when she looked back at Sara, Babe's face was blank. A loud crash in the adjoining room made her flinch. "Bo is another example.''

"I suppose you think Brady and I are, as well,'' Sara said softly.

Babe sighed heavily. "I have nothing against you, Sara. I think you've done a fine job with Brady—he's a delight. But Lawrence has a promising future in politics ahead of him. Thanks to a few high-profile cases, he's become noticed. There's been talk of a possible Senate race. A scandal would destroy all that.''

Nothing more was said, because at that moment Ren walked in carrying Brady, a bright, clean bundle of smiles. "Hello, Mother, I thought I heard your voice.'' He looked at Sara, but she felt too exposed, too vulnerable to meet his eyes. Instead, she put on an artificial smile and held out her arms to Brady. He dove for her.

"Whoa, kiddo, take it easy,'' Ren cautioned. "Your mommy looks beautiful. We don't want to mess with perfection.''

Sara hugged her son fiercely, inhaling his just-bathed smell. Tears clustered in her eyes. Maybe the best thing she could do for Ren's future was disappear, but she knew he'd never let Brady go unless the test came back negative—and in her heart, Sara knew that wasn't likely. These past weeks had confirmed what Sara had feared from the start—Ren and Brady were two peas in a pod, so alike at times that Sara marveled at them.

Nope, if it came down to doing the honorable thing, she knew it would fall to her to leave.

She looked up and saw Ren watching her, his brow knit with concern. She took a deep breath and put on a pretend smile. Any serious decisions would have to wait until after Claudie's celebration.

REN TOOK A SIP of wine, his gaze following the two women as they headed for the rest room. Peripherally he caught the admiring glances of other men. Two beautiful women. One he admired, the other he loved more than words could express.

"What's wrong with Sara?" Bo asked in a low, serious voice. "I thought you said things were working out between you."

"They were—this morning. What'd she tell you?"

"Nothing, but I thought she looked happy. She seemed a little worried about what would happen after the house deal closed... But something's not right. I get the feeling she's faking the smiles for Claudie's sake. What about you?"

Ren slumped back. He'd barely noticed the opulent surroundings that both Sara and Claudie had gushed about. The Stockton Club was fabled for its elegance and exclusivity—only recently had it even started granting memberships to women—but Ren could have been dining at a hamburger joint for all he cared. "I agree. I was giving Brady a bath when she got home. I haven't had a chance to talk to her alone." *Or touch her.* "If you didn't say anything to her, then it had to be Babe."

Bo cursed under his breath. "Claudie and I were goofing around outside. We should have been there when Babe arrived."

Ren straightened. He and Sara had shared more than a kiss this morning—they'd connected. "I should never have let her go to work, but she insisted she needed to run some books by the jail and relieve Claudie."

"Shall we cut this short?" Bo asked, alerting Ren by his nod that the women were returning.

"I don't want to hurt Claudie's feelings."

Bo made a funny face. "I don't think she'd care if you play your cards right. Follow my lead."

Bo rose and motioned for Ren to stand. "Claudie, you are much too beautiful to waste on all these rich old farts. You need to go dancing. Ren's going to take us home to get my wheels, then I'm taking you out on the town."

"Really?" she asked, obviously surprised by the change in plans.

Ren pretended to be offended. "Who are you calling old? I'd dance you under the table, but I know Sara's anxious to check up on my mother and Brady. Right?" he asked.

She nodded. "I don't want to be a wet blanket, but I wouldn't mind making sure Brady didn't decide to disappear on her. What about dessert, Claudie?"

Claudie shifted her gaze from Bo to Sara. Her smile was both real and infectious. "This was the most wonderful meal of my life, and I ate so much

I don't think I'll ever have to eat again. I'm ready for some exercise." She grinned wickedly and said, "Just don't get any ideas, Lester. A graduate like myself has to be careful of her reputation." Her tone was so "Babe" that they all laughed.

Ren paid the bill, and they left. On the way home, Ren handed a small, wrapped gift to Claudie, who was sitting in the back of the car with Bo. "This is just a little something to help commemorate the day, Claudie. I'm proud of you."

Sara shifted to look over the seat. In the lights from the dash, Ren could see her bare knee and smooth calf on the seat beside him. The muted glow gave her an ephemeral appearance—like a magical sprite that might disappear without warning. Silently, he prayed they'd be able to recapture the passion they'd shared earlier.

"Oh, Ren, it's wonderful," Claudie exclaimed, leaning forward to show Sara the opal pendant on a gold chain.

"It's a fire opal," Ren said. "It reminded me of you—lovely and resilient."

While Bo helped Claudie fasten the necklace, Ren glanced at Sara. There were tears in her eyes. She reached out and touched his face, a gentle, loving caress. "That was incredibly kind," she whispered.

He turned his face to kiss her hand. "You are incredibly beautiful."

She pulled back, moving closer to the door.

What did you say to her, Mother? Ren's disquiet intensified when he pulled into his driveway and spotted a burgundy Cadillac parked behind his mother's Lincoln.

"Whose car is that?" Sara asked.

"Armory's."

"I wonder what he's doing here. I hope nothing's wrong."

His rich meal rumbled in his gut. Ren wasn't sure he wanted to find out. He didn't bother to put the car away. Instead, when Bo got out, Ren handed him the keys. "Here. I don't trust your heap."

Bo tossed the keys in the air. "Cool. Are you ready, Miss Graduate?"

Claudie looked at Sara. "It's getting chilly. I think I'll grab a sweater."

"I'll wait for you in the kitchen," Bo said.

Sara spun around. "You can't possibly be hungry."

"I always have room for Revelda's pie."

She rolled her eyes and laughed. "You and Brady."

Together, the group entered the house. Ren ushered Sara ahead of him through the dining room, saying, "Shall we go see what kind of damage Brady managed to do to Babe's self-confidence?" She put on a nice smile, but Ren could tell Sara wasn't looking forward to seeing his mother.

He found Babe and Armory in his office, drinking coffee on the sofa. "Hello, Armory. You remember Sara."

Armory, looking dapper in lightweight slacks and open-collar golf shirt, rose and put out his hand. "Hello, Sara, good to see you again."

"He's brought us the lab results, Lawrence," Babe said.

Armory pointed to a courier's box sitting on Ren's desk. Ren was grateful to see it was unopened.

"They delivered on a Saturday?" Sara exclaimed.

"We paid extra for express delivery," Armory said.

"When he called to tell you it was here, Lawrence, I told him to bring it over directly. No use waiting," Babe said.

Ren reached for Sara's hand and pulled her closer to him. He sensed she wanted to run away. "That was nice of you, Armory, but it could have waited until morning—I'm sure you have better things to do with your time on a Saturday night."

"Well, aren't you going to open it?" Babe asked, standing.

Ren looked at Sara. "Yes. As soon as we're alone."

"What?" his mother croaked. "Alone? The whole point of having Armory here is so you can plan your strategy. Surely you know everything you do from this point on will come under scrutiny."

Ren looked at her sharply. "Mother, thank you for watching Brady tonight. I assume he's in bed—you don't have him tied up someplace do you?" he asked, injecting a bit of humor to soften the frustration he felt at her interference.

He caught Sara's tiny choke of a laugh.

Babe wasn't amused. "Of course, he's in bed. He was a perfect angel. But I didn't drag Armory all the way over here, just so I could leave before you open that."

"I'm afraid that's exactly what's going to happen. The contents of that box concern Sara's future and mine, and we'd like to be able to go over it in private."

Babe looked shocked and angry. She turned toward Armory as if to make him do something. He shrugged sheepishly, then extended a hand to Ren. "Give me a call if you need anything."

Armory's defection seemed to enrage Babe. She grabbed the older man's arm to keep him from leaving. "Armory, talk to him. Lawrence Bishop, do you have any idea what you're doing?"

"Yes, Mother, I think so."

"How you handle this matter will affect your future for the rest of your life."

He squeezed Sara's hand. When she looked up at him, he smiled. "I certainly hope so."

"Lawrence, you and Armory should be discussing a strategy for custody. If that little boy is yours—"

"Mother," he said sharply, "I told you five weeks ago to stay out of this. Sara and I will handle it. Why is that so hard for you to accept?"

She glanced at Sara. Her tone softened some when she said, "Sara is a very nice person, Lawrence, but I think she'd be the first to agree that, given her background, she'd be more of a liability than an asset to your career."

Ren's mouth dropped open. "I can't believe you said that. Where in the hell do you get off acting like some kind of upper-class matron? Good God, Mother, your father was a farmer."

Babe stiffened. "I was referring to her criminal past."

Ren groaned. He didn't know how Babe learned those details, since they hadn't been part of her investigator's report. "She was a kid. She made a mistake. The only reason I don't have a record is Granddad Bishop pulled a few strings."

At Sara's puzzled looked, he said, "When I was thirteen, a couple of my friends and I broke into a neighbor's house and stole some booze. On the way out, one of the guys pocketed a bunch of old coins that were sitting on the bar—they turned out to be valuable collector's items. The next morning, the guy with the coins confessed to his mother, who called my grandfather.''

Babe looked appalled. ''That is not the kind of thing that would come out of the woodwork to affect your campaign, but Sara's record—''

Ren interrupted her. ''What campaign? My re-election? Mother, you know most judges run unopposed. I think it's a little premature to worry—''

She broke in, crying. ''Your senatorial prospects!''

Ren took a deep breath, struggling for patience. Out of the corner of his eye, he saw Armory move into the shadows. ''Mother, we've been over this many times, although you seem to conveniently tune out my feelings on the matter. I have no senatorial prospects, and if I did I would sell them to the lowest bidder. I can't think of anything I'd like less than to be in politics. My current job is more political than I'm comfortable with.''

Babe's face drained of color, and Ren felt Sara flinch as if she wanted to reach out to comfort the older woman. ''But you—''

''No, Mother. *You.* You're the one who's interested in politics. You're the one who loves the game playing and the power. I don't want anything to do with it. And if it turns out that Brady is my son and someone has a problem with Sara's past, then they can have my judgeship, too. It wouldn't be worth it to me.''

''You can't mean that,'' Babe whispered, her eyes wide with fear.

He ran his free hand through his hair. "Mother, I took this job to make you happy. I knew how upset you were when Dad died. His career was the foundation of your life, and I knew it was important to you to have those political connections. But this was never *my* dream."

Babe looked wobbly as if her legs couldn't support her any longer, and Armory hurried to her side, helping her back to the couch.

Reluctantly, Ren let go of Sara's hand. He pulled the armchair close to the couch and sat down facing his mother. "I know what day this is, Mother. I know it's hard for you. It's hard for me, too. I remember it clear as a bell."

She shook her head. "You can't remember that far back. You were only four."

"Four-and-a-half." When Sara's hand touched his shoulder, he took it. "I can still picture it. The minute I woke up from my nap I knew something was wrong. Becky and Jane were crying. Aunt Elaine and Uncle Frank were talking in low voices. When I asked where you were, Frank said you'd gone in the ambulance with Sunny. I knew ambulances meant hospitals. Hospitals were where you went if you were sick." Ren didn't know for sure how much of his memory was real, how much conjecture, but he had a very clear picture of sitting on the step waiting for his mother to return.

"It was almost dark when Dad brought you home. You were crying. I'd never seen you cry before—it scared me. When I reached for you, you pushed my hand away at first, then dropped to your knees and pulled me into your arms. You told me Sunny was gone and I was all you had left."

Babe hunched forward, her face in her hands.

"I've tried to be the person you needed me to be, Mother, but I can't do it anymore. I need to be my own person." Gently, he touched her shoulder. Her body seemed small and frail. She'd aged more than he'd realized, more than she let the outside world know. His heart ached, knowing this would hurt her, but deep inside he knew both Sunny and his father would have understood.

"What does that mean?" she asked in a small voice.

"It means I need for you to go home so Sara and I can talk."

She lifted her chin. "You're my son, Lawrence. I care about what happens to you."

"I know. But I'm forty-two years old, Mother. I think it's time you admitted I can think for myself." He smiled conciliatorily. "I haven't done too badly so far, have I?"

Her eyes narrowed as if weighing his question.

"Granted, I should have bought Intel when I had the chance, but other than that..."

Her face softened, her lips turning up slightly. After wiping her tears with a lacy handkerchief she'd had in her pocket, Babe rose. Ren walked her to the door.

"Armory," Ren said, motioning his old friend to him, "would you please drive Mother home? We'll get her car over to the condo later."

He gave his mother a hug. "Good night, mother. I love you and I hope you can trust me to do what's right—after all, I am a judge."

Her left brow lifted dryly as she took Armory's proffered arm. Her ladylike snort seemed to sum up her opinion of both his wit and wisdom.

With a sigh, Ren closed the door. As he returned

to the office he glanced toward the kitchen, but since he didn't hear any sound, he assumed Bo and Claudie had taken off as soon as the fireworks started.

He hesitated at the threshold of his office. Sara was standing beside his desk, one hand hovering above the courier box as if trying to muster the courage to touch it.

His heart constricted in apprehension. This was their moment of truth. Never had Ren felt more empathy for what a defendant must feel awaiting his verdict. What was in that box would determine Ren's fate: life or an emptiness as hollow as death.

CHAPTER FOURTEEN

SARA'S FINGERS SKIMMED over the cardboard box, but she couldn't make herself pick up the package that would most certainly alter the shape of her future. Turning, she moved to the sofa and sat down, her legs as insubstantial as the craft dough she'd made that morning for Brady.

Her heart pounded in her chest from the turbulent emotions she'd witnessed and felt on Ren's behalf. If she closed her eyes, she could vividly picture him as a child, waiting on the stoop for his mother to return from the hospital.

Poor Ren, she thought, her heart aching for the little boy who loved his mother so much. Babe had manipulated—maybe unintentionally—many of Ren's life decisions, and Ren had every right to resent her for it. But he didn't.

"Tell me what you're thinking," Ren said, plopping down beside her as if drained. He reached for her hand and squeezed it. "That must have been very uncomfortable for you. I'm sorry if my mother hurt you when she said that about your past."

"She was acting in your best interests. I'd probably do the same thing—only I doubt if Brady would be that understanding." She sighed. "I don't think I ever realized what a weighty responsibility the role of parenting is. I don't know if I'm cut out for it."

His smile—so kind and endearing—brought her close to tears.

"As a judge, I see a couple of problems with your theory. Number one, it's too late to back out—you already are a mother. And number two, you're a wonderful mother. Brady will never resent you."

Sara pulled her hand free of his and sat forward. Nervously gnawing on a cuticle, she focused on the courier box. "If those test results prove you're Brady's father, then you'll be the one who decides how much say I have in his life. If you're his father, Ren, you really don't need me in the picture." She felt him jerk and quickly went on before he could say something he might later regret. "I mean, you'd have no legal obligation to me other than as Brady's aunt, and I promise you I won't fight for custody. I know I said I would, but that was before I found out what a great dad you are. He loves you, Ren, and I wouldn't want to come between the two of you."

Sara had tried to keep her tone level and unemotional, so Ren's low oath took her by surprise. He vaulted to his feet and turned to face her. He seemed incensed.

"Did you say I wouldn't need you?" he repeated, his voice shaking with anger. "Do you mean if that test proves I'm Brady's biological father, it somehow negates your connection to him? Your love? Everything you've done for him?"

"I just don't want you to feel obligated to make a place for me in your life."

Swearing under his breath, he threw up his hands. "God Almighty, Sara, don't you know what you are? Who you are?"

She shook her head, feeling as lost and frightened as she had on those nights when her mother hadn't come home, and the only thing standing between her and the big scary world was her twelve-year-old sister.

Without warning, he reached out and pulled her to him, saying fiercely, "Sara Carsten, you *are* Brady's mother." He clasped her shoulders and set her back so she could look in his eyes. "It doesn't matter that you didn't give birth to him. You've been there for him every step of the way, and when he's forty-two and his life is a mess, you'll still be there for him."

Fighting tears, she tried to smile. "Yeah, and he'll probably blame me for it, just like you do your mom."

Ren shook his head. His tone softened. "Even if Babe is to blame for some of my choices, that doesn't mean I don't love her. She's my mother. She's haughty and pretentious and can be extremely shallow at times, but she's also loyal, softhearted and brave—like you."

A little sound slipped from Sara's lips. "If your life's a mess, Ren, it's probably because of us. If we hadn't—"

He cut her off with a small shake. "Don't say it. Don't even think it. I don't know what I can say to make you believe me, but until you and Brady came along, I didn't have a life, Sara. I existed. Period. I had to run away to steal a glimpse of life."

He lowered his head and said softly, "Weren't you listening this morning? Or didn't you believe me?"

Sara's breath caught in her throat. "I want to believe you, but maybe this isn't the best thing for—"

He didn't let her finish. His lips crushed against hers; his arms wrapped around her as if he'd never let her go. This kiss was different. Urgent. A bit desperate—as if he feared rejection and was as unsure of her love as she was of his. The idea radiated inward, connecting with a part of her hidden in a dark abyss. *He needs me as much as I need him.*

She pulled back. Searching his eyes for confirmation, she said, "This *is* the real thing, isn't it?"

His blue eyes lit with joy—the identical look Brady gave her when he hugged her each morning. It was a look Sara couldn't imagine not seeing every day for the rest of her life.

She cupped his jaw and tenderly kissed his lips. "I love you, too, Ren Bishop."

He crushed her to him again, giving her a taste of the passion she no longer feared. In fact, she welcomed it. "Aren't we going to your room?" she asked, when he trailed a string of scintillating kisses down her neck.

Her question seemed to bring him back to reality, because he locked his fingers at the small of her back and sighed. "I hope so, but we still have to deal with that box," he said somberly.

With obvious reluctance, he let her go and walked to the desk. He picked it up, ripped open the tear strip and dumped a sheaf of papers—held together by a large, black metal clip—to the desk. He set the empty box to one side and was reaching for the papers, when Sara cried out, "Wait."

Her pulse raced and a creepy sensation made her shiver. "Do we have to do this now? Couldn't it wait until tomorrow?" Trying to express her fears without making him think she questioned his feelings, she asked, haltingly, "I'm not saying it will, but what if it changes things?"

He placed both hands flat on the desk and gave

her what Claudie called his "judge look." "It *will* change things, Sara. Hell, a part of me wants to chuck this in the fireplace and grab a match, but we can't do that. This is Brady's future, too. He deserves to know the truth." He placed the neatly stacked papers to one side. "But before we look, I have to ask you something."

Sara stepped forward. "What?"

He drew her to his side and took both her hands in his. "Will you marry me?"

She heard the words and comprehended their meaning on one level, but couldn't make sense of them on another. "Marry you?"

He kissed her fingers. "Marry me. Be my wife, the mother of our son." He emphasized the word *our*. When Sara questioned him with a look, he said, "I don't need to see the results to know he's my child. In my heart I know I could never love him more than I already do, but if the test says that biologically he isn't, then he'll be mine when I marry you. If the test says he is, then we did the right thing, because either way you are his mother and that will never change."

Sara's throat was too constricted to speak so she nodded her chin. "I love you," she whispered.

"Is that a yes?" he asked, brushing aside her tears.

She nodded eagerly.

"I'm sorry," he said formally. "You'll have to speak up for the record."

Laughing, she threw her arms around his neck and cried, "Yes, Your Honor. Definitely, yes."

He clutched her tightly, then gallantly scooped her up as nimbly as he would have Brady. "I believe

I'll need proof of that before I can pass judgment,'' he teased, heading for the stairs.

"What about the test results?'' she cried.

"Later. They're not going anywhere, but we are. Upstairs. Now.''

Heart soaring, Sara allowed herself to experiment. She used her tongue to trace the outline of his ear, provocatively exploring every nook and cranny. His step faltered halfway up the staircase.

"Jesus, Sara,'' Ren said, his tone laughing, "watch where you put that thing. You might kill us both.''

Emboldened, she whispered, "Speaking of putting things in certain places, I'm a little out of practice. You may have to refresh my memory about what goes where.''

Ren froze one step shy of the top. His look was dumbstruck, then he put back his head and laughed. "Oh, Sara, you are the answer to my prayers, and I'm going to spend the rest of my life proving how thankful I am.''

Sara felt herself blush, but she didn't contradict him because she knew the same was true for her.

BO CAREFULLY EASED OPEN the closet door. The coat closet wouldn't have been his first choice for reconnaissance duty, but it happened to be where he and Claudie were standing when the proverbial shit hit the fan. Afraid Babe might spot them, he'd hustled Claudie inside and partially closed the door, leaving ample width for air—and conversation—to enter.

Bo might have felt guilty about eavesdropping if the results had been different, but from what he'd gleaned, things were working out right for his friends—and he couldn't be happier. He poked his head out, checking to make sure the coast was clear.

Claudie shoved him from behind. "Move it, garlic breath," she muttered, shouldering past him. "You had to order scampi, didn't you?"

"How was I supposed to know?" he grumbled. He brushed some lint from his jacket sleeve. "I was just gonna congratulate you on being a good sport, and you have to turn into a whiner."

Her eyes narrowed. "I'll show you whining."

A door closed upstairs, and Bo forgot about arguing with Claudie. Ren had finally connected all the dots. Once in one of his beer-hazed moments, Bo had expounded to his best friend the Bo Lester Theory of Life. *"Life is like a connect-the-dots puzzle. You're given this big formless maze when you're born, and it's up to you to make a picture, connecting all the right dots."* Ren had laughed and said that at the rate he was going, he'd wind up with someone else's picture.

Bo bet Ren would change his tune after tonight.

Claudie snapped her fingers in front of his face to bring him back to the present. "That reminds me. We had a bet. I told you he'd propose, and you said he wasn't that spontaneous. Read 'em and weep, Cookbook Man. Time to pay up."

Bo looked at her. "We didn't shake on it."

"Are you going to welsh? I should have known."

Frowning, he grabbed her hand and led the way to Ren's office. "I didn't say I wouldn't. But technically, it wasn't a real bet. Next time, you should make sure you follow protocol."

He saw her trying to keep the grin from her face. If he weren't so happy for Ren, he'd have let that grin get to him. "Just sit down and shut up," he ordered with mock severity.

She settled one hip on the corner of Ren's desk, while Bo walked around and sat down. "Close the doors. This is humiliating enough without disturbing Ren and Sara."

She did so, then quickly returned to her pose, a perfect place from which to watch him make a fool of himself.

"I can't remember the number," he lied, pretending to concentrate on the telephone keypad.

With a sigh of disgust, she leaned over and grabbed the phone, punched out a series of numbers, then handed him the unit. "It's ringing."

Bo rocked back. For a person who valued anonymity above all else, this was torture—which undoubtedly was why she'd selected it as his payment.

When a female voice came on the line, Bo swallowed, then told her what he wanted. There was a slight pause, and then she gave him his cue. He nodded at Claudie, who quickly dashed to the stereo and hit a button, keeping the volume low.

"Now, fellow poetry freaks, we have Bo from Sacramento on the line," a voice said over the airwaves. "Bo is going to share with us a poem he wrote. I get the feeling this is the first time for Bo, so be gentle with him, fellow writers, poets and songsmiths. Remember your first time—a combination of agony and ecstasy."

Bo rolled his eyes. She had the agony part right.

"Go ahead, Bo. You said your poem doesn't have a title, but maybe one will come out of the open-line critique session that follows. Go ahead. Let's hear your poem."

Critique session? Not if I slit my wrists first. He

gave Claudie the blackest look he could muster, ruing the night on his boat when he rocked Brady to sleep by reciting one of the stupid poems he'd written. Claudie had immediately pounced on his weakness, but to his surprise had claimed to like it and had wanted to hear more.

He cleared his suddenly parched throat, then closed his eyes and recited words he'd never before shared with a single soul.

> "White cranes guard the secret palace—a
> reed haven where children of the river live.
> Old men with no allegiance to life—lost souls
> made invisible
> by their need, stumble along slippery banks
> searching for escape from a world that doesn't
> fit right.
> The river children know the evicted ones are
> not the enemy.
> Screaming metal fins churn the water, dripping
> blue poison—
> Toys of smiling ones with bright teeth and oil-
> slick skin.
> Fear them, children, for your home is but a
> playground to those
> who see only a domain to dominate.
> Alert, white cranes. Alert. Forewarn the babies,
> the minnows,
> the polliwogs.
> Children of the river, hide."

He opened his eyes. The first thing he saw was Claudie, sitting frozen, her mouth open. What shook him most was the tears in her eyes. He didn't wait for the DJ's comments. He hung up the phone and jumped up to turn off the radio, blocking out what sounded like a very positive response.

"That was really beautiful, Bo," Claudie said softly. "I'm sorry I made you do it on the radio like that. You should submit it somewhere and have it published."

Bo snorted. "You're just surprised because you didn't think I had it in me. Trust me, it's not great poetry. In fact, it's not poetry. It's just words."

"Words that make sense, Bo. Good words."

He sat back down, pleased by her praise despite himself. He idly fiddled with the stack of papers before him, until it dawned on him what it was. He casually scooted the stack closer and arched his neck to study the writing on it.

"Bo," Claudie scolded. "That's private. Leave it alone."

His curiosity was tempted. "But don't you want to know?"

"No."

She had the grace to blush over her lie.

"Yes, you do," he said, turning it around. "Damn, it's upside down." Using Ren's pen, he wiggled it under one corner and flipped the stack over. "Wow! How'd that happen?"

"Bo, stop it. I'll tell."

He gave her his most shit-ass grin. "Who? I don't think Ren and Sara would appreciate it if you bothered them just now."

She scowled, "But..."

He used the pen to nudge a few pages back until he found one that looked promising. Leaning closer he scanned the words, zeroing in on what he was looking for. He read it twice, then let out a long, low sigh. "Well, I'll be damned. Those condoms didn't fail, after all."

Claudie let out a *yip* of surprise and raced around the desk to lean over his shoulder. "Show me where it says that. I don't believe you."

Bo pointed to the paragraph in question. He knew the minute she confirmed his analysis of the words. She fell back, tears in her eyes. "Oh, my God, I can't believe it. Ren's not Brady's daddy."

Bo spun the chair around and stared at her until she met his gaze. "Let's be very clear about this. Ren may not be Brady's biological father, but he is definitely that little boy's daddy."

A bleak look flitted across her face and disappeared. She took a breath, then smiled. "You're right. It takes more than genes to make a father."

Bo rewarded her with a grin, then jumped to his feet. "Okay. Now that we've got that settled, let's go dancing. We have a lot to celebrate."

REN DREW IN A DEEP BREATH, savoring the fragrance that was uniquely Sara. Curled in the curve of his body, a perfect *C*, she slept as peacefully as Brady did. Lately, Ren had known many a sleepless night that found him leaning on Brady's crib, memorizing his features, watching his eyelids move, his lips pursed in some dreamed response. Ren's heart would fill to the brim, then find room for more images too wonderful to pass up. He'd never imagined one heart could hold so much love and still have room for more—the kind he'd shared with Sara just hours before.

If he closed his eyes and tried to picture the process of their lovemaking, the nuance and texture and taste, his brain became overwhelmed from the sheer joy of remembering. Making love with Sara was like learning to dream in a new language—none of the old words fit. *Wonderful. Perfect. Sensual. Exciting.* All fell short of describing the actual sensations, the giggles, the moans. His only fear was that his face muscles might never go back to normal, since all he could do was grin.

Sara sighed and stretched, bumping his chin with her hand. She started slightly as if suddenly realizing she was lying naked beside him. He waited to see how she would react.

"Umm," she purred, arching back to press more closely against him, "you feel wonderful. Is this heaven?"

"I think so," he whispered, nuzzling her neck. "Only one thing could make it any better."

She caught his implication and a sexy chuckle hummed in her throat. "Hold that thought. I want to check on Brady."

Ren vaulted out of bed and walked to his closet. He pulled out two robes and carried one to her. The moonlight streaming through his windows cast her body in a silver glow almost surreal in perfection. "You are the most beautiful woman I've ever known," he told her, holding the robe for her. When she turned to slip her arms in the sleeves, he reeled her in to his body and closed his arms around her.

She snuggled against him. "You don't have to say that," she said softly. "I love you, anyway. I know I'm not beautiful. I look like a librarian. Always have. My mother told me that when I was ten." She shrugged. "Maybe that's why I like books so much."

Stricken by the memory of his words coming back to haunt him, he turned her around to face him and sternly scolded her. "Sara, you are everything that's beautiful to me—mother, friend, lover. Are we clear on that?"

She began to execute a smart salute, but her hand got lost in the sleeve of the robe. Laughing, she raised up on her toes and kissed him. "I'll try to remember that. Now, let's go check on our little boy."

Ren pulled on his robe and followed her down the hall. The grandfather clock in the hallway read half-past midnight. If Claudie had returned she was already asleep, because her room was dark. Brady's door was partially open and a Winnie-the-Pooh night-light glowed festively near his closet. The blinds on the window let in enough moonlight for them to see without turning on any other lights.

Together they hunched over the crib. "He's a gift beyond all gifts, isn't he?" Sara whispered.

"Then I'm doubly blessed."

She chucked softly. "Try telling that to your mother."

"I will. We will. Tomorrow." When he felt her shrink away, he clapped his arm across her shoulders and squeezed. "Don't worry. Once Babe realizes you're going to be a Bishop—and believe me, that is part of her mind-set, not mine—if you want to keep your last name, hyphenate, whatever, I don't care as long as we're married—she'll take on anyone in your defense."

Sara didn't look convinced.

"Remember on the way home tonight you told Bo and Claudie about my old dog, Freckles?"

"The mutt you preferred over your mother's fancy purebred puppy."

"Freckles was not a mutt. She was a fine dog of

indiscriminate parentage. She was a good friend and an excellent watchdog. And Babe came to adore her. When I went away to college, Freckles and mother became very close. It broke Babe's heart when she died. My point is, no one could ever say anything bad about Freckles because once she became a member of the family, she was no longer a mutt— she was a Bishop.''

Sara's grin made him want to drag her back to bed. ''Freckles Bishop. That has a nice ring to it. But if your mother doesn't mind, I think I like Sara Bishop better.''

His heart jumped, but Ren wasn't worried about his blood pressure. His heart was whole, healthy and incredibly happy. He knew for a fact that love was the best medicine in the world.

He drew Sara into his arms and kissed her. ''I love you, Sara. Thank you for making my world complete.''

She kissed him back with an ardor he'd come to recognize as pure Sara. ''You're what I've been looking for all my life, Ren. I'd almost given up hope, but believe it or not, Claudie inspired me to keep believing in love.''

''Claudie?''

She nodded. ''Even at her lowest moments when she was flat broke and out of work and men hurt her and she didn't have a dram of self-respect left, she'd come to the bookstore and take Brady in the corner and read him a book. Somehow he seemed to sense her need, because no matter how hyper he was, he'd wind down and sit on her lap as if absorbing every word she read. I'd look at them and know that love exists all around us—we just have to let ourselves be more like children. We have to open ourselves up to it.''

Turning, they looked at Brady again. ''He really was the key, wasn't he,'' Ren said, marveling at the miracle of ever connecting with this wonderful woman and her child. *His* child. He thought about the papers on his desk, but shoved the image away.

As if sensing his thoughts, Sara asked, ''Shall we get it out of the way?''

Ren pulled her close. ''You and Brady are mine. That's all I need to know—all anyone ever needs to know.''

He kissed her but sensed the slightest hesitation, and he knew it wasn't that simple. They needed to deal with the results so they could get on with the business of living. He led the way to the study.

His heart was beating faster than normal, but Ren felt confident of the results. He sat down at his desk; Sara stood behind him, bending down to scan the cover sheet. He adjusted the desk lamp and flipped past the documentation garbage to the result sheet.

The result was there in black and white: Negative.

Sara's gasp told him she read the word at the same time. ''Does this mean Hulger was his father?''

Ren shook his head. When he found his voice, he said, ''No. It means Julia and Hulger gave birth to our son. And when Brady's older, we'll share him with them—but for now, he's all ours.''

Sara turned the chair to make room to climb into his lap. She wrapped her arms around his neck and held him tight. ''You are going to be the best father in the world.''

Ren squeezed his eyes tight against the disappointment, the shock. He'd been so sure. "I love him so much," he said, his voice catching on a sob.

"I know. I feel the same way. Sometimes I can't believe I didn't give birth to him."

They held each for a long time, then Ren said, "If it's okay with you, I'll put the file in the safe. Brady will have it if he ever needs it, but this doesn't change how I feel about him. And if Hulger's parents have no objections, I'd like to adopt him after we're married."

"You are a remarkable man, and I love you," Sara said, her eyes shining.

She took his hand and led the way back upstairs. They paused in the doorway of Brady's room. Brady let out a small grunt and rolled to his side. Searching in his sleep, he found his elephant and his fingers closed around the creature's trunk. He hauled the dilapidated beast to him and sighed with complete satisfaction.

"That's his 'funt.' Julia bought it for him that first Christmas when he was only a month-and-a-half old. He loved it from the start." The memory seemed to sadden her, and her expression made him draw her close.

"I'm sorry Julia died, Sara—for Brady's sake and yours. We'll make sure Brady knows the good memories. My father used to say the way to keep Sunny alive was by talking about her. He said, 'I plan to make her the first one I look up when I get to heaven, so I have to keep her close by.' Picturing them together was the one thing that made his death tolerable."

Sara hugged him. "I love you for the man you are and the man you'll help Brady to be, but right this moment I'm in need of the man you were an hour ago.''

She slipped her hands between the gap in his robe and pressed up against his naked body.

''Sara,'' he half choked.

''I'm sorry, but I like making love with you and I'm ready to try something new.''

He hugged her tight and kissed her breathless. ''No problem, but let's go back to our room. I've heard other parents complain about never having private time. We're going to make the most of ours. Starting right this minute.''

CHAPTER FIFTEEN

Four months later

REN TOOK A LAST GLANCE at the election results, then closed his laptop and stretched back in his chair, kicking his feet up on his desk. He couldn't recall the last time he'd spent an election night at home. The sight of his loafers made him smile—one of the perks of being a professor was the casual dress. Another was having the holidays off, and he was looking forward to the upcoming Thanksgiving break with joyful anticipation.

He closed his eyes and breathed a deep, satisfied sigh. Being married to Sara these last three months was a fulfillment that touched every aspect of his life. Her support had enabled him to do what he'd secretly dreamed of doing—teach law. At times he missed the judiciary, but he loved the challenge of inspiring students to look beyond grades to the people, the soul and the character of law.

"Honey, would you bring up that last load of clothes when you come?" Sara called from upstairs.

"You bet," he hollered back. He sat up and took a pen from his desk drawer. *Upstairs laundry room,* he wrote on a notepad. First thing in the morning he'd call Rich, the contractor who had transformed his parents' house into his and Sara's home. It was silly to make Sara cart clothes back and forth upstairs—especially now.

Claudie's old room would be perfect, he thought. Ren started to get up, but sat back down when the phone rang. "Hello."

"Hey, Ren, it's me. Any more calls from you-know-who?"

"Not since Sunday. What about you? Any leads?"

"Not enough to amount to a hill of beans."

Bo had been as perplexed as everyone else had when Claudie suddenly disappeared. Sara had been frantic until Claudie left a message on the answering machine informing them she was on some sort of self-imposed mission.

"I gotta set something right, Sara," Claudie had said. "Tell the Cookbook Man I can handle this myself. It's a family thing, and I don't need him butting in. That's why I took off like I did."

In typical Claudie fashion, she'd added, "Don't worry, Sara, I'll be back in a week or so. Give Brady a kiss for me and tell the girls at One Wish House I'm sorry about abandoning them like this, but they'll understand. Sometimes you get a chance to prevent history from repeating itself and you just gotta take it." With that, she'd hung up, leaving Bo with very few clues to follow.

Now Bo's angry sputtering made Ren sigh. "How one skinny, little ex-hooker can disappear like that is beyond me! I've had my staff working overtime and they're flat-out pissed. So am I."

Ren knew bluster when he heard it. Bo was hurting. "She said she'd be back soon," Ren said. "Maybe you ought to just let her do this on her own."

Bo snorted. "Once I find her, we'll discuss that possibility. Dammit," he added, half under his breath, "I thought we had something going."

Ren grimaced at the pain and frustration he heard in his friend's voice. "You'll find her, Bo. You're the best."

The sigh that came over the line seemed very unlike Bo.

"What's the problem, Lester? Are you getting soft? Can't handle the challenge?"

Bo growled. "Oh, I'm gonna find her and when I do…"

A loud *honk* obscured Bo's words. "Where are you calling from?" Ren asked.

"My car. I thought I'd run by One Wish House and see if I can shake loose a few lips. Those women are as secretive as Claudie."

Bo paused for a second, then added, "I'm thinking about flying to New York."

"Why? Do you think Claudie's there?"

"No. I think she's somewhere in the Midwest, but that's just a hunch at this point. I'm hoping my cousin, Matt, can fine-tune the search. He used to work for the NYPD. Now, he's doing computer tracking for the FBI, and he owes me a favor."

New York. Ren frowned, recalling Eve's last letter. "I don't suppose you'd have time to see Eve while you're there, would you? Sara called her office yesterday, and they told her Eve didn't work there anymore."

"Knowing Eve, she probably found something bigger and better," Bo said.

"Bigger than network news?" Ren asked doubtfully. "Sara said the last time she talked to her, Eve had complained about picking up some kind of flu bug on that trip to Panama. You know Sara; she thinks something terrible has happened to her.'' There was a slight pause. ''I doubt if Eve would be all that thrilled to hear from me. We've never been bosom buddies, you know.''

Ren snickered. ''That's an understatement, but if you have a chance I'm sure a voice from home would be welcome.''

There was another pause, then Bo said, ''I'll let you know once I hook up with my cousin. If Matt's as good as my aunt says he is, I might not be there very long.'' A barely audible ''Thank God'' followed.

Bo's connection started to fade, so they cut the conversation short. Ren replaced the receiver with a sigh then went to retrieve the basket of freshly laundered clothes.

Aside from Claudie's disappearance, things were going fabulously. Ren hoped Bo could solve this case fast. The worry wasn't good for Sara, and he knew Claudie's absence was felt at One Wish House, her halfway house for prostitutes. When he'd first offered Claudie the use of his old Victorian for the project, she'd been reluctant to accept. But Sara and, remarkably, Babe had convinced her to give it a try.

Ren could never have predicted his mother's support of Claudie's efforts, but he credited Brady with having a mellowing effect on his grandmother. Ever since the honeymoon, when Babe and Claudie took care of Brady while Ren and Sara explored New Zealand, Ren's mother had shown a remarkable transformation. She laughed more, joined them on family outings and even volunteered at Brady's daycare twice a week.

After climbing the stairs, he walked to Brady's door and looked inside the room. Sara lay on Brady's bed reading aloud from the book *I'll Love You Forever*. Brady, who would turn two on Sunday, lay beside her, his head pressed against the side of her rounded belly. With solemn concentration he drove a toy car up the incline.

Ren made up his mind not to mention Bo's call until morning. Knowing Sara, she would spend the whole night racking her brain for clues, and the doctor had advised additional rest. "Twins mean double prenatal care," he'd admonished.

Ren was thrilled at the thought of two babies. The news had created quite a stir among the Unturned Gentlemen's reading club, since it fouled up the odds in the betting pool, but at least it eased competition between Bo and Claudie for "god-person" rights.

Sara motioned Ren to join them. He set down the laundry basket and walked to the bed, then tousled his son's hair and leaned over to kiss his wife. Ren couldn't gaze upon her beautiful, glowing face without marveling at his initial blindness. *How could I have called her plain?* he wondered with chagrin.

"Cooties," Brady said, hiding his face.

"I'll cootie you," Ren said, tickling Brady under the arms.

Sara scooted out of the way of the wrestling match that ensued, laughing when Ren playfully tumbled to the floor, carrying Brady with him. She didn't try to stop it—every moment Ren and Brady spent in play was a cherished gift. She knew those moments would be harder to come by once the babies came.

She ran a hand over her belly, smiling with pure

contentment. Marriage was everything she'd ever dreamed it could be—a true joining of spirit and soul. On those rare quiet afternoons at the bookstore when Brady was in school, and Claudie was campaigning to get young girls off the streets, Sara would ponder the quirks of fate. If Julia hadn't gone to Tahoe, Sara might never have met Ren. Why she went remained a mystery, but Sara liked to think her sister would be pleased with how things had worked out.

Sara glanced at the framed photograph sitting atop Brady's bureau—Hulger and Julia beaming with pride at Brady's christening. As a wedding gift, Ren had taken Sara and Brady to Denmark to visit Hulger's parents. Sara doubted that Brady understood how Grandmother and Grandfather Hovant fit into his life, but his gregarious nature seemed to give the older couple tremendous pleasure. Although Sara had worried that Hulger's parents might object to Ren adopting Brady, they'd warmly welcomed Ren into their home and had thanked Sara for keeping Hovant as Brady's middle name. Brady Hovant Bishop. Smiling at her sister's image, Sara silently whispered, *You always said the right middle name would come along.*

"Help," Ren cried, when Brady tackled him. "You're reading the wrong book, Sara. You need *Where The Wild Things Are.*"

"Brady, love, time for bed." She closed her book and rose, feeling awkward and clumsy. By the time she'd put away the book and returned to his bed, Ren had Brady calmed down and tucked in.

Watching Ren kiss his son good-night, she blinked back tears. So alike, so handsome. In unison they looked at her—matching blue eyes, alive with humor, charm and goodness.

Perhaps not genetically identical, she thought, smiling back, but what does science know of love?

HARLEQUIN® SUPERROMANCE®

You are now entering

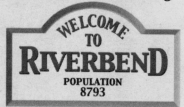

WELCOME TO **RIVERBEND**
POPULATION
8793

Riverbend…the kind of place where everyone knows your name—and your business. Riverbend…home of the River Rats—a group of small-town sons and daughters who've been friends since high school.

The Rats are all grown up now. Living their lives and learning that some days are good and some days aren't—and that you can get through anything as long as you have your friends.

Starting in July 2000, Harlequin Superromance brings you Riverbend—six books about the River Rats and the Midwest town they live in.

BIRTHRIGHT by Judith Arnold (July 2000)
THAT SUMMER THING by Pamela Bauer (August 2000)
HOMECOMING by Laura Abbot (September 2000)
LAST-MINUTE MARRIAGE by Marisa Carroll (October 2000)
A CHRISTMAS LEGACY by Kathryn Shay (November 2000)

Available wherever Harlequin books are sold.

Daddy's little girl... # THAT'S MY BABY! by

Vicki Lewis Thompson

Nat Grady is finally home—older and wiser. When the woman he'd loved had hinted at commitment, Nat had run far and fast. But now he knows he can't live without her. But Jessica's nowhere to be found.

Jessica Franklin is living a nightmare. She'd thought things were rough when the man she loved ran out on her, leaving her to give birth to their child alone. But when she realizes she has a stalker on her trail, she has to run—and the only man who can help her is Nat Grady.

THAT'S MY BABY!

On sale September 2000 at your favorite retail outlet.

HARLEQUIN®
Makes any time special ™

**Don't miss
an exciting opportunity
to save on the purchase of
Harlequin and Silhouette books!**

Buy any two Harlequin or
Silhouette books and save
$10.00 off future Harlequin
and Silhouette purchases

OR

buy any three
Harlequin or Silhouette books
and save **$20.00 off** future
Harlequin and Silhouette purchases.

**Watch for details
coming in October 2000!**

PHQ400

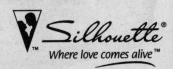

Coming this September from

HARLEQUIN®

A M E R I C A N ◆ R O M A N C E®

You met the citizens of Cactus, Texas, in
4 Tots for 4 Texans when some matchmaking
friends decided they needed to get
the local boys hitched!

And the fun continues in

3 TOTS for TEXANS
BY **JUDY CHRISTENBERRY**

Don't miss...
THE $10,000,000 TEXAS WEDDING
September 2000
HAR #842

In order to claim his $10,000,000 inheritance,
Gabe Dawson had to find a groom for Katherine Peters
or else walk her down the aisle himself. But when he
tried to find the perfect man for the job, the list of
candidates narrowed down to one man—*him!*

Available at your favorite retail outlet.

HARLEQUIN®
Makes any time special ™

HARLEQUIN®

SUPERROMANCE

COMING NEXT MONTH

#936 BORN IN A SMALL TOWN • Debbie Macomber, Judith Bowen and Janice Kay Johnson

Here's what small-town dreams are made of! This is a special 3-in-1 collection featuring *New York Times* bestselling author **Debbie Macomber**'s latest Midnight Sons title, *Midnight Sons and Daughters*. There's also a new Men of Glory title from Judith Bowen—*The Glory Girl*—and *Promise Me Picket Fences*—a return to Elk Springs, Oregon, by Janice Kay Johnson.

#937 HOMECOMING • Laura Abbot

Tom Baines, one of Riverbend's favorite sons, has come home to recuperate. After the year he's had, he needs the peace and quiet. More important, he wants to reestablish a relationship with his estranged children. But he never expects to meet Lynn Kendall, a woman unlike any he's ever met. Living in Riverbend might just have its advantages!

Riverbend, Indiana: Home of the River Rats—a group of men and women who've been friends since high school. These are their stories.

#938 MATT'S FAMILY • Lynnette Kent
The Brennan Brothers

Kristen had known the Brennan boys forever. She'd loved Luke as a friend, but she'd been *in love* with soldier Matt Brennan for as long as she could remember. Then Matt was reported missing, presumed dead. Luke persuaded the young, scared and pregnant Kristen to marry him. Slowly they turned their marriage of convenience into a real one. A second baby was born. Then five years later Matt Brennan—the man she'd never stopped loving—came home.... By the author of *Luke's Daughters*.

#939 SNOW BABY • Brenda Novak
9 Months Later

Two strangers spend a snowy night together. Chantel Miller falls for Dillon Broderick, the man who helped and comforted her during the blizzard—and then she discovers that her estranged sister, Stacy, is in love with him. The sister whose affection she's trying to regain... It's a painful coincidence that becomes devastating when Chantel discovers she's pregnant.

#940 THE NEWCOMER • Margot Dalton
Crystal Creek

Is the town of Crystal Creek for sale? Read *The Newcomer* to find out what happens when an eccentric movie star sends Maggie Embree to put in an offer on her behalf. Maggie runs into stiff opposition from the mayor of the town. Now she has to choose between her loyalty to her boss—the woman who helped raise her—and the man she's beginning to fall in love with.

#941 THE CATTLEMAN'S BRIDE • Joan Kilby

If Sarah Templestowe finds the wide-open spaces of central Australia unsettling when she arrives from Seattle, wait until she meets Luke Sampson! He's part owner of the isolated cattle station her father recently willed to her. Laconic and self-reliant, the quintessential outback hero, he's been managing the station for ten years, and he's about to turn Sarah's world even more upside down than her trip Down Under already has.

CNM0800